LONE WITNESS

Books by Rachel Dylan

ATLANTA ⚖ JUSTICE
BOOK TWO

LONE WITNESS

RACHEL DYLAN

BETHANYHOUSE

a division of Baker Publishing Group
Minneapolis, Minnesota

© 2018 by Rachel Dylan

Published by Bethany House Publishers
11400 Hampshire Avenue South
Bloomington, Minnesota 55438
www.bethanyhouse.com

Bethany House Publishers is a division of
Baker Publishing Group, Grand Rapids, Michigan

Printed in the United States of America

ISBN 978-0-7642-1981-8 (trade paper)
ISBN 978-0-7642-3198-8 (cloth)

Library of Congress Cataloging-in-Publication Data: 2017963677

This is a work of fiction. Names, characters, incidents, and dialogues are products of the author's imagination and are not to be construed as real. Any resemblance to actual events or persons, living or dead, is entirely coincidental.

Cover design by LOOK Design Studio

Author is represented by the Nancy Yost Literary Agency.

18 19 20 21 22 23 24   7 6 5 4 3 2 1

CHAPTER
ONE

Guilty. That's the only possible verdict. Ladies and gentleman of the jury, Felix Sanders, the CEO of Banton Corporation, has been embezzling for five years." Sophie Dawson took a deep breath, then continued her closing argument. She made eye contact with each of the twelve members of the jury who would decide the fate of the crooked CEO.

"Throughout the past week, you've heard testimony not only from other employees of Banton Corporation, but from our forensic accounting experts. Those experts testified that there is no doubt that Mr. Sanders was funneling money from the accounts of Banton investors into his personal slush fund that sits in a Swiss bank account." If she lost this case, then she deserved to be fired. The evidence against Sanders was rock solid. It was rare to have a case this bulletproof.

"The defense would have you believe that every single one of these transactions was made in clerical error, but now that you've heard and seen all of the evidence, I submit to you that there is no way that conclusion could ever be reached. Let me remind you that we're talking about hundreds of transactions over a five-year period. The defense's position asks you to suspend all logic and enter a fantasyland that doesn't exist. While the prosecution has the burden of proof, we have clearly met that requirement with these facts."

This was one of Sophie's first major jury trials since she'd joined the White Collar Crime Unit of the Fulton County District Attorney's office. Moving from the general trial division into the White Collar division had been a promotion, but financial crimes weren't quite as exciting as murder. And the victims in this particular case weren't individual consumers but other wealthy hedge fund types. They still deserved justice, though, because their money had been stolen from them. What Sanders had done was a crime, and she was doing her job as a prosecutor.

Sophie walked the jury through the remaining pieces of evidence. Then it was time for the defense to give their closing argument. Sanders had hired a big shot defense attorney from Peters & Gomez, but even a superstar high-priced lawyer wasn't going to save him from a conviction. Sophie zoned out a little as the attorney droned on and on, trying to poke holes in her case. She thought it was a strategic miscalculation on his part to be so long-winded. The jury had been sitting there all week. They would be ready to start their deliberations and be done with this. But she wasn't a defense attorney and had no desire to ever be one. If that was the strategy he wanted to employ, then who was she to second-guess him?

When her opposing counsel finally sat down, the judge provided the jury with instructions, and the jurors were excused for their deliberations. Now all Sophie could do was wait. It could be minutes, hours, or days before the jury came back with a verdict, although she hoped it would be quick. If it took too long, she'd start to get worried.

She started packing up her stuff as her opposing counsel, John Gomez, walked over to her. Sanders was probably paying Gomez, a founding partner at the firm, over a thousand dollars an hour. A ridiculous sum for legal fees, if you asked her.

"Ms. Dawson, that was a very impressive closing argument." John smoothed his tailored navy suit jacket.

"Thank you." Sophie guessed John was probably in his fifties, and his short dark hair was slightly graying at the temples. She wasn't sure why he was talking to her. She was just one of many Fulton County prosecutors, and he was one of the heaviest hitters in the legal community. Being a founding partner of one of the most prestigious law firms in town was a big deal to most people. But his power and clout didn't impress her that much. She was more moved by other attributes.

John took a step toward her. "You have a great presence, even if you are a bit rough around the edges."

"Excuse me?" This wasn't the first time she had received unsolicited comments about her courtroom performance from her opposing counsel. Being a relatively young female with a baby face and blond hair, she was constantly trying to prove herself.

"It was a compliment. So much so, that I'd love for you to consider making a lateral move over to our firm. I'm sure I could at least triple your current salary, and we can always use top talent with real trial experience. Tested trial lawyers aren't easy to come by." His dark eyes studied her.

What he didn't realize was that she hadn't become a lawyer for the money. She didn't even need to work, because she had a more-than-substantial trust fund set up by her father. She was a prosecutor because she loved it. "I appreciate your kind offer, Mr. Gomez."

"Please, call me John." He gave her a million-dollar smile.

"But I just started this new role in the White Collar Crime Unit, and I really enjoy my work. I can't imagine making the move to private practice." In fact, it was something she'd never consider, but she thought it better to keep her explanations simple and to the point. There was no use in explaining her entire background and career goals.

John nodded. "I understand. But if you change your mind,

you know how to get in touch with me. My door is always open for you." He put his hand on her shoulder. "And I'd love to take you to dinner sometime and discuss it further."

Suddenly uncomfortable, she took a step back, putting a little distance between them. "Like I said, thank you, but I'm not interested. And I'm sorry, but I need to run. I have to handle a few other matters."

"Of course. We'll see how long the jury takes, but it might be next week before we get a decision."

"Let's hope not," she muttered.

He smiled at her again, showing his perfectly polished white teeth, and walked away. She let out a breath. *Well, that was awkward.* Maybe she had misread his signals, but it seemed like he was more interested in her as a woman than as a lawyer. That was also a common response she got from her male colleagues.

Couldn't they just respect her for the work she put in and not always be angling for something else from her? No wonder she still hadn't found Mr. Right, despite her persistent search. She shook off the encounter and headed back to her office to finish up a few other things.

Her caseload was heavy, but not nearly like it had been in the general trial division. She'd been in the courtroom almost every single day for the past seven years, learning the ropes as an assistant district attorney. Now, as a senior ADA, she had a chance to distinguish herself from the crowd.

Once she was settled back in her office, she pulled out her latest case file. She'd just started her investigation into a matter involving Southern Investment Bank, known as SIB. The bank was headquartered in Atlanta, and according to the file, numerous complaints had been lodged against a top senior manager named Glen Shelton.

This was the type of case she could really sink her teeth into. Unlike the trial she had just completed, the victims here were people who truly couldn't afford to be cheated. Shelton was accused of stealing from his clients and charging exorbitant fees on every transaction, in a way that was not clear to the clients that they were being charged at all, much less for what. The complaints were lodged by small businesses and individuals who had used Shelton for personal and small business loans.

These people had trusted Shelton with their finances, sometimes their life savings or their entire business, and now it was gone. Poof! All because of one man's greedy appetite.

There were still a ton of holes to fill in the investigation, but she was definitely ready to tackle this new file. And now that her caseload wasn't as crazy, she'd be able to devote large chunks of her time to this case. A burst of adrenaline coursed through her body just thinking about it. If what she was reading about Shelton was true, he needed to be held accountable for his criminal acts.

It would be a delicate endeavor, though. She'd been around long enough to understand that a case like this could get political. *Very political.* SIB was one of the most respected companies in Atlanta and had tons of influential local connections. The CEO of SIB was one of the most powerful women in the city.

At this point, Sophie wasn't looking to go after SIB as a corporation. Her target was merely one of its employees. Hopefully, that would mean she'd get the full cooperation of the company from the top down, but she wasn't holding her breath. Any type of criminal investigation was bound to make the executives at SIB nervous, and she couldn't blame them for that. But she had a job to do and planned not to let SIB's prestige and sterling reputation hold her back.

Sophie was still settling into her new office. It was marginally bigger than her old one, but still nothing fancy. She chuckled, thinking about her two best friends, who worked at big law firms. They had huge offices in high-rises with plush furniture, views of the Midtown skyline or Stone Mountain, and all the amenities in the world, and here she sat in a stuffy box on the third floor with a tiny window and a view of the parking garage. The office was filled with one lonely file cabinet, a desk, and three basic office chairs. No amenities here, unless you brought them in yourself. Such was the life of a public servant, but she wouldn't have it any other way.

She looked at the clock and realized that time had gotten away from her. That was the story of her life. Many a night she left the office late.

No word yet from the jury, so it would definitely be next week, unless they opted to work over the weekend—which was unlikely, unless they were super close to reaching a verdict. She should just go home.

Once she got to her car and pushed the start button, her stomach started to rumble, and she realized she hadn't eaten anything since that morning. An intense craving for junk food hit her, so she decided to drive to the gas station she frequented for chips and candy bars. At least a healthy dose of salt and sugar would satisfy her cravings. She parked in front of the Quick-Stop and could already taste the mix of salty chips and chocolate. If she was going for junk food, she might as well make it good.

But once she got into the store and started walking the aisles, she couldn't make a decision. Maybe she should try to be healthy and only get one snack, then try to have a proper dinner. She looked at her watch. It was ten o'clock. Too late for a real dinner anyway.

She walked to the back of the store to pick up a flavored tea. As she opened the refrigerator door, debating between raspberry or extra sweet, a sudden commotion began at the front of the store. She turned around and sucked in a breath.

A man was pointing a gun at the cashier, and they were yelling at each other. Her first instinct was to run toward the fight and try to stop a disaster from happening, but she was only halfway up the aisle when a shot rang out. Instinctively, she hit the floor, covering her head, and slid behind one of the popcorn displays. She'd taken active shooter training as part of her job and knew that the best course of action was to try to stay out of sight. She peered around the display, trying to keep most of her body hidden.

The shooter turned around, and she got a good look at his face. He appeared young to her, maybe in his upper teens. He didn't seem to notice her as he sprinted out of the gas station with his gun still drawn.

As soon as he was out the door, she sprang to her feet and ran to the front counter. The cashier lay on the ground in a large pool of blood. Squatting down beside him, she checked for a pulse. Nothing. He was dead.

She heard another round of gunshots and looked outside. The shooter had opened fire on his way out of the store. He was heading toward a midsize gray SUV, but there was another car on the left side of it. One person was on the driver's side, crouched down with her hands over her head, but the person on the passenger side was totally exposed and in the shooter's direct line of fire.

Sophie heard herself scream a warning, but it was too late.

The man fired and hit the woman standing closest to his SUV. Then he jumped into his car and sped away.

Sophie mentally took down his license plate as she rushed outside to check on the victim. The other woman was standing over her friend, crying hysterically.

"It's going to be okay," Sophie said, trying to calm her down. "Call 911 right now."

The woman nodded as tears rolled down her reddened cheeks, and pulled out her cell phone.

Sophie turned her attention to the woman lying on the ground, surrounded by large amounts of blood. Now that Sophie got a good look at the victim, she realized that the petite brunette looked barely older than a teenager. She'd suffered a gunshot wound to the head.

Sophie didn't even have to check for a pulse to tell her what she already knew. This young woman was dead. The head shot had probably killed her on impact.

Dear Lord, so much death. Please help me. Don't let me fall apart right now.

There was nothing she could do for this woman now, so she took the phone away from the woman's friend, who was standing nearby, shaking in shock. Sophie started talking to the 911 operator and gave him the license plate number. The shooter would probably dump the car ASAP, so they only had a small window to try to track him down by the plates.

Sophie wrapped her arm around the woman who had lost her friend. "You're safe. No one is going to hurt you now."

The woman didn't reply, just continued to sob. Soon the blaring sound of sirens filled the air. Sophie was no stranger to crime scenes. In fact, she'd been at more than she could even begin to count. But this was different. Tonight she was not here as a prosecutor, but as a witness.

Thankfully, she recognized one of the two officers who got out of their vehicle. Officer Carlos Wall's dark eyes widened when he saw her.

"Sophie," he said. "How did you get here so fast?" Then his eyes focused on her hands and beige suit jacket, which were streaked with bright red blood. "Sophie? What happened?"

"I was here getting a snack, Carlos. I saw everything." She could hear her voice starting to crack, but she had to stay strong and make sure they had the information they needed. This was no time to get emotional. She had to push through and focus.

Carlos muttered something under his breath and then turned to his partner, who was standing beside him. "This is one of ours," he said. "An ADA."

She didn't correct him about her title and promotion. Now wasn't the time.

"Sophie Dawson, this is Officer Peter Gray," Carlos said. Then he looked at Peter. "You should take Sophie's statement."

"There's another body inside," she said quietly. "He killed two people."

"Then that makes you a witness to a double homicide," Carlos said.

TWO

On Monday morning, Sophie sat in her office, still reeling from the events of Friday night. She'd given her statement multiple times to the officers at the scene before they allowed her to go home. The little she did sleep that night was filled with nightmares about the shooting. Blood was everywhere, and she was always helpless to stop the killing.

She'd also suffered a severe panic attack in the wee hours of the morning. It had been months since her last one, but there was no escaping it that night. At least she hadn't had one at the scene. She'd kept it together until she was alone, and then the world had crashed down on her.

She'd found out that the two women were college students at Georgia State University. The victim was only a sophomore and had just turned twenty years old. The cashier had left behind a wife and three kids.

Sophie's cell rang, and she saw it was her dad calling. He was still completely freaked out.

"Hey, Dad," she answered.

"Sophie, how are you today? I still couldn't sleep much last night. You were on my mind."

"I'm doing okay. Obviously this isn't an easy situation to handle, but I'm taking it one step at a time."

"Are you sure you don't want to come stay with me for a few days? I'd feel so much better knowing that you weren't alone right now."

She loved her father with all her heart, but she feared that if she went to her childhood home, she'd have a hard time leaving. And she needed to be on her own. "Thanks, but I'd rather stay at my place."

"Well, you know you never need an invitation to come home. And if any of this is too much for you, just give me a call, and I'll be right there. No matter what time, day or night."

"Thank you."

She felt tears well up in her eyes. Sophie knew she was a big softie, especially where her father was concerned. He was her rock. And he'd worn multiple hats as she grew up—he'd learned how to braid her hair and had dried her tears when the first boy she had a crush on broke her heart.

She'd never known her mother, though she bore a strong resemblance to her from the pictures she'd seen. A wave of sadness washed over her. Even though she'd lived her thirty-two years without her mom, the loss was always there.

"I love you, Sophie. Stay in touch. I want to know how you're doing."

"Of course. Love you too." She hung up and closed her eyes for a second. The last thing she wanted was to stress out her father, so she was trying to stay composed for his sake.

There was a loud knock on her door, and she looked up to see her boss, Fulton County District Attorney Keith Todd.

"Sophie, do you have a minute?"

"Of course."

Keith sat down across from her. "First, how are you doing? I know you had a traumatic night on Friday."

She looked into his light blue eyes. "It's been a trying couple of days, but I'm thankful to be alive. I only wish I could've done more."

"From what I hear, you did everything by the book and put yourself at risk trying to help. A lot of people would've curled up in a ball at the back of the store and hidden. But you jumped into action. You've made us all proud. Your actions were very brave."

"Thank you." Keith didn't offer praise often, so she was warmed by his compliment, even given the circumstances. He had high career hopes that went beyond being the Fulton County DA. At almost fifty years old, he was setting himself up for the next big thing.

"I want to talk to you about something, so you aren't caught unaware."

Her stomach clenched. "What is it?"

"You'll hear more about all of this, especially as the local news breaks today, but I wanted you to hear it from me first."

She leaned forward in her chair, sensing something big was coming. "Okay."

"The suspect you identified this morning in the lineup for the shooting is a man by the name of Ricky Wade."

"All right." She didn't know where Keith was going with this. "The name doesn't sound familiar to me."

"Ricky is the younger brother of Juan Wade."

That name she knew. "As in the head of one of Atlanta's biggest gangs? That Juan Wade?"

"The very same." Keith ran his hand through his short, sandy blond hair. "So this isn't going to be a run-of-the-mill prosecution. We've got a double homicide linked to a major gang. I don't have to spell all of this out for you."

Her head started to swim. There were a lot of implications. Especially with her being a potential witness.

Keith cleared his throat. "Having said all that, I've decided it makes sense to remove any semblance of bias in this case. I'm assigning a special prosecutor to it."

"Who?"

"Deputy Chief ADA Patrick Hunt from the Dekalb County prosecutor's office. Do you know him?"

She shook her head. "I've heard the name, but I've never met him."

"Good. That way we can put to bed any argument about a conflict of interest. I didn't want one of our own Fulton County prosecutors having to put you on the witness stand. It's just too close. This will be better for everyone, including you."

She looked up to see a tall man standing in her doorway. He had short dark hair and was probably in his mid-to-late thirties.

"Hello," he said. "Hope I'm not interrupting."

"Patrick." Keith rose from his seat. "Nice to see you." He shook Patrick's hand. "Let me introduce you to Sophie Dawson."

Sophie stood and walked around her desk to greet Patrick. "Nice to meet you."

"I know this is a difficult time for you," Patrick said, "but I'll do everything I can to make this process go as smoothly as possible."

"I'll let you two talk," Keith said. "Sophie, if you need anything, let me know. And if your workload needs to be adjusted, that won't be an issue."

She appreciated the offer, but the last thing she wanted to do was give up any of her cases. She didn't want this case against Ricky Wade to impede on her life any more than it had to.

When Keith had left, Patrick leaned against the corner of her desk. "I don't know what all Keith told you, but I'd like to hear everything you can tell me about Friday night."

"Of course." It was going to be a long morning. She stared at her empty coffee cup and thought about a refill. "What about the other woman at the scene? The college student?"

Patrick frowned. "Understandably, she's a wreck. She hit the deck when she heard the shots being fired. Put her head down and never saw the shooter."

"I know she has to be traumatized. It was awful." Sophie had seen many difficult things during her time as a prosecutor, but she could only imagine what that young woman was going through.

"She's seeking counseling." Patrick paused. "Not to add any pressure on your shoulders or anything, but you're the linchpin here, Sophie."

"Don't we have the gas station security cameras?"

He blew out a breath. "We've got nothing. Only one of the cameras was working, and it was at the tanks and didn't capture any useful footage of the shooter. Nothing we can use for identification."

Her heartbeat started to speed up as she thought it through. "So it's literally going to be just eyewitness testimony? My eyewitness testimony?" Her voice cracked.

"Yeah. And I don't have to tell you what that means."

"Because eyewitnesses are often so unreliable."

Patrick nodded. "Plus, on top of that, we'll have to combat the defense's argument that you're biased."

"I know what I saw." She wasn't going to waver on that.

"You're a professional, but you're not used to being on this side of things. It might turn out to be much more difficult than you think."

"I promise I'll cooperate and won't try to play Monday morning quarterback."

"No, that isn't what I meant at all. I'm not concerned about you questioning my legal strategies."

"What is it, then?"

Patrick took a deep breath and looked directly into her eyes. "You have a huge target on your back. And Juan Wade doesn't miss."

CHAPTER
THREE

Cooper Knight hung back and watched as Sophie Dawson walked out of the Fulton County courthouse. The tall, knockout of a blonde didn't look like an attorney, but he'd learned years ago as a cop that you should never judge someone by how they looked.

He'd actually met Sophie once at her birthday party. They were connected through one of his best friends and business partners, Landon James. Landon was marrying Kate Sullivan, who happened to be friends with Sophie. They'd actually gotten engaged at Sophie's birthday party, which was why Cooper had been invited.

Sophie had made quite an impression on him that night. So much so that he almost asked for her number, but then thought better of it. He wasn't looking for something serious and didn't think it best to casually date one of Kate's closest friends, given all the interconnections. He liked to keep things simple.

So he'd decided to play it safe, have a nice conversation with her, and then try to put her out of his mind. But she looked every bit as beautiful today as he remembered. It wasn't just her beauty that had gotten his attention, though. They'd had a great conversation, and he knew she was a woman with depth.

Another reason he'd decided it best not to make a move. Romantic attachments weren't his thing. He wasn't like his buddy Landon. Settling down wasn't an option for him.

Since he'd had that brief interaction with Sophie, he made sure not to get too close to her now. He didn't want her to see him. At least not yet.

He'd gotten a call last night from Randall Dawson, Sophie's father. Randall was very concerned that his daughter was apparently the only witness in a double homicide that involved one of Atlanta's most notorious gangs. Once he'd heard everything Randall had to say, Cooper couldn't blame him for wanting to make sure his only child was protected. Cooper understood how dangerous the Atlanta gang scene was because he'd worked a two-year stint in the gang unit.

His orders right now, though, were to stay under the radar. To not let Sophie know he was keeping an eye on her. Randall had told him that if Sophie found out, she wasn't going to be happy. She valued her independence and wouldn't appreciate his presence.

Cooper got into his SUV, planning to tail her to make sure she safely got either home or to whatever destination she was headed. Since he'd received the phone call from Randall, he'd done some background research. Sophie had attended Emory University for undergraduate and law school. Thirty-two years old, single, and fiercely passionate about her career as a prosecutor.

The most interesting find in his research was that Sophie came from money—serious money that went back generations. Her father was also a highly respected businessman in the community with a thriving commercial real estate company.

His phone rang and he answered. "Cooper here."

"Hey, it's Landon. I'm calling you back."

"Are you alone?" He had to ask Landon something and wanted to make sure his fiancée wasn't around.

"Yeah, in the car on my way home."

"Listen, I got a new client, and it's actually Sophie Dawson."

"Kate's Sophie?" Landon asked.

"Yes, which is why I wanted to talk to you, to make sure you didn't see the file I created for new matters on our shared site and say anything to Kate."

"What's going on with Sophie?"

He filled Landon in on everything he knew as he kept his eyes on Sophie's vehicle, which was about four cars ahead of him.

"Sounds like Sophie may actually need the security," Landon said. "I know sometimes we deal with situations where family or business contacts overreact, but you can't mess around with the gangs. Especially if this is the gang leader's brother we're talking about. This is bad news. I don't like any of it."

"I agree."

"Do you need any help from me?" Landon asked.

"Not at the moment, but I wanted to make sure you were up to speed. I don't know the timetable yet of the trial or whether there's going to be a plea deal or what. For now, I'm just keeping my eyes on her, and we'll take it one step at a time."

"Whatever you need, just let me know."

"I'm so glad you're part of our team now, Landon."

"Me too. It's like I'm right where I'm supposed to be."

Landon had merged his own private investigator business with K&R Security less than a year ago. He had gone through a rough patch after his last army deployment and leaving the military, but was now back on track, thanks in large part to his fiancée. Cooper was so thankful to have his friend back.

"I'll keep you posted. Will you do me a favor and let Noah know what's going on?"

"Roger that."

Cooper ended the call and kept his eyes on Sophie's black Ford Escape. For being so wealthy, it didn't appear that she was flaunting it. She could've been driving a luxury vehicle.

He couldn't imagine what it would be like to come from that kind of money—or any money, for that matter. His parents had barely been able to put food on the table, though a lot of that was because of his father's transgressions. Being raised by an abusive alcoholic had taken its toll on Cooper. He knew it. He didn't need a shrink to explain that to him. No amount of therapy would cure him of his past.

His dad had gotten clean about five years ago, and Cooper was thankful for that. But the damage had been done. And it was irreversible.

Lord, I don't want to think about this right now.

It was a prayer he felt like he'd uttered a million times.

Deputy Chief ADA Patrick Hunt walked into the courtroom, ready for what he hoped would be a run-of-the-mill preliminary hearing. Unfortunately, so far he was learning that absolutely nothing about the Wade case was run-of-the-mill. Starting with the fact that his only witness to a double homicide was a senior ADA. What were the chances of that? It was going to make his job infinitely trickier.

He'd been called in from Dekalb, the neighboring county, so the defense couldn't argue conflict of interest. And once he found out who the defense attorney was, boy, was he glad Keith had asked him to step in.

Ashley Murphy represented the worst of the worst. Gangs, rapists, drug lords, and other violent criminals. He had no idea how she could sleep at night. Ice ran through her veins.

He was facing off against Ashley today. It wasn't the first time, and it wouldn't be the last. He could only imagine what the gang was paying her. It was a hefty sum, that was for sure, because Ashley didn't come cheap. She wasn't representing defendants out of the goodness of her heart, but the desire to pad her pocketbook.

If all went according to plan in the hearing, he'd put the detective on the stand, get the testimony he needed for probable cause, and go about his business.

As Patrick walked to his table at the front of the courtroom, he saw that his eyewitness was seated in the back row for purely observational purposes. Today her name would come out to the defense and to the public at large. There was nothing he could do about that, but it would certainly up the stakes.

He gave Sophie a nod and set his briefcase on the counsel's table. Ashley Murphy was already at the defense table, jotting down notes on her legal pad. When she made eye contact with him, she set down her pen and walked over. Her light brown hair was pulled back in a bun. She always wore wireframe glasses, but for some reason he was convinced it was just for show to make her look more serious.

"You're barking up the wrong tree," Ashley said.

"And hello to you too, Ashley."

She put her right hand on her hip. "C'mon, Patrick. You know how this dance is done. You've got absolutely nothing on my client. This is just a way for you to try, yet again, to make a run at Juan Wade. But it isn't happening. I won't let you smear this young man's good name."

Mixed feelings bubbled up inside him. He wanted to shut her down right then and there. But he kept his emotions in check, figuring Ashley would find out soon enough about his witness. She was going to go absolutely ballistic, and there was a side of him that wanted to see that. He knew he shouldn't think that way, but the utter surprise she was in for when she found out who had witnessed the double homicide would be priceless. Ashley assumed she held all the cards right now, but she was wrong.

"You're way off base, Ashley. Why don't you let us present the evidence against your client first, before you jump to any hasty conclusions that aren't built on the facts?"

Her green eyes narrowed. "What's going on, Patrick? Are you holding out on me?"

His attitude had tipped her off. "Let's just get this done, all right?"

"Fine." She turned and walked away, looking over her shoulder once more at him.

Her client, Ricky Wade, was ushered into the courtroom by an officer. He looked even younger than his nineteen years, with a baby face and big brown eyes. Ricky stood about six feet tall with a lanky frame. Patrick wondered if his looks would make the jury more sympathetic. He was clearly old enough to be tried as an adult, but that baby face might prove to be yet another issue for the prosecution. As if he needed another challenge right now.

Patrick hadn't let on to Sophie just how difficult he thought this case might be. She seemed convinced that Ricky was the shooter, but they would have to overcome a series of obstacles to prove that. And that was under the best conditions, without any interference by Juan.

Patrick pretended to be organizing his papers as he stood and walked around the side of the table, but he couldn't help hearing Ricky say some foul things to Ashley. Didn't this kid realize that she was there to help him? It was mind-boggling that Ashley would put up with that kind of behavior. But she didn't show any signs of distress as she responded in a calm voice and reassured Ricky that she had everything under control.

It was only a few minutes before Judge Edward Turner took the bench and it was show time. Judge Turner was a middle-of-the-road judge who was known for having a calm demeanor. It took a lot to rile him up.

"Call your first witness, Mr. Hunt."

"The state calls Detective Harley Scott." Scott was the lead detective on the case, and he would present the evidence needed to get a probable cause order. Scott was a veteran detective and had done hundreds of these hearings.

Patrick walked the detective through the events of the night of the shooting. "And Detective Scott, you have an eyewitness who will testify to the events that you've laid out today?"

"Yes, sir, I do."

Patrick wasn't going to be the person to name Sophie in open court. He was certain Ashley would ask for the name, so he left it at that and rested. "Your witness, counselor."

Ashley walked up to the witness stand and adjusted her glasses. He figured that was one of her nervous ticks.

"Detective Scott, what is the name of your eyewitness?"

"Her name is Sophie Dawson."

Ashley turned and looked at Patrick, her eyes wide and mouth slightly parted in surprise, before she looked toward the back of the courtroom. "Detective Scott, are you talking about Assistant District Attorney Sophie Dawson?"

Audible gasps went up throughout the courtroom. It wasn't a packed house, but given the high profile nature of the case and the gang involvement, there were local media present.

"Yes, ma'am. Well, let me back up. I'm actually not sure if that is her exact title at this point, but Ms. Dawson is a prosecutor."

"So you're telling me, Detective, that your eyewitness in this case against my client is a Fulton County prosecutor?"

"Yes, ma'am," the detective said without batting an eye.

"How convenient is that, Detective?"

Patrick shot up from his seat. "Objection, Your Honor. I don't think defense counsel's side comments are appropriate."

The judge nodded. "Ms. Murphy, please stick to the questions. There's no need for theatrics at a preliminary hearing. There's no jury here for your performance."

Patrick held back a smirk.

Ashley turned and looked at Sophie before directing her

attention back at the judge. For a moment she didn't say anything, but Patrick could tell she was plotting something.

"Your Honor, since I see that Ms. Dawson is present in the courtroom today, I'd like to call her to the stand and hear the words directly from her."

Patrick rose to his feet again. "Your Honor, it would be highly irregular to have the eyewitness actually testify at a preliminary hearing—and called by the defense, no less."

"Your response, Ms. Murphy?"

"Nothing about this case seems normal, Your Honor. I would submit that I have the right to hear Ms. Dawson's testimony today. She's sitting right there, so it's not like we're putting her or the Court at any inconvenience."

"Ms. Murphy is right on this count. Irregular, yes, but there's nothing prohibiting it. Ms. Dawson, if you are indeed in the courtroom, please stand."

Patrick should have known Ashley would try something crazy like this. He kicked himself for not preparing for such a contingency. He hadn't done any of the typical witness preparation with Sophie that he would normally do before she was called to the stand. Now he could only hope that his case wasn't about to go up in smoke.

Sophie stood up as the judge had ordered, and she could feel every single eye in the room staring at her. While she was accustomed to being in front of the courtroom, it wasn't under these circumstances. Her palms became sweaty, and she felt her cheeks flush. This was no time to have a panic attack.

You can do this, Sophie. You've been in court a million times.

"Ms. Dawson, please come up to the witness stand," the judge said.

Her legs felt unsteady as she made the walk down the aisle toward the front of the courtroom. Never in her wildest dreams could she have imagined that the defense would call her to the stand at the preliminary hearing. To say that was unorthodox was an understatement.

Patrick hadn't prepared her for the possibility, but as a prosecutor, she should've known better. Any contingency was possible, especially when you were dealing with a formidable defense attorney like Ashley Murphy.

Sophie had been opposite Ashley multiple times and had never been able to break through on a personal level with her. She was on friendly terms with many defense attorneys, and she understood the importance of having good lawyers on the defense bar. Everyone needed fair representation. It was a pillar of the American judicial system. But Ashley had built a wall around herself, and they'd never had a personal conversation before, only business. And now Sophie was about to be examined by her.

She shouldn't have come to the hearing today.

Sophie smoothed down her navy suit jacket as she made her way into the witness box. As she was sworn in, she prayed that she would be able to keep it together.

"Ms. Dawson, please state your full name and job title for the record," Ashley said, not wasting any time.

"I'm Sophie Elizabeth Dawson, and I'm a senior assistant district attorney in the White Collar Crime Unit for Fulton County."

"And how long have you been a prosecutor?"

"I'm about to start my eighth year." So far, so good.

"And where were you on the night of October seventh?"

"That's a broad question." Sophie couldn't help but say that, but then she decided it was better to just keep talking. "I left work a little before ten and stopped at the convenience store called Quick-Stop directly off exit twenty on I-85 to get a snack."

"And you contend that you saw my client, Mr. Ricky Wade, at the Quick-Stop that night?"

"Yes, I do. In fact, I saw the defendant shoot and kill two people."

Loud murmurs sounded through the audience. Ashley's green eyes flashed with anger, and a red blotch crept up her pale cheek.

"No further questions at this time." Ashley turned and walked back to the defense table.

Ashley had probably made the strategic decision that as juicy as it was to catch Sophie off guard and create a dramatic scene, the implication of full testimony now, especially with the media present, could actually work against her client. It appeared Ashley wanted a chance to prepare and gather the facts. Sophie knew that Ashley would seek her revenge during the trial, when the jury was present.

"Do you have anything for this witness at this time, Mr. Hunt?" the judge asked.

"No, Your Honor. I think that's best left for another time," Patrick said.

"Ms. Dawson, you can step down, thank you," the judge said.

Sophie realized she'd been clenching her fists as she exhaled and exited the witness stand. She quickly returned to her seat.

"Your Honor, I believe we have more than sufficient evidence for a probable cause order," Patrick said.

"Anything else from the defense?"

"No, Your Honor," Ashley responded.

"Then I agree with the prosecution, and I find that there is probable cause. The defendant will remain in custody."

Sophie let out a breath. Finding probable cause was pretty much a foregone conclusion, since the bar was set so low, but things had gotten a bit hectic there for a minute, and her head was spinning.

"There's one more issue to take up, Your Honor," Ashley said.

"Go on," the judge responded.

"I'd like to request that my client be kept in isolation."

"What?" Ricky exclaimed. "I don't want to be in isolation."

"Do you need a minute to confer with your client?" the judge asked.

"No. This request is made in my client's best interest. I believe, given the fact that he is Juan Wade's brother, that there could be elements inside the prison who would want to do him grave harm."

"I can take care of myself," Ricky shot back.

"One second, Your Honor." Ashley wrapped her arm around Ricky's shoulder and leaned in. Sophie couldn't hear anything being said between them, but she could guess. Ashley was the one doing all the talking. Ricky gave a weak nod.

After a few minutes of discussion, Ashley turned her attention back to the judge. "My client is in agreement, and I would like to make my request again."

"What does the state have to say about this?"

"I don't have an objection," Patrick responded.

"Fine. Then Mr. Wade will be kept outside of general population for his own safety."

"Thank you, Your Honor," Ashley said.

Once the judge called for the adjournment, Sophie was suddenly surrounded by the press.

"Ms. Dawson, what exactly did you see that night?" a man with a bright red bow tie asked.

A woman stepped right in front of her. "Ms. Dawson, did you know about the defendant's gang ties before you identified him?"

The questions kept coming, but Sophie kept her mouth shut. After a minute, Patrick showed up at her side and started to usher her out. "Ms. Dawson has no comment at this time," he yelled over his shoulder.

He held her by the arm and led her out of the courtroom and down the hall. By the time they'd gotten out of the fray, her heartbeat was still thumping loudly.

"We need to get you out of here," Patrick said.

"Let's take the stairs." She knew her way around this courthouse like the back of her hand.

By the time they'd made it back to her office, she was exhausted from all the drama.

"I'm so sorry that happened," Patrick said. "I should've known Ashley would pull a stunt like that. Do you know her?"

"Unfortunately, yes. It wasn't your fault. But now I guess the cat is out of the bag."

"Which brings me to my next issue. You need to be on alert. As I told you when we first met, I wouldn't put it past Juan and his cohorts to try to engage in some type of retaliation against you. Juan will know exactly who you are now."

She brushed his warning aside. "Don't even give it a second thought. They're not going to come after me. It'd be too risky. Everyone's watching."

"I think you're underestimating them. You're on a completely different playing field as a witness than a prosecutor. I don't want you to be lulled into a false sense of security. Their risk analysis is different with you as a witness. And the bottom line here is that you're talking about Juan's little brother. This is about family for him."

His stern warning made her rethink whether she was taking this seriously enough. "All right. I understand."

"And one more thing. I think this goes without saying, but not a word to the press of any kind."

"Obviously not. I'll keep my mouth shut."

"Watch your back, and I'll be in touch about the schedule."

A chill shot down her arms at his words. Was she really in danger?

CHAPTER

FOUR

The past two weeks had flown by as Sophie did everything in her power to cooperate with Patrick and the police officers conducting the investigation. Unfortunately, she'd made the mistake of telling her overly protective father that she'd received some threatening letters in the mail.

Getting letters like that was part of her job, but she couldn't help feeling like this wave of threats, which had started last week, had to do with her involvement in the Wade case. Once it hit the local news that a senior ADA from Fulton County was a witness in the double homicide, the reporters latched onto the story, which put her in the spotlight—a place she didn't want to be. And the letters grew increasingly more troublesome by the day.

Her father meant well. She was his only child, and they had a super tight bond, since it had always just been the two of them. But Randall Dawson worried a lot about his little girl, and she had the feeling he wasn't going to sit back this time and listen to her say that he had no reason to fret.

After a long day in the office, she'd had enough and headed out to her car. She needed to stop at the grocery store on the way home and pick up a couple things. Since the shooting, she couldn't bring herself to go back to the Quick-Stop. She'd just have to buy groceries like a normal person instead of living on snacks picked up on a whim.

When she finished her shopping, she stepped out of the store and started to push her cart out to her car. She had almost reached her car when she saw a man standing beside it. Her heartbeat immediately sped up. What was he doing?

She thought about heading a different direction, but she wanted to get a little closer to see what he was up to. As she moved nearer, the man came into view under the bright parking lot lights. Tall, blond, and very well built.

This wasn't some random guy. Now that she got a good look at his face, she recognized him.

"Cooper?" She rolled her cart toward her car.

"Hi, Sophie. I didn't know if you'd remember me."

How could she have forgotten him? She'd developed a little crush on him the minute they'd been introduced at her birthday party. He'd made quite the impression on her. How could he not, with his all-American good looks. But good looks were only a small part of the equation. She wanted a lot more than that.

"You're friends with Kate's fiancé, Landon, right?" Kate was one of her best friends and also an attorney. Landon had worked with Kate on a case taking on a big pharmaceutical company, and that was how they'd become a couple.

"That's right, and I run K&R Security."

That still didn't explain why he was here. "Is there something I can help you with?"

"Could we go somewhere and talk?"

Her antenna immediately went up. Something was off here, but she didn't know what. "I need to take these groceries home." She trusted Cooper because he worked with Landon, but it was still strange to invite him to her house.

As if he sensed her hesitation, he took a step toward her. "It's actually about your father."

Her heart dropped. "What? Has something happened to him?" She immediately jumped to the most awful scenarios.

Cooper shook his head. "No, no. Nothing like that. Don't worry, your dad is completely fine."

Her skepticism returned. "Then what are you talking about?"

"Your dad sent me here."

And then it all made sense.

Cooper sat at Sophie's kitchen table with a steaming cup of coffee. The prosecutor was fired up. He couldn't blame her, though.

"You're saying my father hired you? To what, be my bodyguard?"

"I wouldn't exactly classify it as a bodyguard." He paused. "At least not at this point. Your father is just concerned about your safety, and rightly so. He cares about you a lot, Sophie—I could tell just from talking to him—and he's really worried." It was a strong contrast to the horrendous relationship he had with his own father. He'd never known that kind of love from his dad—just the opposite.

Her big blue eyes softened. "I know, and I love my father. But you have to understand that it's his nature to overreact when it comes to me. And I think this time he took it too far."

Cooper had a job to do, so he needed to figure out how to convince Sophie that it was in her best interest to hear him out. Randall had warned him that Sophie was going to be very resistant to the idea. She liked to stand on her own two feet. "Can we talk for a minute about the letters you've been receiving?"

Sophie picked up her pink coffee mug and took a sip. "Sure. There have been a number of threatening letters, but in this job, that's not out of the ordinary. After being a prosecutor for going on eight years, you rack up a list of people who aren't happy with you. I did receive them more often in my prior position, but criminals don't follow my career path. There has been a recent uptick, which I suspect is related to the local media attention."

He wondered if she realized how formal and lawyer-like she sounded. "Do you have the letters here?"

"I have copies of them scanned into my email. Let me get my computer."

He waited patiently as she retrieved her laptop from her bag and booted it up. A few minutes later, his eyes scanned through the notes on her screen. "This one says, 'you've messed with the wrong family.' That sounds like a direct link to the Wades to me."

She nodded. "Yeah, but it could just be someone in the gang who supports them. Although I realize that's also a problem."

Cooper took his time and read the remaining letters. One of them specifically said they were coming after her. It included some foul and slang language that seemed like it could also be gang-oriented. The other notes included vague threats of physical violence. "Thanks for letting me see these. I think your father is right to be concerned."

"Hopefully it's nothing."

He needed to understand her change in jobs better in order to gauge the threat of the letters. "Can you explain more about your shifting roles to me?"

"I used to be an ADA in the general trial division, handling everything from assaults to murders to drug cases. A few months ago, I was promoted to senior ADA and moved into the White Collar Crime Unit. I know these letters seem troubling to someone on the outside, but threats come with the territory, and I understood that risk when I took the job."

"Your job as a prosecutor is a lot different than being a star witness."

She raised an eyebrow. "Who said anything about being a *star* witness?"

That was exactly what she was going to be. "Just look at the headlines."

36

She blew out a breath. "What are you suggesting?"

"For now, just let me keep an eye on you. I'll try to stay out of your way, but I'll be around. Not intrusive, but around. I used to be an Atlanta police officer. I know how these gangs work. Let me use that knowledge to help you, so you can keep your attention on your job."

She considered him for a moment. "All right. But if at any time I think this has gotten out of control, I'm going to call you off. I'll deal with my father if that happens, so don't worry about that."

"Like I said, I'll do my best to just let you do your thing. In fact, just so we're starting on an open and honest playing field, I need to tell you something."

"What?"

He wasn't the type to hide the ball, and if this was going to work, he needed to tell her the truth. "I've actually had my eye on you since before the preliminary hearing. I was there in the back, on the opposite side of where you were sitting."

"What? What are you talking about?"

"That's when your father first contacted me and asked me to start this job. But once you received the letters, he wanted me to work more closely with you."

"You've been watching me?" Sophie's voice cracked.

"Yes, just keeping an eye on you."

Her ivory skin turned pale. "Am I that oblivious? I had no idea. No inkling I was being watched."

"I'm a professional. I know how to operate in the shadows when needed."

She held so tightly onto her coffee cup that her knuckles turned white. "I'm still disturbed that I was so clueless."

"A reminder to be more aware, but seriously, if you had spotted me, I would've questioned if I was getting rusty."

"Why did you leave the police force?" she asked.

"I've always wanted to run my own business. My partner,

37

Noah, started talking one day about the idea, and we decided to leave our government careers and give it a try. I haven't regretted it for a moment. I can still help people and companies, but I also get to experience the entrepreneurial angle, which I enjoy."

"What all does your company do?" She seemed more relaxed now that they were on this topic.

"Personal security services like what we're talking about right now. That's my specialty, among other things. Noah is a whiz at all the electronics and forensics. He works with a lot of companies on their security systems, both physical and digital. And Landon came aboard to run our private investigations wing."

"I thought Kate said something about him working with you guys, but I wasn't sure of the details. She's so busy with all the wedding planning, I haven't had time to spend with her. Plus, I've been acclimating to my new position."

"Do you and Kate go way back?"

"We met years ago through the Atlanta Women Attorneys group. When we started working on the same committee, we really clicked. She's a few years older than me, but we have a lot in common because we both represent victims—her on the plaintiff's lawyer side, and me as a prosecutor. She and I became fast friends, and I introduced her to Mia Shaw. Mia and I went to law school at Emory together. The three of us have been a tight-knit group ever since."

"Tell me more about what you do now." He was using this opportunity to gather as many facts about her and what she did as possible. All of that would help him do his job.

"I work in the White Collar Crime Unit, which is basically a fancy way of saying that I deal with economic crimes—embezzlement, fraud, racketeering. But all in the criminal context, because there can also be civil versions of those things. I just secured a guilty verdict against the CEO of Banton Corporation. That was my first major trial in the division."

"Congratulations." This woman was a force to be reckoned

with. She didn't look like your typical trial attorney, but behind her beauty was some serious brainpower. He had to remind himself that she was off-limits for a million different reasons. "Do you like it compared to your old job?"

"I do. It's a different type of challenge, and one thing that's nice is that I get to devote a lot more time to each case as opposed to being on a wild carousel ride of case after case in court. But I wouldn't trade those seven years as an ADA, because I learned how to be a trial lawyer. Now I can use those skills and hopefully take it to the next level."

Sophie stood up to get more coffee, and he was reminded of how tall she was. Probably only a few inches shorter than him.

"What are the next steps?" she asked.

"I'll need your schedule. Basically, I need to know where you plan to be at all times."

"Overkill?" She arched an eyebrow.

"Maybe at this point, but I didn't say I'd be by your side at all times. Just that I need the information. And I'd like to make sure you get home all right each night."

She groaned. "We need to be discreet. I've worked for years to overcome the blond, rich girl stereotype and show that I'm a top-notch prosecutor. I don't want my colleagues to see me as weak."

"Sophie, I don't see a single thing about you that's weak. From what I understand, when the shots started being fired, you ran into danger, not away from it."

"I was acting on instinct. And in the end, I still didn't save either of their lives. I run it through my mind over and over and wonder if I could've somehow stopped him. Done something more."

"You can't second-guess yourself. He was intent on doing harm. And right now, my approach with you is just being cautious. But because I want to put everything on the table upfront, if there comes a time when things do get more dangerous, then you need to be prepared for a change in course."

"You sound like Patrick."

"Patrick Hunt. That's the lawyer prosecuting this case, right?"

"That's him. You really think me being a witness is going to put a different type of target on my back?"

Cooper paused for a second, wondering if he should sugarcoat it or not. But that wasn't his style. "I do. I can't begin to tell you some of the things I experienced with this gang when I was with APD. And I'm sure you've seen enough gang violence as a prosecutor."

She bit her bottom lip. "I guess you're right. But can we just take it one step at a time? Let's not get ahead of ourselves, coming up with dangerous scenarios that don't even exist."

"I get it. In the meantime, though, if you can hook me up with your schedule, that will allow me to start planning."

"Of course. Give me your email, and I'll send it to you."

He pulled out his business card and slid it over to her. "I understand from your father that you have a top-of-the-line security system here, but I'd love to take a look at it before I leave."

This assignment wasn't going to be easy.

Ashley Murphy said a few choice words as her heel got stuck in the sidewalk in front of her law office. She'd opened her own firm a few years ago after practicing at Peters & Gomez for five years. She'd gotten plenty of civil defense experience there, but her real passion was criminal defense. High-profile criminal defense.

No one understood why she took the cases she did, but the adrenaline rush itself was worth it. Not to mention that she only represented those who could afford her incredibly hefty fees. She liked to keep up that reputation, but at the end of the day, the money wasn't her only driver. She thrived on the challenge of taking the most difficult cases. It was what pushed her to get up every day.

She wasn't naïve and knew that the gangs and other criminals she worked for could turn on her at any point. But that was a risk she was more than willing to take. You only lived once, and she intended to make the most out of life.

As she pushed open the door to her office, she called out to her secretary. "Lane, any calls for me?"

"Yes, Juan Wade called. He said it was important."

Ashley looked at her secretary. Lane had a lot of backbone to be able to deal with her. She knew she wasn't an easy person to work for. "Why didn't he call my cell if it was important?"

Lane shrugged. "No idea. I told him I was expecting you in the office before lunch. He said that was fine. I got the impression he might be showing up here for a visit. You know how he is."

"Yes, I do." Ashley had worked with Juan on a variety of cases over the past two years, and he had a tendency to pop up unannounced. "If he comes in, let me know. I'll be in my office, trying to dig out of emails."

Ashley didn't bother waiting for Lane to respond. They had a less-is-more relationship, and so far it had worked. They'd been together for three years, and Ashley paid Lane very well. Having a loyal and competent secretary was worth every penny.

This Wade case was the biggest thorn in her side at the moment. She absolutely hated cutting deals and had a strong reputation for taking cases to trial and winning. But she'd never had a prosecutor as a witness before. It threw a unique and riveting factor into the equation.

She hadn't ruled out the possibility that she could break Sophie on the stand, but the problem was that given Sophie's job, she would have built-in credibility with the jury. This wasn't some vagrant off the street. Sophie was an Atlanta prosecutor. But Ashley had already thought a lot about it and planned to use the fact that Sophie was a prosecutor against her. Ashley intended to show the jury that Sophie was going after Ricky because of his connection to Juan, and that this was a purely opportunistic move on the state's part.

It didn't matter that her client was guilty—the majority of her clients were. That was why she was paid the big bucks. If there weren't people like her around, then the justice system would completely fail.

Ashley had only made it through about a third of her emails before her intercom buzzed.

"Mr. Wade is here," Lane said.

"Bring him to my office." Juan was not the type to wait on anyone.

Ashley noted where she was in her long list of emails and then turned her attention to Juan, who was standing in her doorway. She stood to greet him.

"Ashley," he said. He walked over to her and took her hand.

Juan didn't look like a stereotypical gang leader. He carried himself like a corporate executive. His thick dark hair was neatly styled, and his big brown eyes that matched his little brother's met her own. At almost thirty years old, he controlled one of the most dangerous gangs in Atlanta. And from what she could tell, it was a thriving criminal enterprise that went far beyond street crimes.

"Please have a seat, Juan." She sat back down behind her desk.

"We need to talk about Ricky."

"I figured that's what you wanted."

"I can't let my baby brother go to prison for the rest of his life. Do you understand that? He'll have a target on his back. Rival gang members will kill him!"

"Let's take this one step at a time. The judge ordered that he be kept out of the general population. Everyone in the prison knows who Ricky is. They don't want something bad going down on their watch with all the media attention this case has gotten. So for now, Ricky should be safe."

"That doesn't solve my long-term problem."

"What did you have in mind?" She knew Juan walked on the dark side. The question was how far she would go with him.

"No, the question is what do *you* have in mind? I pay you to make these things go away. And this time it's personal. There's no room to screw this up. How in the world is a prosecutor the witness? How did you let this happen?"

The normally cool Juan was letting his emotions surface. It wasn't something she was used to seeing from him.

"Juan, you're smarter than that. You know I have no control over the fact that Sophie Dawson was at the Quick-Stop that night. It was just bad luck. But we'll work through it."

"Bad luck?" Juan slammed his fist on her desk, causing her to flinch as he let out a string of curses. She was used to dealing with dangerous men, but this particular man frightened her more than most. On the outside he seemed suave and put together, but she knew that behind those good looks was a cold-blooded killer. He probably wouldn't think twice before putting a bullet through her brain.

"You do what you have to do," Juan told her. "Whatever legal machinations you have. Pull a rabbit out of a hat for all I care. I'm giving you an opportunity to handle this your way first. But if your way doesn't work, then I'll take matters into my own hands. Are we clear?"

"Crystal," she said. His way probably involved more bloodshed.

"What do you know about this Dawson woman?" Juan asked.

"She's known as being a straight shooter."

"I took it upon myself to make sure she had some special fan mail. Just trying to get inside her head. Remind her what family she's up against."

Ashley let out a sigh but knew better than to pick that fight as a battle. Letters weren't going to hurt anyone. There would be more battles to come.

"What else do you know about her?" Juan asked.

"Comes from money. Real money. Word is that she doesn't even need to work. She's a prosecutor because she enjoys being a crime fighter and a goody-goody."

Juan groaned. "I'm liking her less and less. She has no idea what it's like to live in my world." He paused. "And you don't either."

"I don't pretend like I do. I know my place and my job. I'm very good at what I do, but having her as an eyewitness is going to make this trial more challenging. Given the stakes, is there any room in your mind to strike a deal?"

"Would the deal include prison time for Ricky?"

"Yes, there's no way around that. It's a double homicide." It occurred to her just how blind Juan was when it came to his little brother.

"Then no. We're gonna win this thing, or like I said, I'll go down other paths."

"Well, whatever paths you're thinking about, don't you dare tell me. Attorney-client privilege doesn't protect future crimes. You got that?" She was looking out for her own hide as much as his. She'd taken off her rose-colored glasses a long time ago.

"Yes. But I'm paying you good money to make this go away."

"Understood. I do have a question."

"Shoot."

"What was Ricky thinking?"

Juan blew out a breath. "He wasn't thinking. Ricky's not supposed to be in the business. *At all.* I have other plans for him, like college. That's what my mama would've wanted. She trusted me with him before she got sick and passed." He took a moment.

Ashley realized that Juan might actually have a semblance of a soft spot where his family was concerned. Although that only made him more dangerous, given the circumstances.

"But some members of a rival gang talked Ricky into it.

Tried to make him feel like he had to prove himself. Taunted him for being my baby brother. Believe me, I'm dealing with them separately. Ricky should've never taken the bait. I thought I'd taught him better than that. I do what I do to make a better life for him and my family."

She needed to make one thing clear for his own good. And for Ricky's. "No more bodies, Juan. Not right now. The microscope is too focused on you. The last thing you need is to start a gang war."

He gave a tentative nod, but she didn't believe her words would deter him for a moment.

"I'm serious, Juan. I'm trying to look out for your best interests here. Don't make the problems worse than they already are. Give me some time to do my work. You'll have plenty of time to get revenge later. Let's focus on Ricky first. All right?"

Juan stood up. "You can't fail me on this one, Ashley."

"I know," she said.

But as he walked out of her office, fear shot through her. How in the world was she going to get an acquittal on this case?

CHAPTER
FIVE

Sophie sat in the courtroom at her counsel's table, waiting to start a status conference on the Glen Shelton fraud case. The other side had requested the conference, and she had only gotten notice of it a few days ago.

"Hello, Sophie."

Sophie looked up, and her stomach dropped. This was the last thing she needed. Leland Kingsley.

"Leland, what're you doing here?"

He gave her a wide grin. "I'm taking over Shelton's defense. He deserves the best."

She held back what she really wanted to say. "I see he can *afford* the best."

Leland cocked his head. "No need to get testy, Sophie. I thought you were always up for a challenge. You were number one in our class, after all, but I was number two. And arguably should've beaten you, if you hadn't become Professor Grimes's teacher's pet and scored that A+ in legal ethics."

She'd earned that grade fair and square. Her law school classmate was known as "the gunner" for being hypercompetitive, and he had made quite the name for himself on the defense bar.

"You need to let that go, Leland. That's ancient history. This case is quite clear," she said flatly. "Your client stole from his clients. Case closed."

Leland patted her on her shoulder like she was a puppy. "Maybe when you were dealing with that half-wit lawyer Shelton had before, you thought this would be a cake walk. But there's a new sheriff in town, and that's why I wanted to have this status conference. I want to get everything calendared and give you and the court notice that I will be filing a series of motions."

"For what?"

"For starters, a motion to change venue." His hazel eyes locked on to hers.

She rolled her eyes. "You're really going to waste our time with that? I know you represent some high-profile clients, but this guy isn't exactly at the top of your list. You won't be able to prove the requisite bias to get this case moved out of Fulton County."

"That's your opinion, and I obviously hold a different one. This is just the beginning, Sophie. Unless you want to save us all a lot of time and effort and give us a reasonable plea offer that I can take back to my client. The operative word being *reasonable*. I don't want to hear any outlandish offers."

Leland had some nerve. "That's not going to happen, so we should get on with it." She would have to convince her boss not to plea bargain, but there was no way she was showing any sign of weakness in front of Leland.

"Then let the games begin." Leland strode confidently over to his table.

Later that afternoon, Sophie pored over the Shelton files, more determined than ever to take him down. The conference had largely been ministerial and uneventful, but it showed her one thing: Shelton was ready to fight hard. Leland wasn't messing around. He was seeking an aggressive schedule and a speedy trial.

Shelton had been arrested but had immediately made bail. He wasn't working, though, because he'd been fired by SIB. Even the hint of impropriety was enough to cause him to lose his job.

She looked at her watch and saw that Keith would arrive at any moment. He was the one who had assigned her to this file. In the back of her head, there were always questions about why Keith had chosen to move her over to White Collar. She worried that he thought she wasn't tough enough to be a senior ADA in the general trial division. That the crimes were too heinous for her to handle. She had a reputation for getting emotionally involved in her cases, but that was the only way she knew how to operate. She'd always been a very empathetic person. Dissociation wasn't in her vocabulary.

She wanted to prove Keith wrong by doing a first-rate job in this new position to show that she could thrive in any unit doing any type of work. And that was exactly what she planned to do.

Keith rapped his knuckles on the doorframe to her office. "Sophie, you wanted to talk?" He shut the door behind him and took a seat.

"Yes. We had a status conference this morning on the Shelton case. He has a new lawyer."

"Who?"

"Leland Kingsley."

Keith groaned. "That guy is one of my least favorite members of the defense bar. What a piece of work."

"Believe me, I know. He was in my section in law school, and I had enough of him to last a lifetime. He's committed to putting on a vigorous defense, but that only makes me want to push harder to take this to trial. Hiring Leland shows me that where there's smoke, there's fire."

"You want to push forward?" Keith loosened his navy checkered tie.

"Absolutely. The evidence against Shelton is compelling. He was cheating a whole group of people—small business owners, entrepreneurs, and individuals. These people trusted him, and he took their money. I think proving theft by conversion and fraud won't be that hard. This wasn't just a side scheme. This was big. And the victims are real people with real life struggles. A jury will be very sympathetic to that. This could be a huge win for us."

He placed his elbows on her desk. "What's your position on SIB going to be? Will you try to bring them into this as a codefendant?"

She shook her head. "At this point I don't know how that would help things. I think Shelton was off on his own, running his illegal scheme. I have no doubt he used SIB resources to further his plans, but I haven't seen any evidence yet in the investigation file that would lead me to believe he had buy-in or support from anyone at the company. Why, do you know something I don't know?"

"No, no. It's just that you can imagine that we have to tread carefully when it comes to a company like SIB. They're one of the cornerstones of the Atlanta community. It doesn't help anyone to sully their reputation."

Ah, Keith. Always thinking about the political issues. That was why he was *the* district attorney, and she was just a run-of-the-mill prosecutor.

"Don't you think a company like SIB would want to support the prosecution and make an example of this guy?" she asked. "Show that they fully cooperated with the prosecution and won't stand for these types of rogue and illegal acts by their employees? They could actually come out of it looking good if they fully disavow his actions and do everything they can to help us."

Keith drummed his fingers on her desk. "Good way to spin it. But if this goes to trial, it's bound to have a negative impact on the company because there will be tons of publicity. People will start to question whether their money and investments are safe with SIB. I'm not saying no to you taking this all the way to trial, but I want to make sure you are completely buttoned-up. SIB thrives on the fact that it's still a local bank. If people get nervous, they may pull their money and go to one of the big national banks. That doesn't help our community at all. The last thing we want is for this to come back and bite us."

What Keith really meant was come back and bite *him*. His political career could be directly impacted. Sophie chose her words carefully because she was treading on delicate matters. "I should let you know that Leland said he will be filing a series of motions, including one for a change of venue."

Keith raised an eyebrow. "He doesn't have strong enough grounds to get this one moved."

"That's exactly what I said. My recommendation is that we can't just let this scumbag go unpunished." She tried to control the emotion bubbling up inside her. The main reason she was a prosecutor was to stop guys like this. He wasn't a murderer or drug trafficker, but he had harmed a multitude of innocent people who had put their trust in him.

"I hear you, Sophie. And I'm not saying that we turn away from this. I just want us to be very careful and methodical in our approach. I'd like to read in the CEO of SIB as soon as possible."

"You know Whitney Bowman?" As she asked, she realized she shouldn't be surprised. People like Keith and Whitney all ran in the same powerful circles in the city. Circles that she could easily run in herself, given her family connections and wealth, but she specifically chose not to.

"Yes. I'll set up a meeting with the three of us. You can talk to her about what you would need from SIB if things go forward. How does that sound? Then we'll go from there."

Sophie didn't have much choice but to say yes. Her boss could put the brakes on anything she was working on, so it would be to her advantage to get him, and hopefully the CEO, on board with her strategy. "Just remember, this isn't about the company. It's about one bad apple."

Keith smiled. "Stop while you're ahead, Sophie." He paused. "One more thing. Given the Wade case and everything going on, I'm assigning Monica Lacey to help you out on your cases and to be your mentee."

"The new girl?" Monica had only been at the prosecutor's office for about six months.

"Yes. It'll be a great opportunity for her to work with you, and you can use the help. Feel free to put her through the paces. I want her to realize what it's really going to be like to work for the Fulton County DA's office. It will also be a good résumé builder for you. Mentoring is important around here."

"Thanks. I'll set up a meeting with her and get her up to speed." Other people had helped Sophie out and shown her the ropes when she had started, so it made sense that she'd return the favor. And it would be good to have someone to help her out with the grunt work.

Keith stood up. "Anything going on in the Wade case I need to know about?"

"It's proceeding as normal. I'm waiting on the scheduling order for the dates, and I'm fully cooperating with Patrick and law enforcement."

"Good. If anything changes or you need something, don't hesitate to ask. I realize you're in a very awkward position, and I need you to be safe and able to work. I know you didn't ask for this, but you have to bear the burden. The office fully supports you."

She nodded. "Thank you."

Keith left, and she decided to go ahead and talk to Monica. She'd spoken with Monica a couple of times, but they hadn't worked together yet. She pulled the directory out of her drawer, found Monica's number, and asked her to come down and chat.

Monica arrived a few minutes later. The young attorney was short and slender, with black hair, big brown eyes, and a bright smile.

"When Keith told me I'd be assisting you, I can't tell you how thrilled I was," Monica said a little breathlessly. "I want you to know that I'm willing to do whatever you need. No matter how small the task. Just say the word." She gushed for a few more minutes, and Sophie thought it best for her to get it out of her system.

"Monica, you've only been here a short time, but you probably realize that this office runs at a very fast pace, and you have to roll with the punches and expect the unexpected. Though it is a little different in White Collar, because our cases are more complex and long running."

"That's one of the reasons I'm so excited to work with you. I'm completely fascinated by economic crimes." Monica's eyes widened as she spoke.

Sophie had to appreciate her pure exuberance. Monica reminded her a lot of herself when she started at the DA's office, hoping to save the world and put the bad guys away. It was refreshing to work with someone who wasn't jaded. Monica hadn't experienced all the ups and downs of working there yet.

"I want to get you up to speed on my top priority case right now. It's the Shelton investigation." Sophie spent almost half an hour telling Monica everything she knew while Monica took copious notes. Monica also asked highly intelligent questions, which made Sophie think the younger woman really had potential. It was actually going to be fun mentoring her.

"What would you like me to do?" Monica asked.

"As a first step, familiarize yourself with the entire file. It's voluminous, but I think it's necessary for you to read it all.

We're going to get additional documents from SIB, but we don't have those yet. We do have a chunk of Shelton's documents."

"And you really want to nail this guy, right?"

"That's the plan. But as you'll quickly find out, sometimes it's not that cut-and-dried."

Monica gathered up her notes. "I'll get right on it."

"Is there anything else I can help you with? I know sometimes adjusting to the office and all the different personalities can be a challenge." Sophie considered her words carefully for a moment, but she felt like she had to say something. "I think most people in the office are great, but watch yourself around Harrison."

"Harrison Westgate?"

"Yes. He's gunning for Keith's job, and he will do anything and everything to get it. Also, he has a bit of a bad reputation among the women lawyers for being a scumbag. I just want you to be aware of that."

Monica took a breath. "Thank you for telling me. I'll keep my eyes open."

"Good. Let me know if you need anything at all."

Sophie watched as Monica left. It felt good to be able to help another young female attorney. And having assistance on the Shelton case would be great. Now she just had to convince Keith to let her take the case forward to trial.

She settled down and reviewed some emails until her phone rang. "This is Sophie Dawson."

There was no response.

"Hello?"

Sounds of heavy breathing filled her ear.

"Is anyone there?"

The breathing continued. She hung up, hoping it was just a wrong number. But the hair on her arms stood up.

The phone rang again. She hesitated and let it ring a few times before picking up again. "Sophie Dawson."

The heavy breathing noises continued.

"I'm hanging up now unless you start talking." She kept her voice steady.

"Watch your back," a deep male voice said.

"Who is this?"

Her only answer was a dial tone.

Cooper decided to do another late-night drive through Sophie's neighborhood, just for his own peace of mind. She'd received a few more letters that he was convinced came from the Wade organization. He'd started doing these random checks at night, and so far, everything had been clear.

He hadn't told her he was doing it because he didn't want to bother her, and he'd promised he would try not to be intrusive. He also didn't want to make her more worried than she needed to be. That was his territory.

As he pulled up closer to her house, he thought he saw something by her side window. A figure.

Immediately, he put his SUV in park and hopped out. He jogged down to her house and scanned the area as his eyes adjusted to the darkness. Sophie's split-level home was set back on a nice-sized lot with a fenced backyard. She had good outside lighting, but there were some dark spots that weren't covered.

Movement caught his eye. A man was lurking in between Sophie's house and her neighbor's. He couldn't be up to anything good at this hour.

Cooper checked his sidearm, which he was fully licensed to carry. He didn't intend to use it, but being a cop had taught him to be prepared for anything.

He walked over toward the man, who was now kneeling on the ground, messing with his shoelaces. "What're you doing?" Cooper asked.

The man jumped up, startled. "Nothing. Just out taking a walk."

"In between these two houses?" No one would believe that.

"Just cutting through to get to the other side of the neighborhood. I don't want any trouble."

Cooper's gut told him this man was up to no good. Was he a peeping tom? The thought sickened him. It was dark, and Cooper couldn't make out much of the man's facial features, but he did seem a bit older than Cooper.

Cooper took a step forward. "I think it's time for you to go."

"And who are you?"

Cooper was quickly losing his patience. The man's combative response only strengthened his resolve. "Don't make me ask you again."

The man stepped forward and took a swing, but Cooper was faster. He blocked the contact, then hauled off and punched the guy in the face, connecting with his jaw.

The man reached into his jacket. Cooper feared he was going for a gun, and he started to go for his.

Before Cooper could get his weapon raised, the man grabbed him and shoved something hard into his ribs. An all-too-familiar sensation exploded through Cooper's body. He'd just been tasered.

The pain knocked him to his knees. As blackness crept into the edges of his vision, he heard the man sprint off into the night.

CHAPTER
SIX

Sophie was sitting at her kitchen table, responding to Leland's latest discovery requests on her laptop. There was no doubt in her mind that he was going to try to make her life miserable to push her into offering a plea.

When the doorbell rang after eleven that evening, she knew something was wrong. She ran to the door and checked the peephole. Cooper stood on the other side.

"What's wrong?" she asked as she ushered him inside.

"Can I have some water?" His face was noticeably red.

"Yes." She ran back to the kitchen and grabbed a bottle of cold water out of the fridge. She found Cooper sitting on the couch in her living room.

"What happened?" She handed him the water.

"I found a guy lurking around outside your house."

She gasped. "Where is he?"

"He ran off after he tasered me."

"Are you okay? Do we need to call the paramedics? Should I take you to the hospital?" She heard the words gushing out.

"No. He didn't have the setting up all the way. The pain will pass." Cooper shook out his hand. "I also landed a good punch before he got me."

"Let me get you some ice for your hand."

She returned a few minutes later with an ice bag.

"Thanks," he said.

"Do you think it was someone from Wade's gang?" she asked.

"It's possible but seems off. I didn't get a great look at the guy, but he seemed older than me. Also, I think it's odd that someone working for the gang would use a Taser. They usually go directly for the guns—or at least a knife. Is there anything you're working on that could have someone interested in you?"

Her mind immediately went to the Shelton case. But would Shelton send a man to her house? "There's something I need to tell you. I got a weird call at work." She recounted the strange phone call.

"That's disturbing. I assume you didn't recognize the voice?"

"No. Just a deep, male voice. I have no idea if the call was connected to Wade or if it's related to something else I'm working on. You're familiar with SIB?"

"Yeah, they're a big Atlanta bank, right? One of the last locals that tries to compete with the big boys."

"Exactly. One of their employees was arrested a couple weeks ago. A senior manager named Glen Shelton. He's out on bail, and I'm in charge of determining whether we're going to pursue a full prosecution or strike some kind of plea deal."

"What are the charges against Shelton?"

"Fraud and theft, as starters. This is all in the public record, so I can talk about it. He was charging his clients extra fees and pocketing that money for himself. He had a solid scheme set up until one of his customers started asking questions when they figured out the irregularities in their account and their statements. When the customer didn't get sufficient answers from Shelton, they went to the local news, and that's how we found out about it at my office."

"What kind of fees are we talking about here?"

"A range of one to three percent for each transaction. For

people trying to run a small business, that type of theft can have a huge impact over time."

"He sounds guilty. So what's the rub?"

Sophie looked away.

"Whatever you say stays between us. I signed a confidentiality agreement."

"It's a delicate situation."

"I'm familiar with those." He paused. "I know the circumstances we're under are strange, to say the least, but having open communication is the best way to make this work. Trust is built over time, and I hope I can build that trust with you."

Sophie decided he was right. She needed to trust him. "Turns out my boss is friends with the CEO."

"You think there's some kind of inside deal between your boss and the CEO to keep the Shelton case from going to trial?"

She shrugged. "I don't know that I'd go that far, but it's a lingering thought in the back of my head. I attended a status conference today on the case. Shelton hired a hotshot defense attorney and fired his former one. His new attorney vowed to make it a tough fight. But still, do you think they'd hire someone to try to scare me off? Keep me distracted?"

"The most likely scenario is that this was a hired hand for Wade. But I don't think we can completely rule out the possibility that this man was connected to Shelton or even SIB in some way."

"I can't believe this. I feel like there are threats coming from all angles."

"That's why I'm going to stick close. If anything, tonight showed me that you have to be careful. And I can't let my guard down."

The next afternoon, Tad Grisham dialed Whitney Bowman's cell and waited for the CEO to answer. Thanks to a stellar referral, he'd recently been retained by the leader of SIB to do some investigative work. His PI business was doing well, and this assignment was going to be interesting for a number of reasons.

When he'd gotten the call confirming the job earlier in the week, he'd immediately jumped on it and had already started his work. He rubbed his jaw. He needed to remember to put more ice on it to stop the swelling.

"Tad," Whitney answered. "How's it going so far?"

"Ms. Bowman."

"Please call me Whitney."

It seemed odd to call her by her first name, but he would try. "I wanted to touch base."

"Did you get my retainer check? My assistant assured me that it got messaged over to your office."

"Yes, I did get the check, and thank you for that."

"Then what's on your mind?" she asked.

"I attended a status conference in front of the judge yesterday. I got to see Sophie Dawson in action."

"And what was your impression?"

"Well, this type of hearing isn't that substantive, but she had a commanding presence in the courtroom even when she was talking about dates and motions and lawyer stuff."

"How focused did she seem?"

"Very. She made the statement a couple of times in front of the judge that she intended to push this to trial. She wasn't pulling punches at all. Shelton's lawyer took a few verbal jabs at her, but she struck back just as hard. If you were thinking that she would be easily manipulated in the courtroom, then you'll need a new game plan."

"I was hoping we'd be able to handle this discreetly through our contacts in the prosecutor's office and get a plea deal. I'm still going to focus on that effort on my side of things."

He needed to get down to the bottom line. "What about

me? Is my direction still the same for now? Just recon and intel gathering?"

Whitney didn't immediately respond. "Tad, I hired you because I was told that you could handle anything and that you had the utmost discretion and judgment. What I need you to do is start making judgment calls. I can't have Sophie taking this case against Shelton to trial. Whatever you can do on your end while I'm working more diplomatic channels, please do it."

"Don't worry, Whitney. You've hired the right man for the job."

Sophie checked her cell. If she didn't leave now, she was going to be late for lunch with the girls. Their schedules had all been so crazy lately, especially with Kate deep in wedding planning, that they hadn't seen each other as much as she would like.

Sophie grabbed her purse and rushed out of the building. Looking over her shoulder, she half expected to see Cooper. But there was no one. At least no one she could see.

He'd made it clear that he was going to operate in the shadows, and she knew for a fact that he had her full schedule, including that she was going out to lunch today. It did provide her with some comfort to know that he was watching her back, especially after the incident at her house.

One thing she knew for sure: at the end of the day, if Juan Wade wanted her taken out, he had his ways. Would he take such drastic action, given the high-profile nature of the case? She hoped the answer was no. The media scrutiny surrounding the case was intense.

All she could do for now was go about her business and rely on Cooper to do his job. But given the unique circumstances, she had to be cognizant of the possible risks. As she started her car, she replayed in her mind the words in the notes she'd received. And then there were the strange phone calls and the creepy lurker.

Whether they were linked to Wade or something else, the bottom line was that she had to testify against Juan's baby brother. That wasn't something she could brush aside. But thanks to her father, she had Cooper on the lookout, so she didn't have to be stressed out about it.

Her mood instantly shifted when she walked into the restaurant and saw the smiling faces of her two best friends—Kate Sullivan and Mia Shaw. She quickly walked over to the table and greeted both women with big hugs.

"Sorry I'm late."

"We're so glad you made it. You have your hands full right now." Kate's hazel eyes zeroed in on her. "We went ahead and placed your usual order."

"Thanks. You know me too well." While her two friends always got salads, she opted for a turkey burger and fries. Her friends had long stopped hassling her about her atrocious eating habits.

"What's going on with this case I saw on the news?" Mia asked. "You were super vague in your texts."

She had purposely not given out many details. Especially via text messages, because those could be discovered in the lawsuit. "I'm in a weird position, since I'm not the lawyer but a witness. I really can't talk about the case to anyone, because Ashley could ask me about those discussions on the witness stand."

"That woman is infuriating." Mia twisted her long dark hair up into a bun. "I haven't even dealt with her on a case, but we work on the same AWA subcommittee, and it's always her way or nothing. She doesn't understand the meaning of teamwork or cooperation. I have to bite my tongue constantly around her. I've given up trying to fight her. It's just easier to let her have her way."

All three of them were very active in many of Atlanta Women Attorneys' programs.

"I've been up against her in court numerous times," Sophie said, "but having her questioning me was unsettling. Getting on the witness stand was surreal. It didn't get too far, because I think she wanted to do her homework before creating a record that she might regret later. It was a bit of a circus for a few minutes, though."

Kate looked at her. "I'm worried about you. From what I've heard, this gang is no joke."

"Well, since you brought that up, you'll find this very interesting. My father hired Cooper Knight to keep an eye on me."

"As in Landon's partner Cooper?" Kate asked.

"Exactly. I guess Landon didn't say anything to you?"

Kate shook her head. "No, but they are careful to keep their cases confidential. Landon doesn't share many details about his work, and I don't ask."

"What is Cooper doing?" Mia asked.

"Right now, I don't see him but he's around. Especially making sure I get to and from work okay. He has my schedule mapped out."

"Have any specific threats been made against you?" Kate asked.

"Some threatening letters and other random things. My dad worries, and if it makes him feel better, I'm willing to have Cooper follow me around. You know how much Dad means to me."

"Cooper is a solid guy," Kate said. "You'll be in good hands with him." She paused. "And it doesn't hurt that he's super cute either."

Sophie sighed. "He is, and the thing is that so far he meets all the items on my checklist. But I'm sure there's something wrong with him that I haven't found out yet."

"There's no such thing as the perfect guy," Mia said. "You want a knight in shining armor along with the happily ever after. You want a smoking hot, muscle-bound, romantic, off-the-charts smart guy with a great sense of humor and a steady job he loves who's ready to settle down like, right now, and start a family . . . and oh, let's not forget he has to share your faith. Did that about cover it?"

"I don't see you in a serious relationship," Sophie shot back.

Mia raised an eyebrow. "I'm not ready. But you are, Soph. All kidding aside, we all know how much having a family means to you. If you hold out for perfection, that will never happen."

Mia was right about Sophie wanting a family. Since she'd never known her mother, being a mom herself had always seemed very important. Like she could somehow make up for a tiny piece of that loss by having a family of her own. And to be able to have a family, she needed a husband.

"I do want a family, but the man has to be the right one, or it's all for nothing. I refuse to settle."

"Not to pile on, but we all have our flaws," Kate said.

"I know I have plenty of flaws, but I believe there is someone right for me. Who shares my values, who can make me laugh. Who can understand my passion for my work. And of course, being super handsome doesn't hurt."

Her friends laughed.

"All the guys I've dated before seem to have some sort of fatal flaw. Some deal breaker I can't get past. I'm not being unreasonable."

"We're not saying you're being unreasonable," Kate said. "Just that you have to give people a chance. You discount people right from the start without getting to know them fully."

"It also doesn't help that you start every date by baring your soul," Mia said. "Guys are easily scared off. You can't hit them with that stuff on a first date—talk of marriage and kids is too much before you even get past the first appetizer together. Makes them want to run for the hills."

"But I'd rather they know up front what my expectations are." She didn't have the time or energy to waste.

"Just keep your eyes open," Kate said. "I certainly wasn't looking or expecting anything when I met Landon, and look what happened." She lifted her left hand to show off her beautiful engagement ring. The diamond sparkled almost as much as her smile.

Sophie wasn't sure she was going to have a happy ending like Kate. As she listened to her friends continuing their conversation, she could only pray that she'd find the right person. But she thought it unlikely that Cooper Knight would be *the one*. Especially considering that right now he was on the clock. It wasn't exactly a romantic situation, and she wanted to be swept off her feet. Was that so wrong of her?

They finished up their lunch, and Sophie checked the time. She needed to head back to the office. She wanted to start preparing for the next SIB meeting. There couldn't be any room for error, or Keith would shut her down. The nagging question was why. Was this a purely political move by Keith, or something more?

A nice fall breeze blew her hair as she made her way to the car. It was still warm in Atlanta in October, but at least it wasn't blisteringly hot. She'd parked in a metered flat lot near the restaurant off Crescent Street. Hopefully she'd put in enough change not to get a ticket. She groaned when she saw that she was literally only five minutes over. The city of Atlanta parking meter attendants were out in force today.

"You've got to be kidding me," she said out loud. That was what she got for talking about her love life at lunch. She yanked the bright yellow ticket from under her windshield wiper and shoved it into her purse.

As she reached for the car door, a strong arm wrapped around her neck, pulling her backward. Immediately, she reacted. Thrashing, kicking, screaming.

The man picked her up off the ground and moved her around to the front of the car. He grabbed her hair and tried to slam her head down on the hood, but she was able to break the impact with her arms. He attempted a second time, and her arms gave way. Her forehead connected with the hood, and she screamed. Anger and rage bubbled up inside her, and she fought back even harder. She would not let this man bash her head in on her own car.

Then she heard a deep male voice yelling, and the next thing she knew, her attacker was gone.

She turned around. Cooper was running toward her, but she could no longer stand as a wave of dizziness swept over her.

She collapsed in a heap on the ground.

CHAPTER
SEVEN

Cooper knelt beside Sophie and pulled her into his arms. It had all happened so quickly. One moment everything was fine. Then out of nowhere, a guy popped out and was attacking her. Cooper had run as hard as he could to get to her, fortunately scaring off the attacker in the process. He'd decided it was more important to stay with her instead of pursuing the man.

He wished with every fiber of his being that he could have taken that guy on. Any man who would beat up a woman was the lowest form of scum. Watching the horror unfold before his eyes had taken him back to an awful place. It was like reliving his father beating up his mother.

"Sophie, can you hear me?"

She groaned in response. She looked up, and her blue eyes didn't seem to focus directly on him.

Dear Lord, let her be okay. He was worried she might have a concussion. "I know your head hurts. Do you feel pain anywhere else?"

"Mainly my head. And my arms a little."

"I need to get you to the ER."

"I hate hospitals."

"We all do, but you have to get checked out. I'm going to pick you up and put you in your car, okay? We'll use your car, since it's right here."

She made a small grunting noise that he accepted as a yes. He pulled her keys out of her purse and opened the passenger side door. Then he lifted her off the ground and helped her around the side of the car.

Once he had her safely in the passenger seat, he jogged around to the driver's side and jumped in. Thankfully, since they were in Midtown, the nearest hospital was only a few minutes away.

"Sophie, I'm so sorry," he said softly.

"It's not your fault," she replied.

He glanced over at her and then turned his attention back to the road. "It is. I should've been closer to you so I could've stopped him before he hurt you."

"You think Juan sent him?"

"Don't worry about anything right now. Let's get you some help first, and then we can figure out all the implications."

"Okay."

The fact that she didn't put up a fight told him how badly she must feel. He didn't say anything else to her the rest of the way to the hospital, and then he focused on getting her checked in.

Later, while Sophie was finishing up with the doctor, he texted Landon and Noah and let them know what had happened. Randall Dawson was going to be seriously ticked off at him for his mistake. Randall had hired him to keep Sophie safe, and he had failed. It occurred to him that Randall might even fire him, and given the gravity of the error, he couldn't blame him if that happened. But he felt personally invested now. There was something about the way Sophie had looked up at him with her innocent blue eyes. He was going to fight to stay on this case and redeem himself.

He'd given Sophie some privacy for the exam, but when the

doctor exited the room, Cooper wanted to hear the prognosis. "How is she?"

The petite, gray-haired doctor frowned deeply at him. She raised an eyebrow. "And you are?"

"A friend," he said. "How is she doing?"

"A very mild concussion. She needs to take it easy. Did you report what happened to her to the police?"

"Yes. I'm actually former Atlanta PD, so I know that's important. An officer is supposed to be here any minute to talk to her."

His words seemed to soften the doc up a bit. "She's going to have a black eye from the impact. I'm giving her a prescription for pain even though she said she didn't want it. Keep a very close eye on her over the next twelve hours. But I'm hopeful that she will be just fine."

"Understood. Thank you, doctor."

A couple hours later, Cooper was at Sophie's house, following the doctor's orders. Sophie had given her statement to the police, and once they realized who she was, they started making phone calls.

When her doorbell rang, he jumped up to get it. "Please stay put on the couch." He didn't want her getting the door for a variety of reasons.

She didn't argue with him as he went to the door and opened it. A man he recognized from the preliminary hearing stood on the other side.

"Is Sophie here?" he asked.

"Yes, she's inside. Come on in."

"I'm Patrick Hunt." Patrick offered his hand.

"And I'm Cooper Knight."

"Sophie's boyfriend?"

"No. I'm actually in private security."

Patrick quirked an eyebrow and followed Cooper into the living room.

"Sophie." Patrick's eyes widened when he saw her. He rushed to her side and sat down close to her.

Almost too close.

"This is even more serious than I was told," Patrick said. "Tell me what happened."

Sophie told him the story, and just hearing it again made Cooper sick.

"If Cooper hadn't been there, I'm not sure what would've happened to me," Sophie finished.

"I only wish I were a minute faster." He was having a serious guilt trip over that.

"We need to reevaluate your security situation," Patrick said. He looked at Cooper. "Exactly what is your current role?"

Before he could answer, Sophie spoke up. "My father hired Cooper to provide personal security. I was the one who insisted that he keep his distance, but I see that may not be practical now."

"Atlanta PD is always strapped for resources, but I don't want them completely in the dark here. Cooper, do you think you could work with them as needed?"

"I used to be one of them, so that isn't an issue."

"Oh," Patrick said. "That's good then. We'll work on trying to track down your attacker, Sophie, but I'm not optimistic. You know how these things go. The bigger picture is that we have to assume for the moment that he was sent by Juan Wade to rough you up as a message."

"Do they really think I wouldn't testify because of that?" she asked.

"It won't end here," Cooper said. "Which is why we'll have to redevelop our security plan."

"Agreed," Patrick said. "I have to admit that I feel so much better knowing that you're going to be around, Cooper. I can't have my star witness harmed, and resources are always an issue for us. As I'm sure you're familiar with."

"All too much." It was one of the reasons he loved having his own business. He could work more efficiently and had paying clients. Being in public service was often a thankless job, and you were always expected to do more with less.

"Sophie, I'm going to go and let you get some rest. But I'll be in touch."

"Thanks, Patrick."

Cooper walked Patrick to the door.

"Don't let her out of your sight," Patrick said.

"Don't worry. I'm on it."

Cooper locked the door and then went back to the living room. He could hear Sophie talking on the phone.

"He wants to talk to you." She handed him the phone. "It's my father. I'm sorry," she whispered.

His stomach sank. "Hello, Mr. Dawson."

"What in the world happened? I thought you were supposed to protect my daughter. That's what I'm paying you for. And now I hear she was attacked in broad daylight."

"I completely understand why you're upset. I'm upset with myself too. I was trying to give her the appropriate amount of space. I was able to intervene to stop the attack, but I wasn't able to prevent it completely, and for that I am truly sorry. I can promise you it will not happen again."

"Let me be clear. One more misstep from you, and you're fired. My daughter is irreplaceable."

He swallowed. "I won't let you down, sir."

"I'm counting on you. I'll check in later to make sure you've developed a game plan."

He heard the dial tone and knew he had been dismissed. He handed the phone back to Sophie.

"I'm sorry about my father," she said. "I told him you saved me today."

"There's no need for you to apologize. You should get some rest. Once you're feeling better, we'll discuss how we're going to move forward."

"Okay. Thank you again. I hate to think of what would've happened if I had been on my own."

That thought bothered him too. Because he wondered if she would even still be alive.

"Are you here to offer a deal?" Ashley asked.

Patrick took a deep breath and for a moment had second thoughts about going to Ashley's office and confronting her directly. But what had happened to Sophie was unacceptable on every level. He wanted to make sure Ashley understood exactly what the stakes were here.

"No, Ashley. I'm not here to talk about that. I have something else on my mind." He looked into her green eyes. She wore her brown hair down today and no glasses. She was a pretty woman, but that was all obscured by her personality and inner qualities, which he found completely unattractive.

She put down her pen. "Well, get on with it, then. I've got things to do."

"Sophie Dawson was attacked yesterday."

"Attacked? Is she all right?"

Either Ashley was a great actress, or she was in the dark. "She's going to be okay, but she was injured. And because I don't like to dance around the issue, I'll just be blunt and put it all on the table. I believe that Juan Wade was directly responsible for the attack, and I came here to tell you to get him to back off."

She laughed. "Do you seriously think I have that much control over Juan?"

He leaned forward in his seat. "This isn't funny. Sophie could've been seriously injured or even killed. I don't think you understand how serious this is. Do you want to be an accessory to this type of action?"

"You can't be suggesting that I'm aiding Juan in any of this. And let's back up for a minute. Do you have a shred of evidence that Juan is linked to what happened to Sophie? Atlanta isn't the safest of cities. Assaults happen all the time."

"You know I don't have direct evidence because Juan wouldn't actually get his hands dirty, but he has the resources to pay someone to do his bidding."

"In other words, you have nothing. You just came in here hurling accusations. I think you should leave." She rose from her seat.

He tried appealing to her very large ego. "Ashley, think about your career. You're better than this."

"Who do you think you are, trying to dictate what's best for me? I make more money in this job than you'll ever see, and I'm one of the most respected defense attorneys in the Southeast. One day that will be the whole nation. You don't get to that place by cooperating with prosecutors and selling out your clients. It's never going to happen, so you're wasting your time and energy."

"You've got this all wrong. I'm trying to help you. And warn you. Juan and his cohorts wouldn't hesitate to turn on you in half a second if it benefited them. Also, if I find out that you were linked in any way, no matter how small, to Sophie's attack, I will bring charges against you. This is your one and only chance to come clean."

She smiled. "Bring it on."

There was clearly no reasoning with this woman. Was she so power- and money-hungry that she'd take such risks? Maybe so.

"I've done all I can do, then." He stood up and walked out of her office.

Ashley picked up the stapler on her desk and hurled it across the room. What nerve Patrick had, waltzing into her office and acting like he knew what was best for her. She dealt with far too many men like that in her life.

She waited until she was sure Patrick was out of the building, then she picked up the phone. But she got Juan's voice mail. She never left details on voice mail, so she just told him to call her.

The thing was that Patrick was probably right. It was very likely that Juan was behind the attack on Sophie. It appeared Juan had become impatient. He hadn't given her much time to deal with Sophie in a more diplomatic and legal way, like she'd asked.

While she'd never say it to Patrick, she did want to have more control over Juan. Client management was a key aspect of her job. Criminal defense attorneys had to have an additional skill set that prosecutors didn't need.

Her phone rang a few minutes later, and she saw that it was Juan. "Juan," she answered, "talk to me."

"What's going on?"

"You tell me. I just got a visit from Patrick Hunt, who tells me that Sophie Dawson was attacked yesterday. Didn't we have this conversation already?"

"I have no idea what you're talking about."

She hated that he was on the phone and she couldn't read his facial expressions and call him out. "I have a sneaking suspicion that you are the one who targeted her. You didn't even give me a chance yet to discredit her. I need time to do my job. If something happens to her, it will only make your baby brother look guiltier. Have you even thought this through?"

Silence.

Then Juan said, "I see your point. Theoretically, though, if something did happen to her, the intent was just to shake her up. I think you realize that if I'd wanted her out of the picture, that could easily be arranged."

Ashley blew out a breath. She knew that all too well. "Yes. I think you've made your point to her loud and clear. Just give me some time to do it my way. Okay?"

"Fine. No need for you to get all up in arms. You work for me, remember?"

How could she forget? Before she could say anything else, he hung up. Typical.

She'd warned Juan, and it appeared that he had deliberately ignored her advice. The last thing she needed was for Sophie Dawson to turn up dead.

EIGHT

Sophie walked down the hallway and pushed aside the fact that she still had a pounding headache and a killer black eye. She'd done the best she could to cover it with makeup, but anyone paying attention could see it.

"Sophie, heard about what happened to you." Harrison Westgate popped up out of nowhere and blocked her way. She was a couple of inches taller than him, and she thought it drove him crazy that she could literally look down at him.

"I guess word travels."

He looked at her closely. "You look awful. Why are you even here?"

Harrison wasn't one to mince words. She didn't trust him, though. Harrison was all about Harrison. "I have a meeting on the Shelton case."

He placed his hand on her arm. "You know I can cover for you if you need me to. You were just physically attacked."

Wouldn't that be perfect? Harrison swooping in on her case. "You're not even in my division."

"We're a team here, right?" His blue eyes glistened. "I'm more than happy to pinch-hit. You know I can handle it."

There was no way she was going to fall for his teamwork act, but she forced herself to be cordial. "Thank you for the offer. I'll be fine today, but I'll keep you in mind for help in the future."

"Perfect." He took a step closer. Way too close for her liking. "One day I'll be running this place," he said softly. "Always good to get in with the boss early." He winked and then turned away.

She felt like she needed a shower to wash off the sleaze, but she put Harrison out of her mind and focused on the meeting. She grabbed Monica from her office so she could be kept totally up to speed. Sophie had insinuated that Monica wasn't to have a speaking role at the meeting. She'd see if Monica had gotten the subtle point. Being able to pick up on cues like that could be very useful.

She could've gotten Monica to take the meeting in her place, given what had happened to her, but a face-to-face with the CEO of SIB and Keith was too important to miss. And she would never pass it off to Harrison.

She'd insisted to Keith that she was up for it. The last thing she wanted to do was give him a reason to reschedule. That would only delay things, and she wanted to continue her pursuit against Shelton.

Monica looked down at her watch. "They're running late."

The young attorney had a lot to learn. "Lesson number one. Be prepared for important people to always run late. It's the nature of the game."

Monica smiled. "I need to work on my patience. It's just one of my many shortcomings."

"Don't do that."

"Do what?"

"Put yourself down. Your male counterparts would never sit here and say those things, even if they had a million more flaws than you. It's good to be self-aware and not develop too big of an ego, but keep thoughts about self-doubt to yourself or those you can truly trust."

"I'm going to learn so much from working with you, Sophie. I'll try to soak everything in."

"Good. Just stay focused on the task at hand, and everything will be fine."

She drummed her fingers on the table as she waited a couple more minutes, and then Keith entered the room with Whitney Bowman, the CEO of SIB. Whitney was a tall woman, close to Sophie's height. She was very thin and wore a stylish gray pantsuit that Sophie assumed was professionally tailored and a strand of pearls, which seemed perfectly southern.

"I'm Sophie Dawson." She extended her hand to Whitney.

"Nice to meet you, Sophie." Whitney's drawl was thick. "Keith has only had amazing things to say about you." She flashed Sophie an award-winning smile, showing perfectly polished teeth.

"Thank you so much for taking the time for this meeting." Sophie's heartbeat started to thump as her nerves kicked in. This was a delicate dance she was about to engage in. Playing politics was not her strong suit. She could do it, but she preferred a more straightforward approach.

Keith introduced Monica to Whitney. "Let's have a seat." He pulled out a chair for Whitney, and they all sat down around the circular table.

Whitney looked directly at Sophie. "I want you to know how seriously I take these allegations against Glen, and I'm willing to do whatever is necessary here. I'm still appalled that one of my employees, especially a senior manager, would stoop to this level."

Was Whitney just feeding Sophie what she wanted to hear? "I appreciate that. I think this is a situation of an employee going off the grid."

"I'm glad you said that," Keith said. "I agree with the assessment that Shelton was acting alone, and I think that's one of the reasons we're having this meeting."

Sophie wasn't sure where Keith was going. "Did you have something specific in mind?"

Whitney cleared her throat. "I know we're all friends here, trying to do what's right, so I'll put my request out for you to consider. Given that this is all based on the action of one rogue employee, would it be possible to resolve this situation through some sort of plea deal? A trial will add work for you, and frankly, provide a lot of negative publicity for SIB when the company did nothing wrong. In fact, we've been one hundred percent cooperative with law enforcement and this office."

Sophie's mind went into overdrive. It was now clear why Keith had set up this meeting—to get her to strike a deal with SIB to only go after Glen Shelton, and on top of that, to negotiate a deal with him. She needed to buy some time. "I completely understand your perspective, Ms. Bowman, but I'm not at a point now in building the case where I can commit to only going down that one path. I'm happy to keep you updated on my progress, however."

Whitney bit her bottom lip before giving a weak smile. "Yes, that makes perfect sense. The last thing I'd want you to do is rush through your work purely on my account. But I wanted you and Keith to understand my position and that of SIB. You have plenty of other things that you can spend your time on that in my opinion would be much more important and impactful than this case."

Whitney might have been smiling, but suddenly something about this meeting felt off to Sophie. Of course Whitney didn't want the bad PR and media circus, but could there be something deeper going on? Whitney was coming on much stronger than Sophie felt appropriate, given all the circumstances.

"Shelton has hired a new aggressive counsel, who has started filing motions. I have a hearing tomorrow on his motion to change venue."

"Shelton wants the case taken out of Atlanta?" Whitney asked.

"Yes, he's arguing that the jury would be biased against him."

"Well, good luck at the hearing," Whitney said. "And if this does go to trial, there's no one else I'd want to take the case. I have faith in your abilities, Sophie. Keith has told me how gifted you are."

Sophie wasn't sure if Whitney was being sincere, but right now she needed to keep Whitney close and use the cooperation to her advantage. "Thank you. I appreciate your time. And like I said, I'll keep you in the loop, and I really thank you for your continued assistance."

Whitney stood and buttoned her suit jacket. "Of course. Anything that I can do—just give me a call, and I will make it my top priority."

"I'll walk you out." Keith left the room with Whitney by his side.

Once the door shut, Monica put down her pen. "She seems nice."

"Yes, she does. I'm hopeful we can all work together on this."

Sophie didn't want to speak prematurely to Monica, but this meeting had told her one very important thing. She needed to dig deeper into this case. Because she couldn't help the nagging feeling that Whitney Bowman was hiding something.

Cooper waited patiently outside Sophie's building, right by the door. She'd insisted that she was well enough to go into the office for an important meeting. He'd tried to convince her to stay home and rest, but he was quickly learning that when Sophie set her mind on something, she wasn't going to budge.

If anything, the attack seemed to make her even more determined to do her work. It made him more determined too. But he had a sinking feeling in his gut that this was going to be his toughest personal security assignment to date. Juan Wade not only had the resources to harm Sophie, he had a strong personal motivation for revenge. And that fact bothered Cooper most of all. Family made it personal, which amped up the threat tenfold.

Not to mention the fact that he didn't like loose ends—and that included the random guy he'd encountered at Sophie's house. It still didn't add up to him that the guy was sent by Wade. And if that was true, could he have been sent by someone connected to Glen Shelton and the SIB case?

Cooper hadn't wanted to scare Sophie half to death, so he'd tried to be balanced with her in his approach about the new security parameters, but the simple truth was that she wasn't safe. As long as she was the possible star witness against Juan's brother, she was in the crosshairs.

Lord, give me the strength to face this challenge. Please protect Sophie and help me do my job. I don't want to let her down.

He saw Sophie opening the door to exit the building and didn't waste any time joining her.

She frowned slightly. "You weren't kidding about sticking close, were you?"

"No. I realize this isn't how you want to work, but the situation has escalated, and we have to adapt to those threats."

Her eyes softened. "I know you're just doing the job my father hired you to do. I'm just grumpy because my head still hurts."

"That's one of the reasons I didn't want you to get out and about so soon. Rest is so important to recovery."

"I know," she said softly.

"Let's get you home." He placed his hand on her back and guided her down the sidewalk.

They were about to cross the street when a loud bang pierced the air.

He knew instantly what it was, but Sophie shrieked, and without hesitation, he wrapped his arms around her. She shook as he held her.

"Sophie, it's okay. It was just a car backfiring." Having her this close to him set off a wave of emotions. Not only his protective instincts, but what he feared could be something more as well.

"Are you sure?" Her eyes were wide with fear.

"Yes, are you all right?" He looked down at her, feeling a stronger connection forming between them.

"Yes." She broke contact with him and took a step back. "Sorry, I feel stupid for being so jumpy." She brushed a lock of hair out of her eyes.

"Don't apologize. It was just a natural instinct. C'mon, let's get out of here."

He quickly walked her to his SUV and got her inside. He surveyed his surroundings before getting into his car, not taking any chances. Even though Sophie was putting up a tough front, she was afraid. And while the last thing he wanted was for her to live that way, a healthy dose of fear was probably just what she needed to keep her safe.

Cooper gave her space on the drive to her house to decompress. They'd have plenty of time to talk once he got her home.

When he pulled up into her long driveway, he stopped the car and looked over at her. "Come in with me, but stay just inside the main entrance while I check everything out."

"My security system is working. There's no way anyone is in my house."

"It would make me feel better to check."

She nodded and did as he instructed. Once he'd cleared the house, he sat with her at the kitchen table. Maybe it would be good to keep her mind on something else for a while.

"How did your meeting go?"

"Strange, actually." She took a sip of water.

"Who all was there?"

"My boss, District Attorney Keith Todd; the CEO of SIB, Whitney Bowman; and I brought along Monica Lacey—she's a rookie who's been assigned as my mentee."

"And how was it?"

"Whitney was pushing for a plea deal for Shelton to put this thing to bed. Of course they're worried about further fallout that could come from a trial. They've already suffered a PR hit from the local news stories and Shelton's arrest. She's making a case for her company, and my boss wanted me to hear it. I have to ask you, though—do you think Shelton or SIB could be behind anything that has happened to me?"

He ran his hand through his hair. "Anything is possible. But given how personal this is for Juan Wade, I think his organization is the prime suspect, at least in the attack against you. I'm still uneasy about that lurker. It's entirely possible that he isn't connected to Wade at all and has to do with this SIB thing. But that's pure speculation. I'd want more evidence before I jumped to that conclusion. Just because the bank might be complicit in some shady scheme doesn't mean that they'd actually come after you."

"Yeah. We know that Wade has it out for me. Maybe I'm just being paranoid about SIB and Whitney Bowman, but something about the entire situation has me on edge."

"What are you planning to do?"

She crossed her arms. "I'm not going to roll over, if that's what you're wondering."

He grinned. "You haven't given me any indication that rolling over would be your style."

"I do this job for a reason." Her voice didn't waver. "To gain justice for those who have been wronged. At the point where I start negotiating away those principles, there's no point in me being a prosecutor."

He didn't know if she was overly idealistic, but he admired her tenacity. "So that's why you chose to be a prosecutor?"

"Absolutely. I didn't go to law school with the idea that I'd become a hotshot corporate lawyer working in Big Law. That was the dream of most of my classmates, but not me. Although since we're in full disclosure mode, I'm in a position financially where I get to make that type of decision. I have a freedom others don't have. I didn't have to take out loans for law school, so I know that I'm privileged to be able to do what I'm passionate about. I don't have to worry about a school loan the size of a mortgage like most of my classmates had. If you take on that kind of debt, you have no choice but to work in Big Law."

Since she'd brought it up, he figured it best to get it all out there. "You don't even need to work, do you?"

Sophie shook her head. "No. My father's inheritance is substantial, and on top of that he has made his own way in the real estate business. But I'm not the kind of person to sit around all day living off a hefty trust fund. I want my life to have meaning. God gave me the skills to make a difference in the courtroom, and I feel an obligation to act. I don't want to sit back. I need to push and challenge myself."

He couldn't relate to her way of life. *Trust fund* wasn't even in his vocabulary. "I suspect we grew up in vastly different worlds."

She took another sip of water. "I realize how fortunate I am. That's one of the reasons I wanted to go into public service. But I'll tell you this—I would give up every penny to have my mom around. The things I want most in life money can't buy."

He knew that Sophie's mother wasn't alive, but he didn't know the full story. "She died when you were young?"

She looked down, and her shoulders slumped. "In childbirth. I never even knew her."

He couldn't even imagine that type of loss. Of never knowing your mother. "I'm sorry, Sophie."

"It's all right. It's not the kind of thing you ever fully get over, but it helps that my dad and I are so close. What about your family?"

He had said open and honest, but he had his boundaries. It probably wasn't the time to air all of his dirty laundry. "I was close with my mom. She passed away a few years ago. My dad and I are not close. Never were, and never will be. We had a rocky relationship growing up." That might be the understatement of the year. "Let's just say that my father is not a very good man."

Instead of prying, she made eye contact with him and gave him a little nod. "Family stuff can be difficult and messy. But I can't wait for the day when I have a family of my own. I love being a prosecutor, but being a mom is really my deepest desire. I know it may sound silly, but not having my mom around has made me want to be a mother even more. Being a mom will be my most important job ever."

"That's not silly at all." He was the strange one who had no desire whatsoever to have a family and couldn't bear the thought of becoming like his old man. He shifted in his seat, eager to talk about something else. "What's next for the SIB case?"

"We have a hearing on a motion to change venue tomorrow. I guess you'll be attending?"

"Yes, I will. Set the alarm when I leave, and I'll be back in the morning to take you to court."

"I guess there's no point at this juncture in me asking if that's really necessary?"

"You can always ask, but I think we both know the answer."

The target was on Sophie's back, and it wasn't going away anytime soon.

CHAPTER
NINE

Sophie walked into the courtroom the next morning, eager to hear Leland's attempt to convince the court of his arguments. She settled in, pulled out her notes, and booted up her laptop.

"Good morning, counselor." Leland popped up at her table. He looked put together as always in a dark navy suit with a checkered tie. He frowned at her. "Sophie, what in the world happened to you?"

She knew he was referring to her black eye. "I was attacked the other day in Midtown."

Leland's eyes widened. "I had no idea. Are you all right?"

He apparently had a bit of a soft side, as it seemed like he actually cared. "Thanks for asking. I'll be fine."

He took a step closer. "Did they catch the guy?"

"No. And they aren't optimistic."

"You gotta be careful out there."

She was ready to shift topics. "You're really going out on a limb on this one. It's a stretch even for you." She enjoyed verbal sparring, and Leland was always up for it. But she had to admit this motion had her scratching her head. It seemed like a total waste of time unless he had a big surprise up his sleeve.

"Things aren't always open and shut, Sophie. Especially on my side of the fence." He walked away to his table.

What an odd thing to say. She had no idea what he was getting at, but she figured she'd find out soon. These types of motions were usually only granted in the most extreme cases, like when the case was so well-known and personal to a huge swath of the community that the defendant couldn't get a fair trial. That wasn't the case here.

Judge Lucy Bernard entered the courtroom a couple minutes later, and Sophie rose from her chair.

"Please have a seat." Judge Bernard was one of the newer members to the bench and a former plaintiff's lawyer at Kate's firm. She'd only been a judge for about two years. Her former life as a plaintiff's lawyer hadn't shown in her decisions, as her record was down the middle. "Mr. Kingsley, this is your motion today on a change of venue."

"Yes, Your Honor," Leland said.

"Then let's get right to it." The judge took off her reading glasses and looked at Leland.

Sophie took her seat while Leland started to present his argument. Judge Bernard was known for a hot bench, meaning she asked a lot of questions. She also wasn't much for procedure. She ran her courtroom as she saw fit.

"I'm asking for Your Honor to consider my motion for change of venue. My client, Glen Shelton, an employee of Southern Investment Bank, simply can't get a fair trial in Fulton County. There's too much connection between SIB and members of the local community."

"Let me stop you right there," the judge interrupted.

Just like Sophie had thought. Judge Bernard wasn't going to let Leland talk for long.

"What is your argument based upon? Pretrial publicity? Because as I look around this courtroom, it isn't exactly a media frenzy right now."

"Pretrial publicity is just one factor. And once the news media do home in on this case, the publicity will be there."

Judge Bernard jumped back in. "But you concede it's not there now."

"I haven't conceded anything, Your Honor." Leland's arrogance oozed out of him. "We have to look at this in the broader sense—the interests of justice. My client deserves a fair trial."

"I still fail to see the connection you're making about why it can't happen in this county and in *my* courtroom," the judge responded.

"Because a large number of residents in this county bank at SIB. They will feel personally affronted, and that will negatively impact how they view my client. That type of bias must be rejected, and you can solve this problem."

"What do you say, Ms. Dawson?" the judge asked.

"I think Mr. Kingsley is stretching. While Your Honor clearly has the power to make such a determination, I don't think Mr. Kingsley has nearly carried his burden here. His position is vague, and it's not clear why jurors would hold any bias against his client. Even if the jurors bank at SIB, they wouldn't be the individuals affected by this lawsuit. I think we have to balance the interests of the citizens of Fulton County here as well. This isn't a one-sided analysis. The bar is high for changing venue, and we're not even close in my opinion, based on what Mr. Kingsley presented in his motion and states here today."

Leland cleared his throat. "But that risk is just too great in a criminal proceeding. Why take it?"

Judge Bernard shook her head. "I'm not in the business of risk mitigation, Mr. Kingsley. That's not my role here. If this is all you have, I'm ready to make my ruling."

"I would caution you not to be so hasty."

Had he really just said that to the judge?

"And, Mr. Kingsley, I would caution you to watch your tone in my courtroom."

He stood tall. "My obligation is to my client. Not to you or this courtroom."

Wow, Sophie couldn't believe he was doing this. Maybe he was trying to intimidate the judge, but she didn't think that was going to happen.

Leland was undeterred. "I want to make sure the Court understands that my client will be irreparably harmed by having his case heard in Fulton County. Jurors will be too close to the case to be objective."

Sophie decided to keep her mouth shut. She was ahead right now, and if she spoke, she only risked the ire of the judge.

"Motion denied. The trial will take place here in my courtroom in Fulton County." Judge Bernard didn't even look at Leland, but instead rose from her seat and exited the courtroom.

Sophie started to pack up her stuff, and Leland approached her.

"Can you believe her?" he asked.

"It's more like can I believe you? Since when do you treat a judge with an attitude like that?"

"I don't like or respect her. I'll be filing another motion for recusal based on her bias against me." He paused. "We have some past history together."

"Like, personal?"

"No. Nothing like that."

"Then are you crazy?" Although the fact that there was a backstory made his behavior make a lot more sense.

"My client has directed me to be as aggressive as possible, and that's exactly what I plan to do."

Sophie stood in disbelief as she watched Leland walk away.

Sophie didn't want to be alone the next evening, and calling Cooper seemed too needy. He was already dedicating a large chunk of his life to her, so she didn't want to intrude any further into his time.

There was also another reason: the way she had felt the other night when he wrapped his arms around her. To protect her. But was that it? She was afraid she might start seeing Cooper in a different light. And being around him so much was only adding to that fear.

So instead of calling Cooper, she invited Kate and Mia over for dinner at her house. That wouldn't violate the protocol, because she wouldn't be leaving the house. After the attack, Cooper had made it crystal clear that she wasn't to go anywhere alone. She kept reliving the moment when that man smashed her head into the hood of the car. Those memories were enough to keep her on her toes and follow the rules. She wasn't the reckless type, but she was a bit lonely and needed her friends.

Mia arrived first, since she only lived a few minutes away. When she walked in the door, she gave Sophie a huge hug. "I can't believe you were attacked. Why didn't you tell us about what happened to you sooner?" Her dark eyes showed her true concern.

"Honestly, it was a whirlwind." Sophie's emotions had run the gamut from disbelief and fear to anger.

"How're you feeling now?"

"My head still hurts."

"And your eye?"

"Yeah, the doctor said it's going to be bruised for a bit." She knew it looked awful, even with the makeup.

A couple minutes later, Kate walked through the door and locked it behind her. "Sophie, my goodness." She gave Sophie a tight embrace. "I'm so glad to see you."

"Come on in, and let's sit." Sophie walked into the living room with her friends beside her.

"Our delivery should be here in about half an hour," Kate said. "From my favorite Thai place."

Sophie smiled. Kate lacked any cooking skills. Sophie was pretty good, but since it was just her, she didn't cook that much.

"Tell us how you're holding up," Kate said.

"I think I've been a bit in shock. If Cooper hadn't been there and stopped things, I don't know what would've happened."

"How is it going between the two of you?" Mia asked.

"Good. He's intense, but I think he was almost as shaken up as I was. He was bothered that he wasn't able to act even more quickly. But I told him that would've been impossible anyway."

Mia grabbed her hand. "Is your dad okay?"

"He's stressed, and I think he chewed Cooper out for not being right by my side. But all of that is in the past, because I almost have a full-time chaperone now. That's why I asked the two of you to come to my place instead of going out to dinner."

"Whatever you need," Kate said. "We're here for you. I can relate to some of what you're going through. If it hadn't been for Landon, I don't know how I would've made it through my ordeal last year. You're right to keep Cooper close. Don't push him away. I know it will be really hard, because you're like me and want to be independent. But if that crazy gang is after you, this is no time to flex your independent side." Kate had prosecuted a big pharmaceutical company last year, a case that wound up putting her life at risk.

"I appreciate your advice. You're both helping just by being here. For some reason, I didn't want to be alone tonight. Normally, that's not an issue, but I think it's all catching up to me."

"How's work going? Are you able to keep up?" Mia asked.

"I'm trying to stay busy on my cases. Harrison offered to help out."

Mia's dark eyes widened. "I hope you declined. That guy is a creep. He will stab you in the back before you can even walk away."

"Believe me, I know." Sophie had replayed their conversation in her head multiple times. "He certainly wasn't acting out of the goodness of his heart. Hopefully he'll leave me alone, and I can keep working on my caseload. I don't want to think too much about the Wade case, except when Patrick calls or needs me to do something."

"Patrick is the prosecutor, right?" Kate asked.

"Yes. He's a deputy ADA in Dekalb. Keith brought him onto this case so we wouldn't face the conflict of interest argument. There are already enough issues to be worried about without having the defense claim that the prosecution is biased."

"At least he's a seasoned attorney who can handle the trial," Mia said.

"I'm thankful for that, but I can't allow the case to take over my life. It's Patrick's case, not mine. I don't want to play the role of backseat driver. I'm taking a hands-off approach for now. I'm still working on that case against the SIB employee that you saw on the news."

"You think you're going to take it to trial?" Kate asked.

Wasn't that the million dollar question. "That remains to be seen. There's politics involved."

Mia groaned. "Isn't there always? We can't get rid of it. No matter whether we're in private practice or government. There's always a political play and powerful people wanting things their way. I know I usually work on the defense side with big companies, but if what I read and saw in the news is true, you should throw the book at that guy. There's no reason he should get off easy. His customers trusted him, and he owed them a fiduciary duty. I'm not telling you anything you don't already know, but I'd think this is exactly the type of case that your office would want to take on. The headline seems clear. 'Big bad bank manager steals from innocent customers.'"

Sophie looked at her friend. "Maybe you should cross over to the prosecutorial side, Mia."

Mia laughed. "I'm still paying off student loans. I'll be in Big Law for at least a few more years."

Sophie had once offered to help Mia pay off her loans, but Mia wouldn't accept the assistance. She wanted to do it all on her own, and Sophie understood that. But sometimes she wished Mia had just taken her help. The two of them had met in law school and become best friends, and Sophie only wanted Mia to be happy. She wasn't so sure that being in Big Law was the best fit.

When they were finishing up dinner, Sophie's phone rang. She looked down and saw it was Cooper. "Let me get this," she told them. "Hello?"

"Hey, it's Cooper. Just wanted to check in and make sure you were all good."

"I'm doing okay. I actually invited Mia and Kate over for dinner."

"Oh, I'm sorry to interrupt. I'll let you go. I was just thinking about you and wanted to be sure you were all right tonight."

She paused. "Thanks for calling. Everything is good."

"See you in the morning," he said.

She hung up and looked at her friends, who were both grinning. "It was just Cooper checking in."

"Is that why your cheeks are bright red?" Mia asked.

Sophie touched her face. "My cheeks are not red."

"Yes, they are," Kate said. "Mia's right."

"C'mon. Cut it out, you two. I told you before that this is all business between Cooper and me." Or at least that was what she continued to try to tell herself.

"Look." Kate walked over to her. "Seriously, you're in uncharted territory right now. You need a professional who can handle situations like this. I'm just glad you have him watching your back."

"Me too," Sophie answered honestly. "I've had plenty of threats before, being an ADA, but I've never been physically attacked." Just saying those words out loud sent a wave of fear through her.

Kate put her hand on Sophie's shoulder. "I'm praying for you."

"Thank you," Sophie said. "I need it." She looked over at

Mia, who didn't say anything. Mia was a skeptic but usually stayed silent during the faith discussions that Kate and Sophie had.

"I think I'm going to call it a night." Mia stood up.

"Me too," Kate added. "Unless you need anything else?"

Sophie shook her head. "Thank you both for keeping me company. I feel like I'll sleep better tonight."

She hugged her friends good-bye and hoped that sleep would actually come.

Patrick pored over the files in front of him, including reading Sophie's witness statement again. Everything added up to him, but he had to anticipate how Ashley would try to discredit Sophie at trial. The first hurdle he'd have to overcome was the basic idea that eyewitnesses were notoriously unreliable. This situation was completely out of the ordinary, since Sophie was a prosecutor, but he could see that cutting both ways.

Ricky Wade had been arraigned, and a trial date was set for next month. Ashley had pushed for a quick date, which made him think she had something sinister up her sleeve. He didn't trust a single thing she did, so he was questioning everything at this point. Although he also knew that Juan Wade was probably pressuring Ashley because he wanted his brother out of jail ASAP.

As Patrick sat there and prepared for his meeting, one thing about Sophie nagged at him. Her background check and investigative research had come up clean as a whistle. It was almost too clean, and he was going to ask her about that when she arrived at his office in a few minutes. It was imperative for him to find out any trouble spots so they could develop a plan to guard against it. Everyone had some sort of skeleton in their closet—including him. Thankfully, he wouldn't be the one on the witness stand. Sometimes lawyers had the darkest secrets, so he was nervous about what Sophie could be hiding. Yes, he might seem paranoid, but in his line of work, it was necessary.

Ashley had called him yesterday to hound him about turning over documents. The discovery process in criminal law was very one-sided. He had to give her everything, and she basically had to give him nothing.

Only a couple minutes later, Sophie walked into his office.

"Thanks for coming in. How're you feeling?" he asked. It had been over a week since the attack.

"Much better. Pretty much back to normal."

"Any other issues?"

"No, but Cooper has been sticking super close, so I'm not sure if that's been a deterrent."

He was relieved that Cooper was protecting her. "I read Ashley the riot act, but frankly, I'm not sure she could control Juan even if she wanted to. I'm curious. What's your relationship like with Ashley?"

Sophie paused, probably considering his question. "I'd characterize it as neutral. I know she has some extremely combative relationships with other prosecutors, but she and I never got to that level. Maybe it's just given the nature of the cases we were against each other on. They weren't nearly as high profile as this case. If I recall, there were a few drug offenses and a simple assault."

"You think it's safe to say that she doesn't have any particular beef with you then?"

"I think that's right. There's never been any obvious personal animosity or anything like that. I've always felt that she has much bigger fish to fry than me."

He opened the manila folder on his desk. "Given the importance of your testimony, I had an extensive background investigation run on you."

Her blue eyes widened. "Really?"

"Yes. It's something I would do for anyone in your position

in a case like this, where the microscope will be on you and the media will be watching every step of the trial. But here's the thing. We came up completely empty. On paper, you look like the absolute model citizen."

She tilted her head to the side. "You say that as if it's a bad thing."

He needed to make her understand why he was pushing this issue. It wasn't to be a jerk. It was because they had to be prepared for whatever Ashley was going to unleash on them. "No. It's not bad. Please don't take this personally, but from my experience, no one could be as squeaky clean as you. And if there's something lurking out there, I don't want to hear it first coming out of Ashley Murphy's mouth in front of the jury."

Sophie let out a loud sigh. "Since you did such a comprehensive background check, I'm sure you know about my financial situation. That's been a source of conflict with other people all of my life. I've never wanted for material things, and I try not to take that for granted. You probably also learned that my mother died in childbirth. What I'm guessing didn't come up in your background check is that I've been seeing a psychologist on and off over the years to help me deal with the lingering loss and grief. There was also a time when I was getting panic attacks regularly."

As he looked into her eyes, he didn't think she was hiding anything. "My goal is to protect you and to protect our case. I know the meetings you had with your psychologist are privileged, but I have to ask you this follow-up."

"Okay."

"Have you taken any drugs for anxiety or anything like that? I'm just making sure we cover all bases here."

Sophie shook her head. "No. I don't have anything against it, but I honestly didn't think any medicine would cure my heartache. The battle in my head and heart isn't cured by a prescription."

"If Ashley figures out that you've been to counseling before, she is bound to bring it up and try to make a huge deal out of it. Anything she can do to put a shred of doubt in the mind of the jurors, she'll do. You need to be prepared for that. And given the type of broad discovery she's seeking, it's possible that she'll find out. That kind of thing is usually in the standard questions for witnesses because it can go toward their credibility."

She ran her hand through her hair. "I get it. But would the jury really hold all of that against me?"

"No. Given what you've been through, I highly doubt it. But Ashley will try to turn it into something it's not. That's why I was asking about the drugs. She'll use any angle she can. I know we covered this, but did you take any prescription drugs prescribed by your doctor for your panic attacks?"

"No. Not once. I made it clear that I wasn't interested in that. I just wanted someone to talk to and hear me out." She took a breath. "I don't know why I'm getting so defensive. I'm not used to sitting on this side of the table."

"My style isn't always the best. I tend to be too direct."

She smiled. "I actually like direct. Much better than playing games. But where does all of this leave us? What do you think Ashley's strategy is going to be?"

He'd given this a lot of thought. "She'll probably argue that you are letting your prosecutor brain take over. That you can't be fair because you're used to being on this side of the aisle, and you want to be able to point your finger at the culprit. And in doing so, you picked the wrong guy because you were overeager."

"That's a decent argument, I guess, but I'm completely confident in what I saw. I know that this wasn't a misidentification. I can promise you that. When I get on the stand and swear to tell the truth, that's exactly what I'm going to do. You don't have to worry about me second-guessing myself on the identification of the suspect. I'm rock solid on that."

"Do you realize how many witnesses have said the exact same

thing and then gotten torn to shreds on the stand? I bet you've had it happen to you with your own witnesses. Ashley is not to be underestimated. She's one of the most talented trial lawyers I've ever seen, and that's what bothers me. It's possible that she'll come up with something that neither of us can predict, but there's nothing we can do about that."

Sophie leaned forward, placing both her hands on his desk. "She *is* good, but we have the truth on our side."

If only it were that easy. "You and I both know that sometimes the truth isn't enough. We have to worry about other factors beyond our control that we haven't even talked about yet."

"Like what?"

"Jury corruption, for one."

"You think Juan would get to them?"

There was no doubt in his mind. "He'd certainly try. And all it takes is him turning one to get a not-guilty verdict."

She frowned. "It's so strange, thinking about it from this vantage point. I always thought I got too emotionally involved in my cases, but this is taking personal to a new level. What in the world do we do about jury tampering?"

"*We* don't do anything." The last thing he needed was for Sophie to start acting like second chair. "Remember, this is my problem. Your only job is to take that witness stand and tell the truth. The rest of it all lies on me. If I know Ashley, she'll specifically ask if you did any legal work on this case. I want you to be able to answer no honestly."

She nodded. "I understand. It's frustrating, but I get it."

"That's really all I need. I just wanted to go through your file and give you an opportunity to tell me about anything I needed to know. If there's something we haven't covered that you think could even possibly come up, now's the time to let me know."

Sophie took a moment. "I don't think there is."

"Okay, I'll be in touch to set up our preparation sessions. We don't have that long before trial."

He hoped Sophie would be as believable on the stand as she was sitting in his office.

Ashley rolled up her exercise mat and exited the Pilates studio. She'd found a couple of years ago that exercise was key to her mental health. It helped keep her centered and focused on reaching her goals. At thirty-five, she still had a long way to go in becoming a nationally known defense attorney.

She walked out to her pearl white BMW and stopped short when she saw she had a visitor. She cursed under her breath.

Juan was leaning up against her car, smoking a cigarette.

"This is an unexpected surprise. How did you know to find me here?" She opened the car door and threw her mat inside. Was he following her now?

"I know your schedule. You're way too predictable." He took a step toward her, but she held her ground.

She'd realized a long time ago that in her line of work, she could never let these men see her sweat. They were used to always having it their way. To being in complete control. But for her to effectively advocate for them, she had to be strong. There was no room for indecision or fear.

"What can I do for you?" she asked.

"The trial date is set, right?"

"Yes. I pushed for it as soon as possible, just like you requested."

He threw his cigarette onto the ground and crushed it with his freshly shined black shoe. "I need Ricky out of jail. He won't last there. I have too many enemies. They can find ways around the security. I can't have his death on my conscience."

He was hoping for some magical solution. He needed a serious reality check. "The only way we'll get Ricky out is if we prevail at trial. I need you to be cooperative and help me in that effort."

He crossed his arms. "And I'm going to work on backup plans."

"Do I even need to ask?"

"You know I'll do whatever it takes."

"Preferably without loss of life, Juan. I don't need to clean that up too. Don't dig yourself another hole in trying to resolve this one problem."

"This *one problem*, as you call it, is my baby brother."

She had to make him understand that he was playing a very dangerous game. "Another reason for you to check yourself and keep your emotions under control."

"Give me some credit, Ash. I know you think you're some fancy educated lawyer and I'm just a kid from the streets who got lucky, but I know how to get things done."

That was exactly what she was worried about. Yes, he had risen to the head of one of Atlanta's most powerful criminal enterprises. But he didn't get to where he was by being a Boy Scout.

"And anyway, if I get in any trouble, I have the best lawyer in town to defend me." He took another step toward her, then reached out and pulled her close to him, wrapping his left arm tightly around her waist.

She had to fight the urge to shrug him off. Juan had often pushed the limits with her, but she thought he saw it all as a game. Another reason she couldn't flinch. Couldn't let him sense an ounce of fear.

He put his right hand under her chin and lifted her head up. She looked up into his dark eyes but kept her breathing even.

"You realize that even most men would be losing it right now if I had my hands on them."

She'd had enough of his tactics. She stepped back, breaking his grip on her. "I have a job to do, Juan. And if you want to win, you need to back off and let me do it."

He smiled, which surprised her. She worried that this man might not only be ruthless but also a little crazy. That only made him more dangerous. She could only hope she wouldn't end up being his enemy one day.

CHAPTER
TEN

Sophie had made her decision, and she wasn't going to back down. Keith had asked to meet with her at the end of the day. She'd been stewing about it since first thing that morning.

She stood in front of the bathroom mirror, preparing for her conversation with Keith. Her black eye had finally subsided with the passage of time. She practiced what she was going to say.

"Keith, I've reviewed all of the evidence and spoken to our investigators. I want to move forward with the trial instead of offering a plea deal."

She let out a sigh when she realized that she didn't sound as convincing as she wanted. Why couldn't she deliver the lines with the command and presence they required?

When she had started this job, everyone assumed she was just a spoiled rich kid who wanted a hobby. There were jokes about why she didn't just become a lady who lunched. It had taken time to build people's trust and to establish her reputation as a top lawyer in the prosecutor's office.

Her father had done a good job teaching her the value of hard work. But she knew she had a hard time hiding her emotions. In this instance, though, she just couldn't let Keith sense her fear. She had absolutely zero political aspirations, but she did want to continue on her path and see what opportunities arose.

It was time, so she buttoned her navy suit jacket, combed her fingers through her hair, and headed to Keith's office. He was expecting her, so she knocked and only waited a second before entering.

He smiled when he saw her. "You're looking much better, Sophie. How're you feeling?"

"Great. Thanks for asking." She took a seat, ready to make her case.

Keith took a big gulp of coffee. He was known for drinking it nonstop. "You've had some time with the Shelton file. What's your decision?"

Here it goes. "I'd like to take the case to trial. I don't believe we should strike an easy plea deal. I want to push for the maximum penalties here. We need to send a strong signal from this office that we're tough on crime—all types of crime, even white collar. Especially since innocent people and small businesses bore the brunt of Shelton's illegal actions."

Keith picked up his coffee mug again but didn't immediately respond.

She had to decide whether to let him sit or keep talking. Now was an opportunity to show that she could be aggressive. "I know you have reservations about it, but I think it's the right thing to do."

He cleared his throat. "It's complicated when you're in my position, Sophie. I have to take all factors into consideration, not just the facts of the case at hand. I have to look at the bigger picture."

"I know you're worried about SIB's reaction, but we don't report to them."

"They're a powerful player in the community."

On a hunch, she asked him something that had been bothering her. "Exactly how well do you know Whitney?"

"We've known each other for years. That's one of the reasons I can guarantee that she's clean as a whistle. You don't find many CEOs with her level of integrity." He paused. "And that's also why I'm reluctant to put her company front and center. We need to go after the real bad guys around town, not a company that's doing its best to do the right thing. You have to trust me on this one."

She needed to close the deal. "But I'm not on a witch hunt here. I'm focused solely on Shelton and his wrongdoings. I can promise right now that he's the target here, not SIB or anyone else who works there."

"Are you sure?"

"Absolutely."

"All right. But I want to be kept fully in the loop here. I think the media is going to have a keen interest in this case, and I don't want it to turn into a complete disaster. That also means all of your actions will be put under a microscope. Do you think you're ready for that?"

Once again, she could feel him doubting her abilities. She had to prove him wrong. "Yes sir, I am."

"Good. Because it's *your* career on the line here."

She took in a breath at his statement—which was more like a threat. "Understood."

"How is Monica working out?"

"Great. She's very eager and inquisitive but not too pushy. I'm enjoying working with her."

"Wonderful. She was near the top of her class at Emory. Just like you. Although I think I recall you were number one in your class. And one more thing. Harrison has offered to help you out if you need it, especially with everything going on in the Wade case. I took the liberty of briefing him on the status of the Shelton investigation. He's completely up to speed and ready to step in on anything you need."

She held back a groan and tried to keep her facial expression neutral. If only Keith knew how hard Harrison was gunning for his job. "Thanks for that. I saw Harrison and told him I had everything under control for the moment."

"All right, but if that changes, know you have help."

"Thank you." She rose from her chair and didn't let out a breath until she was down the hallway.

Later that evening she was sitting on her sofa, reviewing the Shelton file, when she heard a knock at the door. She wasn't expecting anyone, so her pulse immediately sped up. But when she got to the door and looked through the peephole, her heart warmed.

She opened the door. "Dad, what're you doing here?"

"Can't I stop by and say hello to my favorite daughter?"

"I'm your only daughter." She smiled as she looked up into her father's kind brown eyes. He'd had to play double duty for her growing up, but he'd never let her down.

He pulled her into a big bear hug. "I'm just so glad that you're all right."

"Come sit, and I'll make you some coffee." Her father was a big coffee drinker.

"Sounds perfect."

He followed her into the kitchen and took a seat while she put on the coffee. Then she joined him at the table.

"You would tell me if you weren't feeling well?" he asked.

"Yes. I promise, I'm much better. The last thing I want is for you to worry about that."

"I can't help it. You'll see one day when you have your own children."

His words struck her. "I know. And I can't wait for that day. Then you'll be a grandpa."

"Well, I hate to tell you, dear, but you can't get ahead of yourself. You don't even have a serious boyfriend."

She didn't need reminding of that fact. "I know, Dad. I'm working on it."

"That's what you always say. I told you about Jim's son, right?

106

I think the two of you would really hit it off. He's a banker, very stable. A reliable sort of guy who would make a good father."

She had to try her hardest not to roll her eyes. Her father had the absolute best intentions, but he was not a good matchmaker. At least not for her. "I can't really see myself dating a banker. Especially not in the long term."

"Why? Don't you want someone who has a good, stable job?"

"Of course, but I want someone I can really fall in love with." Since her mom wasn't around, her dad had taken on the role of love life advisor many years ago.

"Don't assume that a banker has to be boring. Jim's kid is a great guy. He has a good sense of humor."

She needed to shut this down. "I don't think this is the best time right now, given all that's going on."

He nodded. "You're right. I'm sorry, my head isn't on straight right now."

"Please, I can't have you worried about me. You know the doctor said that stress wasn't good for you."

"He tells everybody that. I'm fit as a fiddle."

She stood up and poured him a cup of coffee in his favorite mug. "Here you go. Just the way you like it." Which meant too much sugar.

He took a sip. "There is one thing I wanted to talk to you about."

"What is it?"

"How do you think it's working out with Cooper?"

"What do you mean?"

He placed his hands on top of hers. "Do you feel safe with him around?"

"Yes. I'll admit I was skeptical at first, but after the attack, I feel much better knowing that he's there."

He blew out a breath. "I still can't believe he didn't get to you in time."

"He did everything in his power. I promise you that."

He leaned in toward her. "If I need to fire him and get someone else, I will do it right now. There is nothing I won't do to keep you protected."

"That will *not* be necessary. I'm getting along fine with him. I don't want to switch. And besides, you realize that he works with Kate's fiancé?"

He smiled. "Yes, I know."

"Another good reason to keep him in place."

"I just wanted you to know that I was more than willing to make a change if you wanted me to. I need you to be comfortable."

"Thank you. I promise that I am. Now, enjoy your coffee and tell me what else is going on."

He took a sip. "Martha keeps asking me and asking me out to dinner."

Laughter bubbled up out of her. "And you keep turning her down."

"Sophie, if I was going to date someone, it would not be Martha."

"I've told you many times before that you shouldn't stay single on my account."

"I've been single for thirty-two years. I don't think this old dog wants to learn any new tricks. I've got everything I need. And then one day, God willing, I'll have grandkids to look forward to. I don't need some woman coming into my life trying to change my ways. My heart still belongs to your mother, and I'm totally fine with that."

"Whatever makes you happy." She smiled at his response. She hated that he was alone, but he was right. He was set in his ways. It would take a special woman to break him down, and he hadn't met anyone yet who fit that bill.

"If only your mother could see you now."

"What do you mean?"

"Maybe I'm getting nostalgic, but I know she would be so proud of everything you've done with your life. I know I am."

Her throat tightened. "Daddy, you're going to make me cry."

"You were always tenderhearted. From the time you were a small child. I worried about that. That people would always try to take advantage. That you were too much of a softie."

"I'm still a softie, but I'm able to be tough now when I need to be."

"You're right. But if someone had told me when you were young that you would become a prosecutor, I would've never believed them."

She laughed. "Me neither. It took me a while to get here. But I love what I do."

"I know you do. And speaking of that, I know I interrupted your work. I saw the files out in the living room."

"You don't have to go."

He stood up from his chair. "I know. Don't worry. I'll visit again soon."

She walked him to the door, and he leaned down and kissed her forehead. "I know I might seem a bit overbearing right now, but it's all because I love you so much."

Sophie nodded. "We'll get through this together, just like everything else in life we've dealt with."

"That we will. Lock up behind me and set the alarm."

She shut the door and then went back to work. It was time to start preparing for the trial against Glen Shelton.

Later that night, Tad sat in a coffee shop across from Whitney. This was only his second time meeting face-to-face with her. She was a very attractive woman, although too thin for his tastes. Even though she was around his age, he was no fool. The divorced CEO was *way* out of his league. He was just a PI. She was a millionaire. They weren't even playing in the same ballpark. But he had bigger concerns than that.

"What's the latest?" Whitney asked.

"A few interesting things to report. First, I've compiled everything I could find on the Wade homicide case that I thought might be helpful. Turns out Sophie is the key eyewitness to the murders. Sounds like a wrong place at the wrong time kind of thing, but she's in the crosshairs of the Wade gang."

Whitney picked up her cup. "How so?"

"The suspect is Juan Wade's little brother. Juan is the head of the gang, so in my opinion, he's trying to spook Sophie off the case. Get her to recant or back out of testifying. I don't know how far he would go, because if something happens to her at this point, it would seem really suspicious. But according to my contacts in APD, Sophie was attacked recently, and they think it's linked to Wade, but they can't prove it."

"Well, that explains a lot. She looked awful when I saw her. A very noticeable black eye that couldn't be concealed with makeup, even though she tried."

"Those guys don't mess around."

Whitney took a sip of her skim vanilla latte. "That does add a wrinkle to everything. I wonder if it works in our favor, though. If she's tied up in this Wade mess, then how focused could she be on our case?"

"We'll find out." He knew it was best never to underestimate a prosecutor.

"She insisted she wasn't coming after SIB, but I have to protect my company."

"Absolutely."

Whitney looked up at him with her crystal blue eyes. "You know, if Wade is after her, that provides us with perfect coverage to act. Do you understand what I'm saying?"

"Completely." It was clear that Whitney was ruthless. She wasn't afraid to blur the lines. And based on what he knew about her, he could understand why.

"Anything else?" she asked.

"A few more tidbits. She has a guy hanging around her. I

110

don't know yet if he's her boyfriend or what. He's around all the time now. I'm trying to run down who he is, but I'm having to be a bit more cautious than normal, because while she seems oblivious, this guy always seems on high alert. If I had to put money on it, I'd say he's had some law enforcement or military experience." He'd experienced that killer right hook firsthand, but he wasn't going to tell Whitney that.

"But you said he might just be her boyfriend?"

"I'm trying to determine that. In addition to that guy, her dad has visited her. She's an only child, and her mother died in childbirth. It's not surprising that she'd be close to her father. How did she seem to you when you met her?"

"She requested our cooperation, and I told her we would fully cooperate. I'm sending her a slew of documents that should keep her buried for a while. But I want you to stay on her. Whatever it takes."

"Understood."

She smiled. "I knew I liked you, Tad."

"I know you hired me to focus on Sophie Dawson, but if there's anything else I can do, just let me know. I'm reading between the lines here that there's something you don't want coming out about your company." He wanted to see how much Whitney would open up to him, because she was clearly hiding something.

Whitney leaned forward. "When the time is right, I might be able to give you more information, but for now, do whatever it takes to keep Sophie in check."

"Understood." This was the most fun he'd had on a case in a long time.

It was Saturday evening, and Sophie had called Cooper over to her house. She said everything was fine, but his instincts had him on edge. He drove there as quickly as he could. He figured if he broke the speed limit, he had enough cop buddies to help him get out of the ticket.

When she opened the door, he walked in and shut the door behind him. "What's going on?"

"Please tell me that you weren't worried. I told you everything was perfectly fine."

Yeah, she'd said that, but he hadn't fully believed her. "Then what is it?"

"I'm going stir-crazy. I'm either locked up in my office or here at the house. And I was hoping, since it's Saturday night, that we could go get something to eat. You said you didn't have any plans."

He let out a huge sigh of relief. So that was why she had asked him last night if he had plans. He'd thought she was just making polite small talk. "You just want to go to dinner?"

"Yes, if you're up for it."

He felt like an idiot. He'd jumped to the worst conclusions when she'd just been restless. "Sure. I'm just glad everything here is okay."

"Cooper, believe me, if something was wrong, I would tell you. We're past the point of me playing tough girl where this is concerned."

He looked at her and realized it was the first time since he'd started working this case that she wasn't wearing a suit. Tonight she wore dark jeans and a blue sweater that made her eyes look even more blue. As he looked at her, he couldn't deny that he was attracted to her. Unlike so many women who caked on the makeup, it appeared she was barely wearing any. Just the hint of pink on her lips. And focusing on her lips wasn't a good idea.

He had to check himself. He'd listened to her talk about her desire to settle down and have a family. He wasn't prepared to offer that to anyone. It just wasn't going to work out that way for him.

"Do you like Mexican food?" she asked.

"Yeah. I pretty much like everything."

"Great, I know a place."

"Can we get in on a Saturday night?"

Sophie smiled. "Yeah, I'm a regular. They'll make it work."

"Don't take this the wrong way, but I wouldn't have expected Mexican food to be your first choice."

She laughed. "Don't judge a book by its cover, right?"

"True."

A little while later, and true to her word, there was a booth waiting for them at the restaurant. It wasn't a dive, but it wasn't fine dining either. It was just the type of place he liked to eat at. He watched as Sophie dismantled the second basket of chips.

"I'm also not the type of woman who eats salads. I hope that doesn't offend you."

He grinned. "Just the opposite. It's a refreshing change of pace."

"My friends get a little mad at me sometimes, because I can eat whatever I want. From what my dad tells me, my mom was the exact same way." She picked up another chip. "He actually stopped by the other night."

"Your father?"

"Yeah. He was checking up on me. And you."

"I can't blame him. I really thought he might fire me."

"I told him I didn't want to work with anyone else but you."

"Really? Why is that?"

"Because I'm comfortable with you, and the last thing I want to do right now is start over with another person. Speaking of which, we need to talk about the schedule tomorrow."

"Sunday?"

"Yes, I want to go to church, but I don't want to impose on you. So maybe we could work something else out?"

He appreciated that she was trying to accommodate him. But on this point, they were on the same page. "I'll go with you."

"Are you sure?"

"Yeah. It's not an imposition. I go to church."

"Where do you go?" she asked.

"Park Hills." He'd been going there for the past few years.

"Oh yeah, I've heard of it. I go to Grace Chapel. You haven't said anything about it before, so I wasn't sure."

Cooper looked at her. "And neither have you."

She swirled the straw in her drink. "I've been told that I'm quiet about my faith. I should probably be more vocal, but that's not my style at all."

"I get it. I'm the same way." It was eerie to him how similar they were in some ways, given what extremely different backgrounds they came from. "What time should I pick you up?"

"It's up to you. We could go to the nine or eleven o'clock service. I usually go to the nine o'clock, but I'm asking for your help here, so I'm flexible."

"Nine is great with me."

She smiled at him, and once again he had to hold himself back. She was oblivious to the impact her sweet smile had on him. Yes, the physical attraction was undeniable, but there was something about her as a person that was also drawing him in.

"Is my case the only thing you're working on right now?" Sophie asked.

"Yeah. I don't want to be distracted."

"Is that a problem? Am I keeping you from being able to take on other opportunities?"

"No. Between me, Noah, and Landon, we have it fully covered. We're also looking to maybe hire someone else into the partnership. Business is strong, so it might be the right time to do it. But we're all very particular and don't want to work with just anyone. We have some additional entry-level employees to help us out, but at our level, we're more cautious on expansion. We're willing to take the time to find the right fit." And each one of them had very strong opinions, so it was going to take someone with a unique skill set.

He ate his entire giant burrito and then felt stuffed. But it had been worth every single bite. She'd devoured her tacos too.

"Thanks for taking me out," she said. "I know you probably could be doing much more fun things on a Saturday night. I really hope you didn't change your personal plans because of me."

"I didn't have any personal plans. I'm unattached and pretty much focus on my job 24-7."

"I can relate to that." She sat back in her chair with a small groan. "You might have to wheel me out of here after all those chips I ate."

"I think you can manage."

She laughed as she stood up from her seat. "You ready to get out of here?"

"Sure." He realized as they walked out of the restaurant that he'd had a nice time with Sophie. She didn't put up any pretenses. He liked that she wasn't into pretending to be someone she wasn't.

They reached the door of the restaurant. "Why don't you wait here, and I'll bring the car around, since it's a bit of a walk to the parking lot." They'd parked in one of the Midtown lots a few blocks away.

"That's nonsense. I'd like the walk, especially after that meal. You should've stopped me after the second chip refill."

He thought about it for a minute, but her pleading blue eyes did him in. "All right. But stay close."

She linked arms with him. "Close enough?"

"Yes." Although, feeling her touch, he started to question whether this was such a good idea after all. What was wrong with him? Why couldn't he keep his cool with her?

"It's such a wonderful fall night," she said. "One of the things I love about Atlanta is the fall weather. It's still warm but not super hot like the summer."

"I like it too. Summer can be miserable."

"Let me tell you, this dinner was much better than my last time coming here."

"What happened?"

"Bad first date. Typical for me."

He found that really hard to believe. "Well, since I've gotten to know you a bit, I can't imagine you were the problem. Did you choose a dud?"

"Totally. All he did the entire time was talk about how important his job was and how much money he made. What a complete and utter turnoff."

They stopped and waited for the traffic light to change so they could cross the street.

"Guys tend to have big egos," he said.

"You seem more grounded than that."

"Sometimes, but don't be fooled. I definitely have my moments." The walk sign flashed bright white, and they started to cross.

Cooper took one step with her out into the street just as a black SUV came barreling toward them. Rapid, loud gunfire filled the air.

Sophie's piercing screams echoed through his ears. Instinctively, he pushed her back onto the sidewalk and dove on top of her, using his body as her armor. Tires screeched, and time felt like it was standing still.

More shots rang out, and he reached for his sidearm. But before he could return fire, the SUV sped away.

"Sophie, are you all right?"

She didn't speak, just stared at him, her face pale under the bright Atlanta streetlights. Then her mouth dropped open and her eyes widened. "You're bleeding! You got shot!"

He looked down at his left arm and started to feel the pain. "Not a direct hit. It just nicked me. We need to get you out of here."

"No. We need to get you to the hospital."

"Don't worry about me. Come on, let's move." He grabbed on to her with his right arm and pulled her close. "How fast can you walk?"

"I can do better than that." She broke into a jog. "Good thing I didn't wear heels tonight."

He matched her pace. "This was an act of escalation."

If there was any doubt in his mind that Sophie was in danger, it was completely erased. Juan had just thrown down the gauntlet.

ELEVEN

Sophie sat in her living room, supercharged from the events of the night. The police had finally left, but she was still surrounded by Cooper and Patrick.

"I think we need to get Sophie out of her house and somewhere safe until trial," Patrick said. "Given what happened this evening, the risks are too high."

"And what exactly do you mean by that?" She envisioned being stuck in a small dark room with armed guards, unable to do anything but sit. That was not an option.

Cooper looked at her. "I think what Patrick is getting at is that you're in danger. Juan showed tonight that he's willing to put a hit out on you. Those guys weren't just trying to scare you, Sophie. This has gone beyond mere threats or trying to get you to back out of your testimony. They're trying to eliminate you so you can never step up to that witness stand."

Eliminate sounded so ominous. And final. "Your solution is to lock me up for the next few weeks?" She wasn't sure if everyone was really thinking this through.

"More like have you work out of a secure location. And if you do have to go anywhere for work, you'll need security. I was hoping that Cooper and his team could come up with an alternative place for you to stay," Patrick said. "And fast. Keeping you here isn't an option, in my opinion."

She didn't like any of this. "I have a job. A job that needs me."

Patrick gave her a sympathetic look. "I knew you would be concerned about that. I spoke with Keith on the way over here, and he was very supportive. He can get your caseload covered by Harrison."

An alarm bell went off in her head. Yeah, she was probably paranoid, given the fact that she'd just been shot at, but was Keith using this as an opportunity to get her to lay off the Shelton case? She wasn't willing to bring that up in front of Patrick. She thought he was a good guy, but she hadn't built that level of trust with him yet.

"I know that Keith is cooperative, but I have a say in this matter," she said firmly. "I think I should get to decide what lawyering I do and what I hand off to others. Besides that, I don't want to go dark for the next couple weeks. I'll lose my mind if I don't have something to keep me occupied. I don't think that would be very good for my testimony."

"What if we come up with a compromise?" Cooper said. "You keep doing your regular caseload at an off-site secure location, and we'll provide security for any court appearances. Then at least for your day to day, you wouldn't be in the office or at your house."

She blew out a breath. Both men had her boxed in. And as much as she hated to admit it, they had a point. There was a difference between completely taking time off versus working outside of the office. "Okay, the only way this could be a viable option is if I can keep working the Shelton case. The trial date will be here before we know it."

"I don't see why that would be a problem," Patrick said. "But you'll have to keep an extremely low profile. Mandatory court appearances are one thing, but going out to dinner in the city is off the table. Do you understand?"

She nodded. At least it wasn't for long. She could handle it if it was the best thing for her safety.

"I'll work on a plan," Cooper said. "And, Sophie, you know I have to bring your father into this, given all the circumstances."

"I figured as much." She worried that her dad was going to lose his mind if he found out exactly what had happened. "Do you have to give him all the details of tonight? Is there any way to sugarcoat it just a bit?"

"I'll do my best."

Patrick stood up. "I've got to run. You're in good hands with Cooper. Keep me posted on where you end up and what the ultimate plan is."

Cooper walked Patrick out. She could hear the two men talking in hushed tones, but she couldn't make out what they were saying.

When Cooper returned, he took a seat on the couch right beside her. "How're you holding up?"

"Well, I've never been shot at before, so I have nothing to compare it to." She paused. "But all things considered, I think I'm doing all right." She heard her voice shake a little, but didn't want him to see how afraid she really was. She wanted to prove that she was tough enough to handle anything. The last thing she needed right now was a panic attack, but if she wasn't careful, it might creep in on her.

"Sophie, it's okay to be worried and fearful. You don't have to put up a front with me."

She met his eyes. "Is it that obvious? I'm not very good at hiding my emotions."

"And you shouldn't have to. The fact that you wear your heart on your sleeve isn't a bad quality."

He took her hand in his, sending a jolt of warmth through her body. His strong but caring touch was starting to have a major impact on her. She could see herself falling hard for Cooper if she didn't put on the brakes.

"I'm actually more worried about my dad finding out and being worried than I am about myself."

"Let me handle your father."

"How's your arm?" She still couldn't believe that he'd been grazed by a bullet. It could've been so much worse.

"Just a tiny nick. Nothing to worry about."

"I hope you're right." When they'd gotten to her house, Cooper had attended to his arm with her first aid kit. He wouldn't let her look at his wound, which made her suspicious, but he insisted that he wasn't really hurt.

"And one more thing." He paused. "I know we talked about church in the morning, but I'm afraid that's just not safe right now."

She knew he was right, but it still bummed her out. "I get it." She also got something else that hit her squarely in the gut. The man in front of her right now seemed to be ticking off all of her checklist requirements, and he didn't have the least idea that she had started to consider him in that way. It was crazy, given everything that was happening, but she couldn't help what she was starting to feel.

"I need to make some calls to figure out a solution for you," he said. "You should start packing."

"This is really happening, huh? I'm going to a safe house?"

"Yes. I don't think there's any other way."

She looked down and realized that he was still holding her hand. Butterflies floated through her stomach. "I trust you."

Sophie's simple words rolled through his mind like a tidal wave. She trusted him. The fact that she was counting on him both encouraged and scared him. He couldn't let her down.

Cooper had told himself that his relationship with Sophie was purely professional. She wanted things he couldn't give her. But for some reason, he still found himself thinking about her. The way she looked at him got to him every time.

Which brought up an even thornier issue—was she developing feelings for him?

His current plan was to keep things platonic. He'd taken her hand tonight because he was trying to reassure her, but he probably shouldn't have let his touch linger. He knew he was playing with fire.

Pushing those thoughts out of his mind, he focused on the next steps. Noah had been able to secure a safe house through his extensive network of contacts. Now Cooper had to make the call he was dreading to Randall Dawson. There was no getting around it. And while he told Sophie he'd do the best he could, he wasn't sure how he was going to tell Randall the truth but do it delicately.

Here goes nothing.

He dialed Randall's number and waited.

"Hello," Randall said.

"Randall, it's Cooper."

"Is Sophie okay?"

"Yes. I'm here with her now, and she's perfectly safe." He took a breath. "But we did have an incident earlier tonight."

"What kind of incident?"

"A rather serious one." He knew that wasn't going to fly, but he was trying to build up to it.

"You've got to give me more than that."

"Sophie and I went out to grab dinner. When we were walking back to my car, another vehicle approached and shot at us."

"What?" Randall's loud voice boomed through the phone.

"I know it sounds dangerous, and it is. Which is why I'm taking Sophie to a secure location where she will stay until the trial begins."

"You're worried that they may come to her house?"

"I can't rule it out. If they're willing to take action like they did tonight, then we have to presume they won't stop. They probably already know where she lives. I'll take her someplace where Juan will not be able to find her."

"This is even worse than I could've ever dreamed. I think you need more manpower."

"I've got my partners helping me out, and they will do whatever is necessary to protect your daughter—as will I."

"I want real-time updates. Do you understand?"

"Yes, sir. I will keep you posted."

"No matter the time, day or night. There is nothing more important than my daughter's safety. You have my full resources at your disposal. Don't let expenses stop you from taking all necessary precautions."

"I understand. I'll keep you fully in the loop."

"Good. Now get out of there and take Sophie somewhere safe."

"We have to stop meeting like this." Ashley eyed Patrick with suspicion. Yes, he was supposedly clean as a whistle, but she didn't trust him. She didn't trust any man, for that matter. "You really should make an appointment before you pop up at my office."

"Do you know what happened last night?" Patrick asked.

"No. Should I?" She had no idea what he was talking about, but he was staring her down.

"Sophie Dawson was almost gunned down in the streets of Midtown."

She kept her facial expression neutral, but inside she wanted to scream. Why had Juan defied her yet again? "What do you mean by 'almost gunned down'?"

"I mean your guy put a hit out on her, and there was a full-out, drive-by gang shooting."

"Is she okay?" She didn't want Juan to kill Sophie. That wouldn't help anyone.

Patrick rested his elbows on her desk. "Yes, but that's beside the point. I'm ready to go to the judge on this. This is a courtesy visit to let you know my intentions."

He was stretching. "That's preposterous. You have nothing to take the judge except a theory. You have no evidence, do you?"

"C'mon, Ashley. Stop it with the gamesmanship. Who else would be trying to shoot Sophie in cold blood?"

She couldn't help but smile, because she had the advantage here. "You do realize that she's been a prosecutor for what, seven or eight years? That woman has made *plenty* of enemies. There's no way you can tie the events of last night to my client."

"And exactly who is your client? Ricky or Juan? Or both?"

"I represent the interests of both brothers. You know that, and there's absolutely nothing wrong with that. There is no conflict here."

"You know, I've dealt with some pretty difficult defense attorneys over the years on a variety of cases. But I can say without a doubt that I've never seen anyone as ruthless as you."

"I take that as a compliment. My job is to zealously defend my client, and I'm doing it. If you want to drag me before the judge, then so be it."

"Will you be singing the same tune when Juan turns on you?"

"And why would he turn on me? I'm his advocate."

"Because men like that aren't loyal, Ashley."

She put up her hand. "Are you going to give me another paternalistic lecture? Because I really don't want to hear it. Do what you have to do, and I'll see you in court. I have other work to do."

"Fine. But this wasn't a veiled threat. I'll be filing something with the court later today."

"I look forward to it."

Patrick let out an exasperated sigh and left her office.

There was no point in even talking to Juan about this again. It was clear he was going to act in whatever way he wanted, regardless of her legal advice. It would now be her responsibility to convince a judge that he had nothing to do with the threats against Sophie.

She started doodling on her legal pad as she thought about

her strategic approach to handling this situation. Playing dumb or oblivious wasn't going to cut it. She would have to go the route she'd told Patrick. Hopefully, she'd be able to dig up some plausible scenarios from Sophie's prior work and try to use those examples to cast doubt on Patrick's allegations.

Given the severity of the situation and the fact that Sophie was a prosecutor, it wasn't going to be easy to convince the judge that her clients were blameless.

Well, at least she loved a good challenge.

When Sophie awoke in a strange bed the next morning, it all came flooding back to her. She was in the safe house. Cooper hadn't been exaggerating. She'd packed a bag, and he had brought her to this new location. He'd taken a very circuitous route and made sure they weren't being followed. She'd decided it was better not to ask too many questions—like how Noah had found a place for them so fast.

The two-story brick house tucked deep into a private cul-de-sac of a Buckhead neighborhood wasn't what she'd envisioned when they'd told her they were taking her to a safe house. But she wasn't going to complain, because it was much nicer than she had expected.

It all seemed a bit cloak-and-dagger to her, but she understood why Cooper had to take the precautions. Never in her wildest dreams had she thought she could be killed because of her witness testimony. Threats were one thing, but this had gone well beyond mere threats.

If only she hadn't stopped that night for a snack. But then, she told herself, Ricky might have gotten away without being punished.

Now she sat with her laptop and a stack of files at the table in the living room, ready to work. It was a welcome distraction from the Wade case. And she was actually excited to dig in.

She was surrounded by banker's boxes filled with documents provided by SIB that one of the guys had been able to get transferred from her office.

Cooper was so squarely in his element that she let him do his thing. It was her job to concentrate on her cases, and it was his to concentrate on her. Well, at least her safety.

She hadn't forgotten what it was like holding his hand last night. She could sense something inside herself, a longing for more with him. And she wasn't sure what to do with those feelings. Everything was so amplified right now. Was she crushing on him because he was being so protective and kind? Or was there something deeper going on? She didn't know the answer yet, but she intended to find out. The spark between them was undeniable and unlike anything she'd ever felt before.

Cooper was in the kitchen with Landon and Noah, talking shop, so she was free to turn her attention to the case against Glen Shelton. Keith probably wasn't going to be happy that she planned to put all her time and energy into building this case while she was sequestered so she'd be ready to go to trial. But she'd come to the realization that her interests and Keith's wouldn't always be aligned. She planned to do the right thing, regardless of the impact to SIB. They were a big company and could withstand this lawsuit, that much she was sure of. She wasn't a politician and didn't have those aspirations, which allowed her a freedom to do her job that Keith simply didn't have.

She'd also received a troubling email from Harrison, once again offering his help—specifically to review any files and help her with trial strategy. Not only was she highly suspicious of his ulterior motives, there was no way she'd work with him on this. Harrison was playing a long political game, and she couldn't afford any of that. It also tugged at her mind why he was so insistent on being involved in the Shelton case. It made her wonder if Harrison had some relationship she didn't know about with SIB. She was definitely dealing with a tangled web.

She'd politely thanked him again for his offer and declined the help. Hopefully he'd get the point.

Sophie pulled a stack of files from a folder that she had previously reviewed. It was all the transactions Shelton had executed over the past three years. She'd analyzed and categorized them as best she could to isolate all of the excess overcharges. She'd also received a document dump from SIB that included a lot of other transactions. Her first order of business was to go through the new documents.

She'd told Keith that she wasn't after SIB, and she wasn't. But she still had to do her due diligence to see what else was in the files. SIB had been cooperative about turning over a ton of documents, which made her think that they knew they were clean, or they wouldn't have done that. Regardless, she was going to take a look. She needed to confirm for herself that the illegal activity stopped with Shelton.

It was a good thing she'd made coffee, because this type of document review was very dry. Page after page of financial records needed to be reviewed, and it was up to her to connect the dots. In a law firm, an entire team of associates would review documents like this, but in her world, it was just her and a rookie prosecutor. This task was so important, though, that she wasn't going to delegate it all to Monica. She needed to put her own eyes on these documents, because Monica wasn't seasoned enough to understand all the intricacies.

As she was going through each page in painstaking detail for fear of missing something, she stopped short for a moment. She reread the top of the first page, which indicated whose account this was. It was definitely Glen Shelton's account. His personal account, one of a few he had with SIB. But she'd never seen these particular transactions before.

The statements listed multiple cash deposits that were all just shy of ten thousand dollars. That set off a big red flag because banks were required to report transactions that amounted to ten thousand or more. But these deposits appeared to be spaced out to ensure that the rule wouldn't trigger. So whoever was making these deposits understood financial regulations, and they were purposely trying to avoid the reporting requirements.

This was strange. What was she missing? How did these deposits interact with what Shelton was doing otherwise?

"Why the frown?" Cooper walked into the room and took a seat across from her.

"I'm reviewing the documents I received from SIB."

"Not finding what you're looking for?"

"More like finding things I didn't expect. Are the guys still here?"

"No. They just left, but we're all good. We've got state-of-the-art security here, and we've kept the circle really tight about who knows where we are. And by really tight, I mean only me and the guys. No one else."

"Not even my father?"

"No. And he was fully on board with that strategy."

Suddenly, an awful thought struck her. "Do you think my father is in danger?"

"Why do you ask that?"

"Maybe they'd use him to get to me."

Now he was the one frowning. "I'll be honest, we haven't considered that yet. I don't think that's really Juan's MO. They're more the brute-force type, as evidenced by the drive-by."

"But it's possible. They could threaten him and blackmail me to try to get me not to testify."

"Good point. I'll call the guys and we'll figure out a plan." He pulled out his phone and left the room.

Sophie turned her attention back to the papers and started highlighting individual entries. Shelton's illegal activities looked like they ran much deeper than she'd expected.

Cooper returned to the room a few minutes later and sat

back down. "Landon's on it. He's going to have a chat with your father right now."

"Good. I'll feel better knowing that we've covered every angle."

He smiled. "You could have a future in security consulting."

She laughed. "I think I'll stick to the courtroom." She paused. "I know this may seem odd, but I'd like to hire your company as a consultant for my Shelton case."

"What for?"

"I'm seeing some things in the documents that I need your help with. And I think it could have potential implications for me too. Would you be interested in that?"

"Sure. You've piqued my interest."

She took a few minutes to update the confidentiality agreement he had previously signed, and they worked out some logistics. Once that was taken care of, she was ready to explain why she needed his help.

He turned toward her. "Tell me about what you're finding in the documents."

"Shelton has made a series of sizeable deposits to multiple accounts over the past two years. They're all under ten grand, so they wouldn't have been reported. But I'm trying to figure out how those deposits fit into his scheme."

"And his scheme was siphoning off money from his clients by charging them excessive fees, which he would pocket, right?"

"Exactly. But these deposits don't fit within that model, because I've already traced those funds. These are completely separate. Which makes me wonder what else he was involved in, and with who. Someone had to be making these cash payments to him. The question is what was he doing to get paid these chunks of money, and whether this is some type of money-laundering scheme." Her adrenaline started pumping. "Maybe I'm just looking at the tip of the iceberg. I've got to see if he's moving these chunks of money out at different intervals. And that's where I could use your help. K&R Security has more technical ability to analyze data like this than I do."

"Yes, I can have Noah start to work on it. If anyone can find out what's happening to that money, it's him. I have to say, though, that if you're looking at a bigger situation than you thought, that could lend credence to the idea that SIB might have someone keeping an eye on you."

"You're talking about that random guy at my house?"

"Yeah. SIB would probably have a strong motivation to keep a lid on this. If their employee stole from customers, that one's thing, but if you start talking about Shelton running a money-laundering operation, that's a different ball game."

"You're right. I'd like to think that Whitney is on the up-and-up and that I don't have anything to fear from her or the company. But I also know that when you're talking about this kind of money, it can make people do crazy things."

"Yes, unfortunately, I think that's the reality of the situation."

"Well, that's another reason I'm thankful to have you around. But how is this going to work on a day-to-day basis?"

"Someone will be here at all times. If it's not me, it will be either Landon or Noah. We can't risk you being alone right now, and with each day we get closer to trial, the risk amplifies."

"Thanks for the reminder," she muttered.

"There's no need for you to stress. I promise you that Juan has no idea where you are."

"For now," she said softly.

CHAPTER
TWELVE

True to his word, Patrick filed an emergency motion with the court, and Ashley was forced to appear and face what was likely going to be a very unhappy bench. Judge Turner wore a deep frown as he walked into the courtroom to take his seat. Ashley didn't like that Patrick was being so aggressive. She needed to shift the balance of power back to her side.

Patrick's motion was highly inflammatory and based largely on conjecture rather than evidence. But she'd be fighting a difficult battle, given that Judge Turner was going to be protective of Sophie since she was a prosecutor. Ashley had no idea what the judge was going to do about Patrick's claims. His motion left her a bit confused, because he hadn't asked the judge to enter any specific order or even do anything, really. It was more just Patrick airing his grievances in a formalized way. She figured he had something else up his sleeve.

"Mr. Hunt, I have your emergency motion for a hearing, and your allegations are deeply disturbing. But before we get into the substance, I fail to see what type of relief you are seeking from this Court."

Bingo. At least she and Judge Turner were on the same

wavelength. She'd wondered herself what Patrick was going to ask the judge to do.

Patrick glanced over at her and then made direct eye contact with the judge. "Your Honor, I'll be the first to admit that this situation is highly unusual, but I also believe that there has to be some action by the Court, given the circumstances at hand."

"What I'm hearing you say is that you're not even sure what type of relief is appropriate here, Mr. Hunt?"

"You're right, Your Honor. I think that is up for discussion."

"I'll cross that bridge in a minute, then," Judge Turner said. "You make some very serious claims. What evidence do you have supporting your allegations in the motion?"

Patrick cleared his throat. "Everyone knows that Ms. Dawson is the lone witness the state has in its case against Ricky Wade. We're not talking about one isolated or random incident here. There have been two attacks on Ms. Dawson, with the second being an attempt on her life in a drive-by shooting. That type of MO is textbook Juan Wade."

Ashley had to jump in. "That's a ludicrous assertion, Your Honor. All Mr. Hunt has is some fantasy theory that he's constructing to obscure the real issue here—that my client, Ricky Wade, is innocent until proven guilty, and he deserves a fair trial in this Court. This is nothing more than a sideshow to distract from the core issue. Further, my client is still in jail. There's no way that the prosecution can link him to these attacks. He's been in lockdown."

The judge shifted in his seat. "Mr. Hunt, a response?"

"Ms. Murphy is correct about her client, in this case, being in jail—for double homicide. But the defendant's brother, Juan Wade, who is also Ms. Murphy's client, has the motive and the means to come after my witness. Ms. Dawson could've been killed in cold blood if not for intervening circumstances. I don't have to tell the Court what implications that would have for my case against the defendant."

Judge Turner crossed his arms. "Mr. Hunt, I'm sympathetic to your general premise here, but it almost sounds like you're starting an opening statement in a case against Mr. Juan Wade. Wouldn't your arguments be better suited for a case brought against him, assuming he was ever brought up on charges for what happened to Ms. Dawson? And let me make clear, that hasn't happened yet, as I understand the facts."

"And I would make these arguments in a case against Juan Wade, but my priority right now is getting this issue in front of you so that you can determine if anything can be done about it in relation to the case against Ricky Wade."

Judge Turner thought for a moment. "There are two issues here, as I see it. One is the underlying factual issue about who is behind these attacks and if there's anything I can do about it now. Second is the actual physical security of your witness. Let me tackle the second point first. Are you asking for court-ordered protection for your witness?"

Patrick shook his head. "No, Your Honor. That is already being taken care of."

"Then I'm afraid my hands are tied. The matter before me is the case of the state against Ricky Wade. I can't take any action against someone who isn't even a named party. But I will say this. Ms. Murphy, I suggest you have a frank discussion with your clients—both of them—about these events. And if either of them had anything to do with the attacks on Ms. Dawson, either directly or indirectly, I'm sure that's a fact the state will try to argue at your client's upcoming trial. That's all for now. The state's motion is denied."

The judge stood up and exited the courtroom, and Ashley's mind swirled with thoughts. The judge went way easier on her than she had expected, but Patrick didn't seem fazed by any of it.

She walked over to his table as he shoved papers into his large black briefcase. "What was your play here, Patrick?"

He turned to face her. "What do you mean?"

135

"You don't seem that upset or even surprised that the judge didn't give you anything today. Was this just a move on your part to annoy me and suck up my time?"

He gave her a dazzling smile, showing his bright white teeth, and she clenched her fists tightly at her side, fighting back her anger.

"Patrick, I fail to see why you're smiling."

"I got everything today that I needed." He glanced over his shoulder at the courtroom gallery.

Then it hit her. How could she have been so stupid? She'd been thinking about it completely the wrong way. "You were trying to get this story out into the media to hurt Ricky's case."

He shrugged. "Those are your words, not mine. I was just making sure the judge was fully apprised of the situation."

"You're a weasel, do you know that? You like to play it like you're all about truth and justice and all of that, but really, you're no different than me. You just want to win. So you can take the self-righteous routine and use it on someone else."

His dark eyes narrowed. "Really, Ashley, is it worth you getting so worked up? What's gotten into you?"

He really knew how to push her buttons. She took a few breaths and tried to get back under control. The last thing she wanted was for him to realize how much he had gotten under her skin. "I'm not worked up. I'm just a bit surprised that you would stoop to such tactics by using the media this way. You think Sophie is going to charm the jury, but once I'm done with her, you'll be wondering why you even put her on the stand."

"You can tell yourself that all day, Ash, but you and I both know it's not true. She's solid as a rock."

"Don't call me Ash."

He put his hand on her shoulder. "Lighten up. There's no judge or jury here now. It's just us."

She'd had enough. "I'm going back to work. Thanks for a

complete waste of time." She turned away from him and walked out of the courtroom.

Today had taught her one very important thing. She'd vastly underestimated Patrick Hunt. That was a mistake she'd never make again. It was time to turn up the heat.

Just when Tad thought things couldn't get any more interesting, Sophie Dawson appeared to have gone off the grid. He sat at his favorite downtown diner, eating biscuits and gravy. At almost fifty, he knew he should start watching what he ate, but he couldn't give up southern comfort food. Born and raised in Georgia, there was no other eating, in his mind. As he took a swig of his sweet tea, another guilty pleasure, he started to put the pieces together.

At first he couldn't figure out why Sophie was AWOL, but he had attended a court hearing today in the Wade case that made things make a lot more sense. He hadn't had eyes on Sophie since Saturday afternoon. The last place he'd seen her was her house, and now it was clear to him that she was no longer there.

The hearing had been highly informative. In his opinion, the gang had tried to take her out. A drive-by shooting fit the gang MO perfectly. Although he had to admit, a tiny piece of him wondered whether Whitney had gone behind his back and ordered a hit on Sophie. The gang angle would be perfect cover for her, and she'd said as much to him. But he didn't know how extensive Whitney's contacts ran for her to be able to pull off something like that.

At the end of the day, he thought Wade was behind this attack. Tad had gotten the message from Whitney loud and clear, though, that she wanted him to be aggressive in his handling of this case. If Whitney only understood just how complicated this all could be—and dangerous. One thing he knew for certain: ominous threatening phone calls weren't going to stop Sophie

Dawson—and it appeared a drive-by wouldn't either. Which meant he was going to have be more aggressive.

This job was important to him, and he wanted to keep Whitney happy. He also wanted to keep his referral source happy too, because that ultimately meant more business. Whether Whitney was going to come clean and tell him exactly what she and the bank had been up to remained to be seen. But he planned to push her until she told him everything. It was critical that he got all the information he could to be able to take the next steps and play his hand correctly. He wasn't naïve. He knew what corporate America was like, especially a bank like SIB struggling to compete with the megabanks. Just how far would Whitney Bowman go?

Sophie walked into the family room of the safe house and found Cooper sitting on the couch, writing in a notebook.

"Hi," she said.

He looked up and smiled. "I didn't want to bother you because you seemed hard at work in the other room."

"I was, but now I'm ready for a break. How're you doing? Are you going stir-crazy?"

He shook his head and gave her a half smile. "It's my job. I've had to spend time with much worse people before. Trust me."

"I guess that's a positive?" She took a seat on the sofa beside him.

"Definitely."

"I did need to ask you something."

"Sure."

"I got an email from Patrick. He needs to do some witness preparation with me. Where is that going to happen?"

Cooper ran his hand through his hair. "Good question. Let me think about it, and I'll coordinate with Patrick. Also, tomorrow Landon is going to be here for a bit while I handle a few things."

"All right." She looked into his bright blue eyes, and her stomach tightened. It hit her that she didn't want him to go. It wasn't that she had anything against Landon, but she was starting to form a bond with Cooper. He'd proven that he was able to protect her.

"I take this work very seriously, Sophie. I hope you know that."

"I know." How could she even begin to describe her emotions?

"What is it? Talk to me."

"I'd like to get to know you better." She blurted it out before she could stop herself. She didn't break eye contact with him, and she noticed the hint of concern that crept across his handsome face.

"I don't know if that's such a good idea." He moved slightly away from her on the couch.

His response stung. Was she completely misreading him? She thought she could feel an intense spark between them, but right now he seemed ice cold. Maybe she was delusional. No wonder she was still single and pining for Mr. Right. She had the absolute worst instincts when it came to men.

"I'm sorry," she said. "I'll go back to the other room."

Sophie stood up, but then Cooper was right beside her. "No, I'm the one who should be sorry. It's just that, given all the circumstances, I think it's best for us to keep this relationship strictly professional."

"Can't we be professional but friendly? I just want to know more about the man I'm spending every waking minute with." As she said the words, she didn't believe them, because deep in her gut, she knew that was only the tip of the iceberg. She wanted more from him. Friendship was just the starting point.

He sat back down and patted the sofa. "Please sit, then. Ask me whatever you want to know."

She took a seat beside him. "Well, now you're putting me on

the spot." She clasped her hands together. "How do you do this job? It seems like it makes it impossible to have a normal life."

"What do you mean?"

"You have to dedicate all your time to protecting me. I assume once my problems are over, you'll move on to something similar. Another person who needs you to protect them from whatever dangerous situation they've found themselves in. Don't you want to have more control of your life? More time to yourself for your own friends and relationships?"

"You have to remember that I work with my two best friends."

She hadn't thought about it that way. "I guess that's true. I just don't want to be a burden on you or make you stop living your life."

"That isn't anything you need to worry about. Promise me you'll put that thought out of your head."

Something else had been on her mind. "Speaking of friends, I assume I won't get to see Kate and Mia until after the trial?"

"That's probably for the best. For your safety and for theirs too."

She figured that would be the answer. And the last thing she wanted was to put her friends in harm's way. "I get it. My plan is still to put my time and energy into the Shelton case except when Patrick needs me."

"What's your read on him?"

"I like Patrick a lot. He's a straight shooter. He doesn't dance around difficult issues with me. What do you think about him?"

He didn't immediately respond. "He's taken a very strong interest in you."

That was no surprise. "Of course he has. I'm the linchpin to his case."

He raised an eyebrow. "Is that all you think it is?"

"Yeah." Had she missed something with Patrick? She hadn't felt like he was interested in her beyond her being his witness. "Do you trust him?"

He placed his hands on his knees. "Right now, I only trust my team, but we have to work with Patrick, so I'm being extra cautious. I can't be sure what anyone's motives are, given the danger that you're in. If that means I'm operating with everyone under a cloud of suspicion, then so be it."

She blew out a breath. "I'm ready to get my old life back. I know I shouldn't complain. Two innocent people lost their lives, but this is not how I envisioned things."

"I'm sorry, Sophie. This life can be tough. As you know."

"Yeah, I'm living through it right now."

"I'd hate to know that my comments caused you pain."

She shook her head. "It's not you. I have to admit, I've asked God many times in my life why He has tested me, and this challenge is no different. While I have so many things in life, they're no match for the hole in my heart. It's hard not to ask, why me? I really don't want to be *that* person. The person who has it all and still complains. But there are things money can't buy. I wonder why God has chosen to keep those things from me. I wrestle with that every single day. It doesn't seem fair. And knowing life isn't always fair doesn't make it any easier."

"I think we've all asked questions of God. I know I have many times in my life. Different questions than yours, but still questions. I know we can't see the whole picture, and sometimes what we can see looks so distorted. But there's nothing wrong with questioning. I can tell just in the short time that we've known each other that your faith is strong. You might not say much about it, but it shows in how you live your life."

Her heart warmed at his kind words. "I could say the same thing about you." In fact, that was one of the qualities that drew her to him so strongly. She moved in closer to him on the couch.

This time he didn't move away from her, but he didn't move toward her either. An awkward silence filled the air. She told herself that she refused to be the one to make the first move.

She had to let Cooper do it. This meant too much for her to mess it up.

But before anything else could happen between them, he stood up, ending the moment. "I'm going to do a security check."

"All right," she said, swallowing her disappointment.

It was clear that Cooper was holding back. What she didn't know was why.

Cooper moved through each room of the safe house, breathing deeply with each step he took. It was like when he was around Sophie, he couldn't catch his breath. The way she had looked at him tonight solidified in his mind that she was starting to feel something for him. And that was a big problem.

As much as he wanted to, he couldn't allow himself to be drawn in by her big blue eyes and kind heart. His problem was on multiple levels. The first and most obvious was that he was in charge of Sophie's safety. He couldn't permit himself to be distracted by emotions. And they were pretty strong emotions brewing inside of him. Besides the intense physical chemistry he felt, he also was forming an emotional connection with her. That combination was dangerous.

But even beyond that, he was the wrong man for Sophie. The problem wasn't attraction. He was clearly attracted to her on every level. She was smart, kind, and beautiful. But she needed a man who had the same hopes and dreams as her. The white picket fence, multiple kids, and a dog.

That wasn't him. Maybe he could swing the dog, but that was about it. How could he make her understand that their connection didn't matter because he had a different game plan than her? A plan entrenched deeply inside of him based on everything that had happened in his life.

She'd made her plans clear to him. She hadn't had a mother, and it was a top priority for her to be one. The last thing he ever wanted was to hurt her. As much as he dreaded having this conversation, it was necessary to keep things between them simple and easy so both of them could stay focused on the task at hand. He was worried that if he didn't say something now, the situation might get out of control.

He found her where he'd left her, sitting on the sofa, except now she had her laptop out and was typing away.

"Is this a bad time?" he asked.

"No. What's up?" She set the laptop on the coffee table.

He took a seat beside her and readied himself for what was sure to be an awkward discussion. "I want to talk to you about something."

She tilted her head to the side. "All right. Is everything okay?"

"Yes, everything is fine." As he prepared himself, he questioned whether this was a good idea, but he felt like he needed to have this talk. It was the right thing to do. *Lord, help me. I want to do what is best for Sophie. Not act based on my own selfish desires.*

"Maybe I'm way off base here, but I feel like there might be a connection forming between the two of us."

As he said the words, her eyes lit up, and he knew this was going to be even more difficult than he had expected.

"I'm so glad you said something. I was beginning to feel like maybe I was crazy and completely misreading the situation." She smiled and leaned in a bit closer.

"You're not crazy. That's why I wanted to talk to you. The thing is, I think you're amazing. I do." He stopped, trying to find his words.

"Uh-oh."

"It's not easy to say this." He took another breath.

She moved away from him. "I think I know where you're going with this. You're not comfortable exploring what there is between us while you're working for my father."

"That's definitely part of it. A big part, in fact, but if I'm

143

being completely open with you, there's more than that. A lot more. And that's what I want to tell you, to explain, because I don't want there to be any confusion."

"What else is there?"

Once he opened up about his past, there was no going back. Things between them would be changed. "I think I mentioned before that you and I had very different family situations growing up."

"Yeah, but you didn't elaborate."

Could he do this? Could he tell her about his past to spare her from developing any more feelings for him? "First I have to say that I loved my mother. She was my mom, and I would've done anything in this world for her, but she had issues. She did the best she could when I was growing up, in a very difficult situation, because my father was a complete beast of a man."

Sophie's eyes widened. "How so?"

He didn't like talking about this. He'd confided in Noah and Landon years ago in college, but it was never a topic of conversation after that. It was so much easier to keep it locked up in a dark place inside him. Somewhere he never liked to visit. Like a pitch-black jungle.

"My father was physically and emotionally abusive both to my mother and me. He was an alcoholic." He steadied himself and continued. "I grew up in the midst of complete chaos. My house was a turbulent place where the only ounce of love and protection I ever received was from my mother, and she struggled even to provide much of that, given that she was continuously targeted by my father." The words seemed to rush out of him once he started talking.

Sophie took his hand in hers, and given the subject matter, he didn't break away. He needed her strength and support right now to get him through this.

"There was always so much yelling and fighting. Violence and misery. Some of my earliest childhood memories are of

144

my father coming home late at night after a drinking binge. I'd hear the front door slam shut, and I would know that he was on a tear. The sad thing is that it almost became second nature to me. There were more nights like that than nights of him being sober. And when he was drunk, he became violent." He almost choked up but steadied himself with another deep breath. "I'd wake up and hear him attacking my mother. At first, she'd scream. But after a while, she wouldn't even do that. Her spirit was completely broken. She wouldn't fight back."

He watched as a tear slid down Sophie's cheek. But she didn't say a word.

"For years, I didn't know what to do. But once I got older, I started confronting him. I hit a growth spurt as a young teen, and all of a sudden I was taller than him. And by the time I was a senior in high school, I was also stronger. I defended my mother the best I could, but she always told me that he didn't know what he was doing. That it was the drinking and not the man she fell in love with. Frankly, I wasn't having any of that. I hated the thought of leaving for college, but she insisted that I did. She said that she wanted me to get out and have a better life. It was really the only thing she focused on—helping me get out of that house."

"What happened after you left?" she asked softly.

"It was bad for a couple of years until my mom got sick. When she got diagnosed with cancer, something happened, and my dad stopped drinking. But as far as I was concerned, the damage had already been done. I'd spent twenty years of my life with him being an addict. And it impacted every facet of my existence."

"And what about now? How is it between you and your father?"

"We don't have a relationship. I know the right thing to do would be to forgive him and move on, but, Sophie, I'm not a strong enough man to do that." How could he? He couldn't

145

even speak to his father. "I've prayed about it, and the Lord has given me some measure of peace, but I'm not ready to try to go back to my father. I doubt I ever will be. I know what I should do, but I'm also just a man. I pray for strength, but I'm not strong enough."

He waited for her to say something. To counter his words and say that he was strong enough. To suggest that he make amends with his father. But once again, she didn't say anything. She just listened.

"The reason I'm giving you all the awful details is because I know I'm messed up. And because of it, I have zero interest in getting married and even less interest in having a family of my own. Growing up, no one on the outside had any idea what was happening, and people always told me how much I looked like my dad. How much I acted like him. It made me sick. But it also made me realize that I couldn't turn into him. Wouldn't turn into him. I'd never take the risk of putting a child through what I went through. What happened just shows that people can change for the worse."

She squeezed his hand and broke her silence. "But you would never do that. I know you, and I know you aren't that type of man."

"How can you be so sure? My mother told me my father wasn't like that until after I was born. Then he started getting stressed about everything. That led him to start drinking heavily. How do I know that I couldn't be tempted to go down a similar path if put under those circumstances? It's in my blood, Sophie."

"I can't pretend to act like I know what you lived through and how it still follows you every day. But I wouldn't be a very good person if I didn't point out the differences. The man I've gotten to know sitting beside me right now would never physically attack a woman or a child. Never." She was fierce in her defense of him.

"That's a risk I just can't take, and I'd never want to put

146

you in a bad position. The last thing I'd ever want is to start down a path and then disappoint you when I couldn't give you all that you wanted. And all that you should have." He shook his head. "I won't do that to you. It would be utterly unfair."

She closed her eyes for a moment and then opened them. Another tear streamed down her cheek. "I don't even know what to say."

"You don't have to say anything right now. I just had to get that off my chest, because I do care about you and would never want to mislead you. Now you understand why I haven't been as open about my past as you have. And I ask you to also understand why we need to keep things completely professional and platonic between us."

She gave his hand one more squeeze before letting go of it. "Please excuse me." She walked out of the room.

It hurt to watch her go, but he hoped and prayed that he'd just spared them both a lot of pain in the future.

THIRTEEN

The next afternoon, Sophie sat at the kitchen table, waiting for Patrick's arrival. Cooper had decided after consulting with the guys that it was best for Patrick to come to the safe house to do her witness preparation. From what she understood, one of the guys would pick up Patrick and make sure they weren't detected on their way to the safe house.

As much as she wanted to focus on her testimony in the Wade trial, her mind kept going back to her troubling discussion with Cooper last night. His words played like a sad ballad over and over again in her head and broke her heart.

She almost had to laugh at the irony. This man had come into her life and seemed to be the perfect fit. Then she found out that the thing she wanted most was the thing he had no interest in. *Lord, is this some sort of test?*

She honestly didn't know. Cooper opening up to her only made her feel more connected to him, but his revelation did shake her. Because as much as she was starting to develop true feelings for him, she simply couldn't give her heart to a man who was so strongly opposed to having a family.

Cooper walked into the kitchen and took a seat. "You ready for your meeting?"

"Yeah."

"Noah just called. They're two minutes out."

"Is everything okay with that? I know you were concerned about the security risks."

He nodded. "Yeah. Noah is very good at what he does, and Landon was also involved to ensure that no one was following them. We're still locked down tight. You don't have anything to worry about."

"Good. I'm ready to get started whenever Patrick gets here."

"One thing, really quick." He paused. "Are we good? I feel like I really dumped a lot of stuff on you last night, and that was probably pretty selfish of me, especially given all the other things you have on your plate right now."

"It wasn't selfish. It helps me understand you better." She considered how much she should say right now. She feared that if she told him how she really felt, he would not take it well. She needed to figure out a way to open his mind to the idea of a future together. "I want to talk more about it, though, when we have the time. I have some thoughts."

He broke eye contact with her. "I don't know if that's a good idea. Maybe we should just let it go. Put it behind us and move on."

She shook her head. "You can't tell me all that stuff and expect me to have no reaction."

His phone buzzed. "They're here. We'll finish this conversation later. I'll go let them in."

Sophie let out a big sigh. At least now she understood why he was trying so hard to push her away. Especially after she had been so open about her desire for a family. There she was, talking about how important being a mother was for her, and all the while it was like a big flashing warning sign for him.

Lord, what is your plan here? Is there a plan?

She couldn't help but question God, because she had no clue what she had gotten herself into.

But regardless of how she felt, it was now time to get to work. The innocent homicide victims deserved her full attention.

Patrick entered the kitchen and made eye contact with her. "Do you want to work in here?"

"This is a good spot, but if you want to go somewhere else, we can."

He looked the part of a prosecutor, wearing a traditional dark suit and navy striped tie.

"You came from court?" she asked.

"Yeah. I had a few hearings this morning." He set down his bag and started to unpack his things—a laptop, a legal pad, and a stack of documents. "Before we get into the nitty-gritty, how are you doing?"

"Obviously, being locked up in a safe house isn't ideal, but I know it's for the best, given the circumstances. And thankfully I've been able to get work done on my own case, so at least I don't feel like I'm getting too far behind. I'm not the type of person who likes to sit around and do nothing. This way I can keep being productive."

He pulled a few pens out of his bag and set them on the table. "I imagine your caseload is a bit different in White Collar than when you were a general ADA?"

"Yes, it's much lighter. I can actually spend good chunks of time on each file instead of just grabbing something and hitting the courtroom. I feel like I'm developing a different skill set, and that should help in me in the future."

"Do you miss the daily courtroom grind, though?"

She considered his question. "You know, I don't think I really have. I've enjoyed being able to take a deep dive on some issues. I like the research and case building. There was absolutely no time for that in my prior role. Everything felt like it was off the cuff, and there was barely time to catch your breath. This position allows me time to think through issues in a way I've never been able to do before."

Patrick nodded and took a moment to organize his materials in front of him. "Let's get down to business, all right?"

"Sounds good." The sooner this trial was over, the sooner her life could get back to normal.

"Let's start with the rules of the road. I'm going to do my best to treat you the same as I would any other witness. I don't want to presume that you're going to act one way or the other just because you're also a prosecutor. I think it'll be best if I try to keep things as normal as I can under the circumstances."

"All right. But I think we both know this is going to be unique. Ashley will treat me differently. I think she'll come at me in a much more aggressive fashion because of who I am."

"And we'll get to that. But let's go through the basics of testifying first, just like any other witness. You may need this even more than other witnesses, because you have a specialized level of knowledge."

She knew what he was getting at. The fact that she was a lawyer might make her a worse witness. She was going to do her best to stay open-minded and focused. This was too important for her to have an ego. "I'm listening."

"You'll be called after the law enforcement officers. I want them to set the stage from their perspective, just like a regular case. That's going to be my theme here. Then I'll put you on the stand, and I want you to play the role of a true eyewitness. No lawyer speak. None."

She laughed. "I'll do my best, but some of it's just built into my vocabulary, and it has become who I am. But I realize it's important not to play prosecutor."

"Good. I'd like to practice some of your direct examination to see how you'll answer things. But remember, for this trial, you're just Sophie Dawson—a thirty-two-year-old woman who was at the Quick Stop to grab a snack after a long day of work. Got it?"

"Yes." She had relayed the series of events that took place

that evening many times, but as the trial drew nearer, it was all starting to weigh on her.

As Patrick led her through what he envisioned to be the examination, she answered him to the best of her ability. They spent over an hour on that portion of the preparation.

"Now let's turn to preparing for your cross-examination," he said. "This is going to be tough, and I want to say upfront that this may become uncomfortable. But I'd rather we hash this out here than in the courtroom with Ashley. Just remember that I'm on your side, even if I'm role-playing as Ashley."

"It's your job to prepare me for what might be coming. I'm ready. Please don't hold back." It wouldn't do either of them any good if he was too gentle with her. He needed to go all out so she'd have the best chance of actually handling Ashley's cross-examination.

"I'm going to try to stay in character through a series of questions. Then we'll stop and talk about them."

She readied herself for Patrick's attempt to become Ashley Murphy.

He looked down and then back up at her. His dark eyes focused in on hers. "Ms. Dawson, you testified that you had just finished up a trial earlier in the day of the shooting. Is that right?"

"Yes." She knew she needed to keep her answers short and to the point. Make Ashley work for everything. One of the first rules of testifying—don't volunteer.

"And after the trial, you had more work to do, and you didn't leave the office until late?"

"Yes."

"Had you slept much the night before?"

"I think I slept about the normal amount."

He raised an eyebrow. "Even though you had closing statements the next day? You didn't stay up late preparing for that? For your first big trial in your new job?"

She clenched her fist by her side as she started to see where

Patrick was going with this. "I had completed the preparation work for my closing statement. I don't recall how much I slept, but I know I did sleep."

"Ms. Dawson, just a moment ago, you testified that you slept the regular amount. Now you're saying you don't recall. Which is it?"

"I don't specifically recall."

"But it might have been less than you normally do?"

Patrick was using leading questions, which would be perfectly allowable on Ashley's cross-examination. "It might have been. I can't remember. What I do recall is that I definitely slept that night."

Patrick leaned forward. "Okay. Let's pause for a moment." His eyes softened. "You're sounding defensive already, Sophie. There's no reason for you to get your back up against the wall on this topic. I need you to take a few deep breaths and put all of this in perspective."

"I'm sorry. I'll do better."

"That's why we're going through this exercise. I know you will end up being a strong witness, but just like any other person testifying, it's helpful to go through it and practice."

Patrick was being very diplomatic. He was good at his job, and she could probably learn a few things from him. "Do you think she's going to argue that I was too tired to make an accurate witness identification because of the trial?"

"It's one of many paths she may go down." He lifted his legal pad, showing his chicken-scratch handwriting. "Unfortunately, I have a whole list of possible lines of questioning she may pursue. I've spent a lot of time going through all the scenarios I could come up with and tried my best to put myself in Ashley's shoes. Although she's so different than I am, it has been a challenge. We have to be prepared for the fact that she doesn't have a strong moral compass guiding her. She will do anything—and I mean anything—it takes to win."

Hearing those words gave Sophie pause. "I really don't re-member how much I slept that night. Yes, I was preparing for trial, but I definitely didn't pull an all-nighter. I rarely do. It just doesn't stand out to me, because there's no reason for me to remember exactly what happened then. Especially given what did happen the next night. I can tell you that I did not sleep much the night of the shooting. That I remember very clearly."

Patrick set down his pen. "Let's stop for now. I don't want to overdo it in one day."

"Whatever you think is best. I can keep going as long as you need to."

He started gathering up his papers and looked down at his watch. "No. This was good for today. I'll make arrangements with Cooper and Noah for the next session."

"Thanks."

He leaned in close and put his hand on her shoulder. "Don't obsess over this tonight."

She looked into his brown eyes and felt a bit reassured. But she also saw that he had some concern about her performance today.

Cooper and Noah walked into the kitchen, and she noticed that Cooper's gaze went directly to Patrick, who removed his hand from her shoulder.

Patrick straightened. "Great timing, guys. We're done for the day."

"I'll get you back to the office," Noah said.

Sophie rose from her seat. "Thanks, Patrick. I'll be better tomorrow."

"Remember, don't worry." Patrick gave her shoulder a pat before he exited the kitchen with Noah.

She took a few breaths. If she couldn't handle that set of sample questions from Patrick, how was she going to respond when all eyes were on her at the trial? She needed to get her head on straight and do a lot better than that.

Her stomach churned at the thought of letting down the families of the two victims. Closing her eyes for a moment, she prayed. *Lord, I am not strong enough to do this on my own. I need you.*

Cooper walked up to her. "Are you all right?"

"Yeah." She looked up at him.

"What were you talking about with Patrick?"

"We're preparing for cross-examination, and I fumbled the first set of questions. It was not good."

"Just tell the truth, Sophie. You'll be fine if you do. I have all the confidence in the world in you."

His words were meant to comfort her, but she was too wound up. "Ashley will do everything in her power to discredit me. And if I perform in the courtroom like I did today, it will not be good for the prosecution. I can't give the jury anything to have a shred of doubt about."

"I think you're being too hard on yourself."

"Two people were murdered, Cooper. There is a lot on the line." She tried to keep her emotions in check, but she wasn't doing a very good job. A wave of exhaustion washed over her. "Maybe I should lie down for a bit."

"Are you sure you're all right?"

"Yes. There's nothing you can do right now."

She needed to be alone. Maybe Cooper was right. She shouldn't be consumed with him and their relationship right now. She had bigger problems.

Patrick sat in Noah's truck and started to process his meeting with Sophie. Unfortunately, she'd not been as strong of a witness as he had expected. Even on the direct examination, she'd seemed too lawyerly, too measured, too guarded. How was he going to break her of those habits? That was the big question.

"How did it go?" Noah asked him.

"Okay for the first prep session. It's just an extra challenge, Sophie being a trial lawyer. I worry that she might get too much inside her own head. That won't work well in front of the jury."

Noah glanced over at him before focusing on the road. He seemed like a good guy. Not a huge talker, but serious about his work. Noah had taken the lead in making sure Patrick would be able to visit Sophie at the safe house.

"Sophie seems like a smart woman. I think with a little practice, she'll probably come around," Noah said. "It has to be hard on her after witnessing the murders to relive it over and over again."

That angle hadn't occurred to Patrick. "That's a good point. I was so preoccupied with the legal aspect of things that I didn't take the emotional impact into account. Maybe you should go to law school."

Noah laughed loudly. "I'm perfectly content in the private security business."

Patrick smiled. "Tell me about your business."

"What started as just Cooper and me has turned into a growing security company. Landon came on as another partner, and we've been able to expand and hire some additional employees to assist us. We operate in the personal security and tech space."

"Have you always been in that line of work?" Patrick figured he'd be spending a lot of time with this guy, so he might as well get to know him a bit.

"No. Before I opened K&R Security with Cooper, I was at the ATF."

"Remind me not to get on your bad side." The revelation didn't surprise Patrick one bit. Noah had a strong law enforcement presence about him. Patrick worked with the law-and-order types every single day, so he was very familiar with the vibes they gave off. "You like the private sector better?"

"I enjoy running my own business. The ATF was a great

experience, and the work they do is important. But in this phase of my life, I feel like I'm in the right place."

"That's great," Patrick said.

"Are you going to be a prosecutor for the long haul?" Noah asked.

"Maybe. I don't like the politics involved in moving up the chain, but you learn to work within the system because you have to. I get up most mornings excited about going to work. Not many people can say that."

"Isn't that the truth. How do you feel about the case?"

"It's always tough in situations like this. Especially when you throw in the Juan Wade factor. We can't guarantee the integrity of the jury."

Noah tapped his fingers on the wheel. "You think Juan would go after the jury?"

"Yeah. He's ruthless, and he has the money and power to back it up."

"How much do you know about his attorney?"

"Ashley Murphy has quite a reputation with my side of the bar."

"How so?"

"She's open about the fact that she wants to be a famous criminal defense lawyer. She wants to represent a celebrity and hit it big. She hopes to be the new face of high-profile criminal defense lawyers—showing up on all the TV shows."

"Maybe I should do some digging into her background."

"It wouldn't matter. She's not the type to be rattled by anything, as far as I can tell."

"If you change your mind, just let me know. And if you need anything in the meantime, just call one of us."

"I should be fine. Focus your efforts on Sophie. If something happens to her, my case is toast. And we can't have Ricky walking out of that courthouse as a free man."

Patrick planned to do everything in his power to hear the jury say one word: *guilty*.

FOURTEEN

I don't like this." Cooper looked over at Sophie as she sat in the passenger seat of his SUV.

"It's going to be fine," she said. "You have Noah as your backup, and we're going to the courthouse, where there is plenty of security. There is nothing to worry about."

Leland had filed an aggressive pretrial motion to suppress evidence in the Shelton case, and she refused to let Harrison argue it, even though he had made a pitch for it.

She'd finally worn down the guys and convinced them to take her to the courthouse. It was too important to outsource. Besides, she certainly wasn't going to relinquish control to Harrison, and Monica wasn't experienced enough to handle it.

"Remember the plan we discussed." Cooper's hands gripped the steering wheel.

"Yes. You'll be by my side the entire time. I do the argument, and then we leave. No hanging out. I get all of that." She thought Cooper was a bit too on edge, but when she replayed the night when they were shot at in her mind, it all came flooding back to her. "I promise I won't take any chances."

He gave her a rare smile and then turned his attention back to the road. When they arrived at the courthouse, she saw Landon and Noah standing at the curb. Landon was going to handle parking Cooper's SUV so Cooper and Noah could escort her directly into the courthouse.

"You ready?" Cooper asked.

"Most definitely." She was actually happier than she'd been in days, because she was going to be in the courtroom again as a prosecutor instead of someone else's witness.

"I'll come around to your side and let you out," Cooper said.

He exited the car and paused when Landon and Noah stepped over to meet him. She waited patiently while they talked. No doubt reiterating their plan. Cooper walked around the vehicle a moment later and opened the passenger door. She grabbed her laptop bag and placed it over her shoulder.

"Stick close."

She did as instructed and noticed that Noah stayed a few feet behind them. They walked up the steps and into the courthouse, where they'd have to go through metal detectors. She would be able to bring in her electronics because of her bar card. She also knew almost all the security officers who worked in the courthouse, but they still always did their jobs and checked her credentials each time.

Cooper started a side conversation with one of the officers, and she realized they knew each other. Despite this, she knew Cooper couldn't carry a weapon into the Fulton County Courthouse. Pretty much no one got a weapon into the courthouse these days unless they were active duty.

After getting through security, she made her way down the long corridor toward the elevator bank. "See? Everything is fine here."

"Just focus on your argument. I don't want you preoccupied with the security stuff." He placed his hand on her back as she walked into the elevator.

Right before the elevator door closed, Leland stepped his black designer shoe through the door.

"Ah, counselor, good morning. You ready for this?" he asked. He had gone a little overboard on his hair product today. His thick blond hair wasn't going anywhere, even in the event of a windstorm.

She glanced over at Cooper, who wore a noticeable scowl. "I doubt the judge is going to be too excited to hear your motion, Leland."

The elevator dinged, indicating their arrival on the fourth floor.

"Ladies first," Leland said.

She stepped off the elevator and glanced over her shoulder. Cooper's gaze was locked onto Leland's back. He was skeptical of everyone at this point, but she didn't have anything to fear from Leland.

They walked into the courtroom for their scheduled hearing. The judge had specially set this motion, and she looked down at her watch.

"This should be fun," Leland said. Then he walked over to his table, leaving her alone with her thoughts. She had a minute to organize her notes.

She flipped through her legal pad and pulled a copy of Leland's motion out of her bag, along with a copy of her response. His motion had been brief and to the point, but she certainly expected his presentation today to have more dramatic flair.

Judge Bernard entered the courtroom. Interestingly enough, Leland hadn't yet gone through with his threat to file a motion for recusal. Sophie wondered if he was going to keep that in his back pocket.

"Mr. Leland, we have before us today a pretrial motion to suppress evidence," the judge said. "I'm ready when you are."

"Thank you, Your Honor." Leland rose from his seat. "I'm moving to have all evidence taken from Mr. Shelton's personal laptop be excluded from the trial."

"And the basis?" Judge Bernard asked.

"It was illegally obtained. The search warrant was written specifically to cover my client's work computer and did not say a word about his personal electronic devices. In fact, the search warrant explicitly stated, and I quote, all *business* electronic devices."

"I am looking at that language right now." The judge studied the search warrant.

Leland nodded. "My client's personal laptop was clearly marked as personal. A sticker stating so was on the front of the laptop. The cases back me up here."

"Yes, I've read them." The judge turned to look at Sophie. "What's your response to that, Ms. Dawson?"

"Mr. Shelton conducted some company business on his personal laptop, thereby making it fair game—and I have case law on that exact point. In addition, SIB company policy makes it clear that personal electronic devices are not to be used for company business, and in the event the employee does use their personal device, it is subject to collection in litigation."

"The policy cited by Ms. Dawson is best understood in the civil litigation context," Leland countered. "This is a criminal trial. Therefore, different rules apply. My cases on the scope of search warrants are clear. Your Honor cannot overlook the explicit language of the warrant—which, by the way, was written by the Fulton County prosecutor's office. This is a problem of their own making."

Sophie felt this argument slipping away from her. "There is highly relevant evidence on Mr. Shelton's personal laptop."

"But you wouldn't have known that if you hadn't illegally obtained his laptop in the first place," Leland said.

"You're banking on a technicality."

"It's your technicality, though. Your office wrote the warrant too narrowly." Leland stood tall. "The personal laptop should be excluded. It wasn't included in the search warrant and therefore was illegally obtained. The case law backs me up. It's pretty open and shut. Ms. Dawson's cases are distinguishable from the facts here."

As Sophie listened to his reasoning, she realized she was in trouble. She should have had Monica do more research, but instead had wrongly thought that the judge just wouldn't buy it. Now she may have made a strategic miscalculation.

"Anything else from the state, Ms. Dawson?"

"No, Your Honor." She had nothing else.

"Then while I'm sympathetic to the state's position on this, Mr. Leland is correct. I have no choice but to exclude the personal laptop."

"Thank you, Your Honor," Leland said.

The judge didn't respond but instead turned to her clerk to talk about the order. The hearing was over.

Doubt crept into Sophie's mind. Maybe her head wasn't fully in the game.

Cooper walked up to her table. "Everything okay?" he asked.

"That didn't go as planned."

"I assume his personal laptop isn't key to winning the case?"

She shook her head. "No. But I don't like losing. I'm not sure why the search warrant was written like that. It was written by someone else before I started on the case."

"Don't let it get you down. This is just one small piece of the greater puzzle. From everything I've seen, you'll be able to get this guy based on the official documents from SIB."

Cooper was right. But there was still a nagging in her gut that made her question how this had gotten mishandled from the start.

Once they were back in the car, she started strategizing her next steps. This setback today only made her more determined.

After they drove for a bit and got off of I-85 north, she looked over at Cooper. His eyes where darting back and forth between the street ahead and the rearview mirror.

"What's wrong?" she asked.

"Nothing yet. But I think we might have a tail."

"Why?"

"This dark blue Grand Cherokee has been on us for the past six minutes."

The fact that he had been watching the clock upped her anxiety level.

"Where are the other guys?"

"Noah is a few cars back. Landon went ahead to ensure the safe house was still secure."

She turned and looked behind them, but she didn't see anything or anyone out of the ordinary.

Cooper took a sudden left turn. "If he follows us through this neighborhood, we know we have a problem."

"Do you have any idea where you are?"

"Not exactly, but I'm winging it. Take my phone and call Noah. Put him on speaker."

She did as he directed and listened as Cooper recounted what had happened.

"I saw you turn off," Noah said. "The Grand Cherokee did not pursue."

Cooper let out a breath. "Maybe I was just being paranoid."

"Better that than to take any unnecessary risks," Noah replied.

"Okay. Then the plan is to continue to the safe house."

"Roger that. Let me know if anything else comes up. But the Grand Cherokee is not on your tail. I've got eyes on it right now."

The call ended, and Cooper visibly relaxed, no longer gripping the wheel. "We'll be back to the safe house in no time."

"Good. And don't worry about the detour. I appreciate you being so careful." She knew he was only doing what he thought was best to keep her safe. It was one of the many qualities she found so attractive in him. If only there wasn't that one insurmountable obstacle. But there was no point in wallowing in that right now.

Cooper turned back onto the main road, and something caught her eye from the right. A black truck was barreling toward them. She screamed and braced for impact.

By the time Cooper saw the truck, it was too late. It rammed into the passenger side, jarring him. He managed to bring the SUV to a stop and watched as the truck sped away, tires screeching. He wanted to get the license plate number, but his first concern was Sophie.

"Sophie, are you all right?"

She looked at him, her expression dazed. She had a cut on her face from the shattered window. "Yes. My right arm hurts a little." She gingerly lifted her arm.

"Don't move it." He quickly dialed 911 and asked for assistance. "They'll be here soon."

"Did he get away?"

"Yes. I missed it. I never saw the truck coming, and then I couldn't act fast enough."

"He was targeting us. Targeting me." Her words broke as she said them. Her breathing began to speed up.

"Yes. But it could've been much worse."

"You think?"

"He punched the brakes right before impact."

"What do you think that means?"

"That he wasn't trying to kill you."

"That doesn't make a lot of sense, does it?"

"Not if it was one of Wade's men. But I think, given the facts, we have to seriously consider that this has something to do with your work on the Shelton case. Your inquiry is expanding, and you started digging into SIB. You were just coming back from a hearing on the Shelton case. He could've tracked us from the courthouse. This could all be connected to that. Plus, you've shown Leland that you're going to be aggressive in prosecuting the case."

"You make a good point."

"The police will be here soon."

"And they will probably assume Wade is behind this. Are we going to bring up SIB?" she asked. She was breathing more steadily now, and some of his worry subsided.

"That's up to you."

"I'd prefer not to at this point. If we're wrong, I'd create a really difficult situation for myself in continuing the prosecution. I can't risk that."

The next day, Cooper stood in the foyer of the safe house and watched as Sophie quickly typed on her laptop. Thankfully, she hadn't been seriously injured in the hit-and-run. She sat on the sofa with her legs up on the coffee table and the computer on her lap.

It felt like a storm was brewing deep inside him. He had told her all about his past and how he planned to live his life, figuring that would be the easiest way to send her running.

Well, she hadn't run away yet, but he had sensed some hesitancy on her part, and rightly so. The problem was that he was just as interested, if not more, in her. But he'd lost sleep trying to figure out if there was a way forward for them. A way to at least see if there could be something there.

He kept coming back to the central problem. The two of them wanted very different things out of a relationship. He couldn't change her and didn't want to. Whether she thought she could change him was another issue. She'd been resistant to his fear that he could end up like his father.

Just thinking about his father made his stomach churn.

"You just going to stand there?" Sophie asked.

"Sorry, my head was somewhere else."

"Come on in. I could use a break." She patted the spot beside her on the sofa.

He hesitated for a moment, because he knew he should just walk away and let her get back to work. But instead, he took one look into her blue eyes and started walking.

She laughed. "I'm not going to bite."

The way she looked at him only twisted him up more.

"How're you feeling?" he asked.

She stretched out her right arm. "A bit sore, but I've been diligent with the ice. I just keep thinking back to what you said about it likely not being Juan behind the crash."

"We have to start considering that possibility. Noah hasn't been able to trace the exact movement of funds out of Shelton's account, but he has flagged some additional suspicious activities. He's going to email you a report."

"Thanks. I know there might be something going on here. And if SIB is involved, then that provides motive."

"You still need to get through the Shelton trial. Who knows what you'll uncover there. That could lead to even more problems."

"If we get to that point. I'm worried Keith might intervene and pull the rug out from under me. I'd like to think that if I take my concerns to him about the additional suspicious cash deposits, he would have to back me. But we'll see." She paused. "Enough about all of that for now. You've been avoiding it, but we never got to finish the conversation we started about everything you told me."

"Yeah, but that may be for the best. Don't you think?"

She frowned. "Why are you trying so hard to push me away?"

"Isn't it obvious?" It was to him. She was so bright that she had to have figured it out for herself.

She studied him for a moment. "Can I say something brutally honest to you?"

He didn't know what to expect from her, but how could he argue with honesty? "Go on."

"I think you're afraid of letting someone into your life. That's why you've concocted this protective mechanism about your father."

He sucked in a breath. Her words were like a punch to the gut. "I don't know if that was honest, but it was brutal, that's for sure."

"I'm not trying to be hurtful, but I think you're selling yourself short by relying on your past as a reason not to have a full and thriving life. Are you just going to be alone forever?"

"You're questioning me, but what about you?"

Her eyes widened. "What do you mean?"

"If you're really so gung ho to get married and have a family, then why are you still single?"

"It's not for lack of trying," she shot back. "I don't think you realize how hard it is to find someone who is right for me."

"There has to be something holding you back," he said.

She shook her head. "No, but I want to make sure I'm with the right man. Of course I want someone I'm attracted to who is smart and kind. But I also want someone who shares my beliefs. That takes out a big chunk of guys right there. And not just faith in name only. I want a man who lives it every single day."

"And you think that's me? Because we haven't even had that many discussions about that."

"We haven't needed to. I've seen God's love through you in all of your actions."

That was a good thing, but hearing her say those words scared him. What if she thought that God was bringing them together? He needed to dispel that notion right then and there. "Sophie, just because we share our faith doesn't mean anything beyond that."

She sighed. "Cooper, you are lying to yourself if you think our common faith is the only thing drawing us closer to each other. Yes, I think it's part of our connection, but if that was all there was, then you could be any random guy that I've dated from church. But you're not. You're different. Way different.

What I feel for you is not what I've felt before. You have your opinion about what you want, and you've stuck to it for years, but what if there's another way?"

"And I'm telling you that I'm not the right guy for you. You're the type who would try to change my mind, but I'm not one of your cases. You can't win me over or argue me into being someone I'm not. I'm obviously attracted to you. I'd have to be a fool not to be, but there's so much more to this picture. And like I said before, the last thing I want is to hurt you."

She was quiet for a moment, then said somewhat stiffly, "I respect your opinion."

"I appreciate that." He knew she wasn't going to give up even if she said so. But for now, it was best to act like that was going to happen.

She looked down at her computer. "I should get back to work."

That wasn't how he wanted to end the conversation, but it was better to let it go. For now.

―◁◇▷―

Ashley sat in a booth in the back corner of the diner, waiting for Juan to arrive. He'd summoned her to talk pretrial strategy. She still had to let him think he was in control, but she had a bone to pick with him too.

Juan walked in and immediately made eye contact with her. As he approached her table, she plastered on a fake smile. She didn't like him, but right now he was one of her most important clients. She didn't have to like any of her clients to reach her goals.

Juan had his security entourage with him, but they hung back as he took a seat.

"What's on your mind?" she asked.

"I want to make sure I have all my bases covered."

What he needed to do was let her handle things. "I hope

that doesn't mean going after Sophie directly again. There's way too much risk there. In fact, the police are investigating a hit-and-run incident involving her. You wouldn't happen to know anything about that, would you?"

His nose crinkled. "No."

"Cut the crap, Juan."

"Seriously, you know I own up to what I do. At least with you, anyway, since you can't rat me out."

She'd need to push him to get to the bottom of this. "You're saying you had nothing to do with the hit-and-run?"

"Absolutely nothing."

"And to be clear, you didn't tell any of your crew anything that would have led them to do it?"

He shook his head. "You told me no more violence, and for now I'm listening."

"Let's keep it that way." She wasn't sure whether she really believed him or not, but he seemed like he was telling the truth. That led her to a bigger question: Who else would be targeting Sophie?

Juan nodded. "But I have other ways to reach the same results. Do you have any dirt on the lawyer?"

"Who?"

"Hunt," Juan said bluntly.

"I don't know him extremely well, but I think he's clean."

He cracked his knuckles. "Everyone has skeletons. I plan to figure out what his are."

"I don't think he's susceptible to bribery."

His eyes widened in amusement. "Like I would ever consider that. I prefer more direct pressure points."

"I think you're barking up the wrong tree by focusing on him. He's just the prosecutor."

He slammed his fist on the table. "Just the man who's going to put my baby brother away for his life."

"Keep your voice down. You'll draw unnecessary attention."

Juan was like a ticking time bomb. She wondered if he was strung out tonight.

"You need to be careful in your jury selection."

She hated when he tried to play lawyer. "I always give ample thought to the makeup of the jury. As you know from your vast experience, sometimes we get a dud that we don't want on there. That usually works both ways, though." It was difficult to keep her sarcasm in check.

"We only need one to get an acquittal."

She held back a smirk. "Juan, you are aware that I am the lawyer here? I understand how this all works."

"I'm just reminding you of where your attention needs to be. Discrediting that woman and getting me the right jury. If you do that, I can handle the rest."

She wasn't going to ask what he meant by that. The less she knew, the better.

He reached across the table and grabbed her hands. "We don't have a problem, do we, Ash?"

"Why would you even ask that?" She took a deep breath to remain calm. She'd already told him not to put his hands on her, but she refused to let him know that he scared her.

Juan glanced over his shoulder and then back at her. "I have enemies lurking around every corner. A rival gang is taking credit for Ricky being in jail. I need him out, or some of my men may consider defecting. This is so much bigger than just my brother's freedom. It impacts my entire business."

Of course. She should've known all along that Juan's primary concern was his own business empire, not the well-being and safety of his little brother. But she held her tongue on that issue. "I realize that you're in a complicated situation and that you have your business to be concerned about." People didn't realize how wealthy and powerful gang leaders really were.

"You're not going to call Ricky to the stand, are you?"

She couldn't hold back her laugh. "Are you really trying

to tick me off, Juan? I'm not a first-year attorney, bright-eyed and bushy-tailed, right out of law school. I know how to be a defense attorney. That's why you pay me. If we're done here, why don't you let me do my job?"

"Should I attend the trial?" he asked.

"My gut reaction is no. We don't need to remind the jury about Ricky's association with you. The gang connection can only hurt him. We're going to go hard on the misidentification argument. Let the state push the gang card. I'll be working against that."

He pushed back his chair. "Then if we're done here, I'll walk you out."

"That's not necessary."

She stood up and walked away, glancing over her shoulder before she pushed through the main door. Juan still sat at the table. He gave her a wink that sent a chill down her spine.

CHAPTER
FIFTEEN

The next afternoon, Sophie decided to talk to Keith about SIB. If only for a minute, to take her mind off her witness testimony.

"Keith, I wanted to update you on a few things." Sophie held the cell phone against her ear. It wasn't her phone but a burner phone provided by Cooper. He had said it was too dangerous to keep her phone on because it could be tracked. "Shelton's attorney filed a motion for suppression of his personal laptop, and the judge granted it. It appears the initial search warrant only covered his work devices, not personal electronics."

"You don't need the personal device to make your case."

"No, but I don't understand why someone there would have written the search warrant that way. Do you know who worked on the initial draft?"

"Yeah. Harrison did it. We were understaffed in White Collar at the time, which is one of the reasons I transferred you over. He offered to pinch-hit until you could start."

Wonderful. The thought crossed her mind as to whether Harrison had done that on purpose, knowing he wouldn't be the attorney to see the case through. But she hoped he wouldn't stoop to that level. "The other thing I wanted to let you know about was that there's weird stuff turning up in the documents. It turns out that Shelton had additional personal accounts at SIB that I was not aware of. It hadn't come up before, but I have documentation given to us through SIB that shows he does have these other accounts."

"And what's the significance of that?"

"The various accounts contain multiple cash deposits over time, all under ten thousand dollars."

"Hmm. What's your theory? Are you thinking that Shelton was laundering money?"

"I'm not sure. I think he was engaged in something even deeper than what we previously thought, but I haven't put all the pieces together yet. Someone was paying him real money or using him to funnel money, and I don't know why."

"Sophie, I think you're wasting your time chasing shadows."

Keith's voice had turned stern, and she thought it better to let it go for now. "I understand your concern."

"All right. Where are you on witness prep for the Wade trial?"

"I've worked with Patrick the past few days, and the prep is ongoing."

"We're a week out. Take as much time as you need to prepare. Your cases will still be waiting for you."

"Believe me, I'm taking the preparation seriously."

"You'll be representing the entire office. Everyone will know you're a Fulton County district attorney. I just want to make sure you put your best foot forward. How you perform will reflect on all of us, including me."

No pressure or anything. She suddenly felt a bit nauseated. "Remember, sir, it's not like I asked for this. The entire chain of events was far beyond my control."

"Oh, I know that." His voice softened. "I just want to make sure you take all the time you need to get your head on straight and be the star witness I know you can be. Wade's conviction would be big for us. Even though Patrick is from

Dekalb County, we're all on the same team here—fighting for justice."

"Of course." There was a piece of her that wondered if Keith was right. Should she take a break from the Shelton case this last week before trial?

"If you need anything, just call," he said, wrapping up the conversation.

"Thanks, Keith." She ended the call as Cooper walked into the room.

"How's it going?" he asked.

"I was just providing Keith with an update on the Shelton case. He shot me down. I think I need to bring him a more concrete theory. He also told me that for this last stretch, I should put all of my effort into the Wade trial."

"And how do you feel about that?"

That was a good question. "I'm conflicted. In a way, I totally see his point, but I also worry that I may go a bit crazy if I'm thinking about my testimony 24-7. I'll talk to Patrick when he gets here."

"And he'll be here any minute. Noah called about half an hour ago." Cooper took a seat next to her. "Things seem to be really intense between you and Patrick lately. Is everything okay there?"

Intense was an understatement. Their latest session had gone totally off the rails. Patrick had raised his voice at her when she didn't directly answer his question and instead tried to hedge. That was not a good legal strategy, and she knew it, but it was harder to be a witness than she had imagined.

Patrick's vocal frustration had obviously gotten Cooper's attention. He looked ready to pounce. All she had to do was say the word. "Patrick's under a lot of pressure to win this case, and I'm under the same type of pressure to perform."

"If he gives you any trouble, just let me know."

Just as she suspected. Cooper was protective of her even

when it came to Patrick. "I'm not worried about Patrick. He's just trying to do his job and get the result we all want and need. I can take tough preparation sessions, because let me tell you, there's no way that Ashley's going to hold back."

"Well, I'll be here if you change your mind."

Cooper ran so hot and cold it was beginning to drive her crazy. In one instant he was pushing her away, and then in another moment he was rushing to be her protector. That told her that he might have convinced himself to stay away from her, but it wasn't really what he wanted.

The problem was that she was still completely conflicted about what *she* wanted. She feared opening up her heart only to get it crushed. Because as much as she wanted to believe that Cooper would change, there was a piece of her that told her banking on that was a terrible idea. Especially on something that meant so much.

Sophie walked into the kitchen and got set up at the table, then waited for Patrick to join her. It wasn't long before he rushed into the kitchen.

"Sorry I'm late," he said. "You know how it is."

"All too well."

Today he wore a black suit and red striped tie. Patrick should've been the type of guy she was attracted to—very driven, smart, not to mention tall, dark, and handsome. But she wasn't into him at all. He could've been a good diversion to get her mind off of Cooper, but the spark wasn't there.

"Ready to get down to it?"

"Yes."

He met her eyes. "I should also apologize for getting heated yesterday. That's not the most productive way to deal with a witness, and I lost my cool."

He had gotten agitated with her yesterday, but the pressure was mounting. The trial was about to start. "No need to apologize. Maybe I needed a good kick to get me going. You were covering a sensitive topic about my mother and her death and the counseling. It's hard to relive that. But I'm glad you prepped me on it, and today is a new day. I'm ready to go."

Patrick cross-examined her for the next two hours straight. When he finally leaned back in his seat, she let out a breath.

"Well?" she asked. "How did I do?"

He smiled. "Much better. If you keep this up, I have no concern about you being able to go toe-to-toe with Ashley."

"Good. It may sound crazy, but I've been rehearsing questions in my mind."

"I actually think we're in a great place, and I don't want you to overdo it and become rehearsed or lapse back into the legal mindset. I think we'll be fine with just doing one more session before your testimony."

"Whatever you think is best." She was going to let him drive this train, since it was his case.

"There is one more thing I want you to think about."

"What?"

"What you should wear."

Had she heard him correctly? What did her clothes have to do with anything? "Excuse me?"

"I know it sounds silly, but your appearance could reinforce the idea in the jury's mind that you're a prosecutor."

"That can be a positive, can't it?"

"Yes. But they're already going to be hit over the head with that so many times. I was wondering if you'd be open to dressing more casually. Not totally casual, but also not a suit. To reinforce the story that you're just a young working professional who ended up in a dangerous situation. Maybe a nice top and slacks. Something that makes you seem approachable, to soften you up."

Ouch. Did she really come across that way? "You don't think I'm approachable?"

"Your normal power suit thing gives off a different vibe. Perfect if you're the one prosecuting the case, but I really want the jury to be able to envision you as one of them. Remember our theme— you're just a woman getting a snack after a long day at work."

She hadn't even thought about this. But then again, her mind had been on other things lately. "I'm sure I've got something suitable to wear."

"Perfect." He put his hand on top of hers. "I don't want you to worry."

She let out a breath. "Easier said than done." She noticed Cooper standing in the foyer, but he walked away when she made eye contact.

Patrick squeezed her hand. "You're ready, Sophie. Don't psych yourself out."

"Thanks." She could only pray that she would be ready when the day came.

Cooper wished he had his punching bag, because right now he needed to let off some steam. In his opinion, Patrick Hunt was getting way too cozy with Sophie. The problem was that he had no right to think that, especially given everything he'd told her. Heck, his confession may have pushed her right into that prosecutor's arms.

His gut reactions were visceral and real. That told him he had building feelings for her even if his head told him it was the worst idea on the planet. The bigger issue was how he was going to handle it. Was he strong enough to keep his distance and maintain a cool air of professionalism?

He didn't know the answer to that.

Lord, how have I gotten myself into this situation? You know how I feel about my father and what that means for my future. It's just not my path, and I've come to terms with that. I don't want to drag Sophie into my world of problems. A past that is almost unspeakable.

He'd had this conversation with God often. But right now it seemed like it was more important. Because there had never been a woman who interested him like Sophie. Yes, he'd dated in the past, but it was easy to keep his distance and not get too serious. And lately, he'd thrown all his time and effort into his business. Then Sophie came into his life.

Sophie walked into the living room. "I saw you lurking around the kitchen earlier."

"Was just checking on things, but it seemed Patrick had everything under control." He couldn't quite keep all the sarcasm out of his voice.

She raised an eyebrow. "If I didn't know better, I would think you were jealous of him."

He shook his head. "No. I just think it's odd that he's so touchy feely with you."

She sat down beside him. "He's trying to be reassuring." She grabbed his hand. "Just like I'm trying to do right now. Reassure you."

Only her touch didn't reassure him about anything. It scared the living daylights out of him. He knew he needed to pull away from her, but he couldn't do it. He wanted to see how this played out. "There are different kinds of touches, Sophie, and it's hard for me to think that Patrick hasn't developed a thing for you."

"You're wrong. I can tell when a guy is interested in me. He's focusing on me because of my role, not because of any romantic interest. And even if he did like me, I don't have any feelings for him."

"That's your business if you do."

She reached out with her other hand and placed it on his cheek. "Cooper, what's going on here between us?"

The simple touch of her hand made him crazy. "I've been completely honest with you about my situation. I haven't tried to hide the fact that there's a spark between us. A huge spark. But I've explained why it's a bad idea to explore it any further."

"And you think it's right for you to make that decision unilaterally without my input?"

"I'm doing it to protect you from getting hurt."

She dropped her hand from his cheek. "I already have one man in my life who thinks he always knows what's best for me. I don't need a second one."

"See, we're already arguing over this. It's not worth it. I don't want to hurt you. That would be the worst scenario of all."

"Then don't hurt me, Cooper," she said softly. She squeezed his hand.

As she looked up at him with her big blue eyes, he leaned down toward her. He could imagine kissing her right now. But where would that leave them?

She started to lean into him, and he knew he had to move back. Break away from the situation.

He stood up from the couch and placed his hands in his pockets. "I'm going to go call the guys and check in."

Sophie didn't say anything. She didn't have to. Yes, he was running away, but it was for the best. For both of them.

Tad walked into the tall Midtown office tower that was the headquarters for SIB. The building was everything you would expect from a swanky bank. He couldn't even imagine what Whitney's office was going to look like.

She'd called and asked for a face-to-face meeting at her office, and of course he'd cleared his schedule. The two cheating-spouse cases took a back burner, because this was his primary assignment. There was a lot riding on this case.

He approached the receptionist in the main lobby. The pretty young brunette looked up at him and smiled. "How can I help you, sir?"

"I have an appointment with Ms. Bowman." Since he was coming into the bank today, he'd decided to look his best. He'd chosen his dark suit and a conservative tie to match. If he wanted to get more work from SIB, he needed to look like someone who could work for the bank—not someone off the street.

"And your name?"

"Tad Grisham."

The receptionist quickly typed something on her keyboard. "Yes, I see that in Ms. Bowman's schedule. You'll need to take the elevator up to the twenty-fourth floor. There will be another receptionist there who will be expecting you."

"Thank you, ma'am."

He went to the elevator bay and proceeded to the twenty-fourth floor. When he exited, his breath caught. If he thought the main lobby was nice, then this floor was on a different level. Everything about it screamed money, from the plush furniture to the high-end artwork hanging on the walls.

Another woman, a bit older than the one in the lobby, greeted him. "Ms. Bowman is ready for you, Mr. Grisham. I'll take you to her office. Can I provide you with any coffee or water?"

"Coffee would be great." Heck, he planned to take advantage of getting pampered. He could certainly get used to this.

"How do you like it?"

"Cream and sugar."

"Wonderful. I'll bring it in to you."

"Do I hear Tad?" Whitney walked out of her office to greet him with a hearty handshake—or as hearty as a hundred-pound woman could offer. "Please come in and take a seat."

He did as she requested and sat down in a large navy armchair. He imagined the chair cost a pretty penny—just like everything else in her office. Her large window showcased the Atlanta skyline and puffy white clouds. "What's on your mind?"

"You've been doing great work so far. Doing everything I've asked of you, and I appreciate how discreet you've been. I'm sure you can appreciate that in a relationship like ours, it takes time to build trust."

He had an idea where she might be going with this. "I'm glad you're happy with my services. I strive to do the best job I can for you and the company."

A sly smile spread across her frosty pink lips. "I think it's time we had a heart-to-heart."

"Please go ahead." He'd been waiting for the juicy information on SIB since the day he was hired.

"I have sources telling me that Sophie Dawson is expanding her investigation in the Shelton case."

"Expanding how?"

"She's starting to look into possible money-laundering activities undertaken by Shelton."

"That's not good."

She shook her head. "No, it's not."

"Are you worried that Shelton's actions could implicate SIB?"

"Yes, which is why we need to find a way to shut down her investigation before things get out of control. I know you've been monitoring her situation and engaging in, how should I say it, certain efforts against her. But I need you to step it up. Really step it up."

"I've taken some actions. I think you'd prefer to have plausible deniability, so I won't go into details, but she has started to feel the heat. I can guarantee you that."

"Well, it hasn't been hot enough, apparently. Take it to the next level. You're not the type of guy who is afraid to get his hands dirty, are you?"

"That won't be a problem for me." If only she knew just how dirty his hands could get.

"Good. Then I need you to work fast and come up with a plan for handling her. I can't have this situation getting out of control on my watch. Are we on the same page?"

"Most definitely."

Just when he thought things couldn't get any more interesting.

CHAPTER
SIXTEEN

Patrick looked over his outlines for the last time. He needed to go home and get some rest. The trial started tomorrow, and he didn't like to pull all-nighters. Being fresh and on his game was the most important thing.

A few minutes later, he walked out of the building, and the fall breeze hit him. He started to practice his opening statement. He liked to have chunks of it memorized. Reading off of notes could only get you so far. It was his goal to form a connection with the jury from the moment he walked into the courtroom.

"Talking to yourself, counselor?" Ashley appeared out of nowhere and started walking with him.

"Are you stalking me now?"

"No. Just wanted to see if you were ready for the big day."

What was her angle this time? She always had one. "Of course I'm ready. But I assume you are too. Neither one of us is the type to just wing it."

She grabbed his arm, stopping him. "Patrick."

He turned to face her. "What is it?"

"Be careful. That's all."

He took a step, closing the gap between them. "Are you threatening me?"

She shook her head. "Just the opposite. I'm warning you. But if you ever say this conversation happened, I'll deny it."

Thoughts swam through his mind. "What do you know, Ashley?"

Her eyes narrowed. "Nothing specific. I just don't have a good feeling. I shouldn't be doing you any favors after that stunt you pulled in court, but I also don't want anything to happen that could've been prevented."

"Security will be tight."

"Yes. But you know there are always risks in our jobs."

"More so in mine." Prosecutors were much more likely to be targeted than defense attorneys. He put bad guys away for a living. That came at a cost.

"I know that."

Her coming to him confused him. It didn't seem to fit what he knew about how she operated. "Why warn me? What's in this for you?"

"Do you really think I'm that calculated? That I have no sense of right and wrong?"

"Ashley, I've never seen you show one ounce of compassion. You make it clear that your job is about the bottom line."

She tilted her head. "You shouldn't always judge a book by its cover, Patrick. I'll see you in court tomorrow."

He watched as she walked away. Her words echoed in his ears. Was Juan Wade going to try to take him out? That would be a bold move. But the fact that Ashley had come to him made him realize she was at the very least worried that Juan may try to take some drastic action. He figured she didn't want that on her conscience.

But did she even have a conscience? Regardless, he wasn't stupid. It was a good idea for him to watch his back. At least there would be beefed up security tomorrow at the courthouse.

At the end of the day, if Juan wanted him out of the picture, there wasn't much he could do about it. Juan had the resources and power to take action. He just had to hope Juan wouldn't want to risk that kind of publicity. It would look highly suspicious if the prosecutor was killed right before or during the trial.

He wondered if he would be able to sleep tonight after all.

The next morning, once they'd finished jury selection, Ashley gathered up her notes and tried to remain calm and focused. It was game time, and she had to do her best to advocate for her client. Opening statements were when she got to tell her version of the story.

Regardless of what she thought about Ricky's innocence, or lack thereof, her job as his defense counsel was to fight as hard as she could. It didn't matter who Ricky was, or that he was Juan's brother. Even though most people thought she was only in it for the money, that wasn't true. Yes, she did care about money and fame, but at the most basic level, she believed that every person was innocent until proven guilty, and that she had a moral obligation to fight that good fight. The American justice system couldn't function without people like her. And yes, if she could get wealthy along the way and have her time in the spotlight, then it was worth it all the more.

Her eyes locked onto Patrick's, and she quickly looked away. She'd had a moment of weakness last night when she went to talk to him. If Juan found out she had done that, she'd be the one in danger.

But there had been this nagging feeling in her gut that told her she had to speak up. She didn't want Patrick to be harmed. As much as he annoyed her, she had a bit of a soft spot growing for him.

To the rest of the world she might seem like a fearless force of nature, but deep inside, she wasn't as sure.

She turned to Ricky, who had been very quiet since being brought back into the courtroom. "Remember what I told you.

The jury will have their eyes on you at all times. You need to be on your best behavior."

He cursed under his breath and refused to look her in the eyes. This kid had no idea how fortunate he was. He had her as a defense attorney—someone who would do anything in the world to protect him and advocate for him. Many others in his position wouldn't be so lucky. And yet he always viewed her with such disdain.

"Ricky, I don't care what you think or feel about me. This is your life on the line, and if you want a fighting chance to actually live your life, you need to listen to me."

He didn't respond. That wasn't good enough for her.

"Understood?" she pushed again.

"Yeah," he mumbled.

Ricky was acting like a petulant child, but she was used to dealing with difficult clients. She'd just have to keep him on a tight leash.

Patrick would give his opening statement first, since he was the prosecution. She had no doubt he would give an impressive argument. It was her job to create doubts. Patrick had the burden of proof.

"Mr. Hunt, are you ready to proceed?" Judge Turner asked.

Patrick stood up. "Yes, Your Honor." He walked over to the podium that stood directly in front of the jury. The twelve people—seven women and five men—who would determine her client's fate.

"Ladies and gentleman of the jury. Your presence and attention here today and throughout the trial are greatly appreciated. I will do my best to make this process as efficient for you as possible while at the same time ensuring that the state gets to present all of its evidence. I know from the jury selection process that some of you are familiar with this case. As the judge has previously instructed, you're supposed to put all of that knowledge in a little box and set it aside. Try your best to focus only on the evidence you'll hear in this courtroom to make your determination."

He was setting the ground rules, which was standard. Ashley was interested to see what his overall strategy was going to be. How hard would he go after her client?

"Jackie Destin and Ronnie Thomas. Those are the names of the two innocent people who lost their lives on the night of October seventh. The evidence will show that they were both gunned down by the defendant, Ricky Wade. My job as the prosecutor is not to answer the question why. Why did the defendant take those two lives that night? We may never know the answer to that question. I'm here to ask you another question—a much simpler question. It requires a yes or no response. Was the defendant, Ricky Wade, the man who shot Ms. Destin and Mr. Thomas? I will submit to you that the answer is a resounding yes."

Ashley studied the faces of the jury members. Some of them eyed Ricky warily, while others were focused more on Patrick. But they were all engaged so far. And she knew that the prosecution would always score points. They got to go first, set the stage, and at the end of the day, there were two people dead. Her job was to make the jury unsure as to who actually killed those people.

It was interesting to her that Patrick was trying to take motive out of the equation by removing the *why*. He was trying his best to make this case as simple as possible.

"The evidence I will present during this trial will leave no room for doubt. The state will be presenting an eyewitness who was at the Quick Stop that night and saw the defendant shoot both victims in cold blood."

She shot up from her seat. "Objection, argumentative."

"I'll allow it," the judge said, "but watch yourself, Mr. Hunt."

Patrick probably knew that Ashley would object, but he was trying to set the stage. She listened attentively as he continued his opening statement. Sophie was the linchpin to everything. If she could discredit Sophie, even in the least bit, then she had a good chance of getting an acquittal from this jury.

And that was exactly what she planned to do.

The next morning, Sophie felt like she might be sick as they entered the courthouse. Cooper had a tight grip on her arm, and she was actually thankful that he was there to steady her.

She'd been up most of the night, going over the mock questions in her head, and now she was fit to be tied. She'd taken Patrick's advice and worn a light pink cardigan with black pants. No power suit for her today, and she felt naked without her usual suit jacket.

"Sophie, talk to me," Cooper said.

"I'm okay."

"Your face is pale."

"I'll be better soon. It's just the initial wave of nerves." She saw the concern in his eyes, but she wasn't sure if he was worried about her or whether she might buckle under the pressure.

Just outside the courtroom door, Patrick walked toward her, a frown pulling at his lips. "Sophie, what's wrong?"

"I'll be fine by the time I testify." She prayed that would be true.

Patrick looked down at his watch. "That's mere minutes from now. I'm calling you as the first witness today."

"She'll be fine," Cooper said.

She appreciated that he stepped in for her. She wasn't sure she could have spoken just then.

Patrick placed his hand on her shoulder. "Okay. Take a minute and compose yourself. Then head on into the courtroom." He walked through the door, and she stayed outside with Cooper by her side.

Noah was also there, and Landon was somewhere in the

vicinity. Plus, there was a greatly enhanced police presence. She wasn't worried about her physical safety at the moment. She was worried about failing the victims. She closed her eyes, praying for the ability to get through this day.

"Sophie, it's natural to be nervous. Just remember how much you prepared. Don't doubt yourself." Cooper gave her arm a reassuring squeeze.

His words gave her a boost of confidence. He was right. She had worked hard to be ready for this day. She'd been in a courtroom hundreds of times before.

The next fifteen minutes passed in a blur. She was seated in the courtroom. Noises all around her. People coming into the room to take their seats. But when the bailiff's loud voice reverberated throughout the room, she was jerked back into reality.

The judge entered the courtroom, and the jury was brought in. She watched intently as the twelve members took their seats.

"Please proceed, Mr. Hunt."

Patrick rose from his seat. "The state calls Sophie Dawson."

As she stood up, her legs felt like gelatin. She tried to stand tall and take deep breaths as she walked up to the witness stand. When she raised her right hand to get sworn in, the full gravity of the moment hit her.

"Ms. Dawson, will you please state your full name for the record?" Patrick asked.

"Yes, I'm Sophie Elizabeth Dawson."

"Thank you. Ms. Dawson, I'd like to start by asking you some questions about the night of October seventh."

"Yes, I remember that night." This was just as they had practiced. Patrick was making a concerted effort not to lead with the fact that she was a prosecutor. Ashley had already brought that up in her opening statement, and it would surely come up again. But first Patrick wanted to make the jury relate to Sophie.

"Did you stop at the Quick Stop on your way home?"

"Yes. I was hungry and had a craving for a snack. I have

a weakness for junk food." She noticed that a couple of the jurors smiled.

"Did you enter the store?"

"Yes, I did. I was really hungry. The only question was whether to get a healthy snack to try to offset the chocolate and chips. So I was debating with myself, and then I opened up the cooler to get a tea." She took a deep breath. "And that's when I heard loud voices coming from the front of the store."

Patrick kept his eyes locked on hers. "And what did you do when you heard those loud voices?"

"I turned and saw that a man had pulled a gun on the cashier. They were yelling at each other. I started to go try to break it up, but before I could get there, the man with the gun shot the cashier."

"What did you do?"

The events of that night played before her eyes as if she was right back there. "When I saw him take the shot, I hit the ground. Then the shooter turned around."

"And did you get a good look at the man with the gun?"

"I did, yes."

"And is that man here in the courtroom today?"

"He is."

"Can you point him out?"

She took a deep breath. "He's the defendant. The man sitting beside Ms. Murphy."

A few murmurs could be heard from the audience, but Patrick didn't break his stride. "What happened after you saw the defendant shoot the store clerk?"

She couldn't believe Ashley wasn't objecting but knew the defense attorney had to have a plan of attack. "The shooter ran outside, and I went up to the front of the store to check on the clerk. He was on the ground. There was blood everywhere. I checked for a pulse, but there was nothing." She could hear her voice start to shake, but she had to remain strong. The families of the victims deserved justice. She was the one who was still alive and could tell the truth of what happened that night.

"What did you do after you checked for the clerk's pulse?"

"I heard more gunshots coming from outside, and I saw the shooter firing. I watched as another person fell to the ground before the shooter got in his car and sped off."

"Did you call the police right then?"

"No. I ran outside and tried to see if I could do anything to help. There was another woman with the woman who was shot. I checked on the victim first and told the woman to call 911."

"Did you know at the time that the woman who was shot had been killed?"

She looked at Patrick and then at the jury. "Yes. She had sustained a gunshot wound to the head." After she said those words, she realized she had added that information off script.

"Then what did you do?"

"I tried to talk to the surviving woman, and we waited for the police to arrive at the scene."

"And you said the shooter drove away?"

"Yes. He was long gone by the time the police arrived a couple of minutes later." She knew Patrick planned to leave her testimony there. He would clean up any additional points in the redirect.

"No further questions," Patrick said. He turned and looked at Ashley. "Your witness, Ms. Murphy."

Ashley gracefully rose from her seat. Today she wore a black skirt suit with a dark purple blouse. Her hair was pulled back in a low ponytail, and she wore her signature glasses.

Sophie had no doubt that Ashley was going to go in for the kill. The only question was how direct she was going to be about it.

"Ms. Dawson, I'd like to fill in some information that Mr. Hunt didn't quite get to in his examination."

"All right." *Remember, stay calm. Don't let her rattle you.*

"You're actually one of Mr. Hunt's colleagues, aren't you?"

"No. I work in a separate office and for a different county than he does."

Ashley took another step forward. "And tell the jury exactly what you do."

"I'm a senior assistant district attorney." *Keep it short. Don't volunteer. Make her work for it.* Patrick's words echoed through her mind.

"So that's a fancy title for saying you're a prosecutor, right? You work for the state of Georgia just like Mr. Hunt?"

Sophie had to resist the urge to point out that Ashley was asking her multiple questions at one time. Instead she tried to take the high road. She had to remember that the jury was listening to her every word. "We are both prosecutors."

"You put bad guys behind bars for a living, right?"

"That's one way of putting it." Ashley was starting to weave in the bias argument. Clever.

"In fact, it bothers you greatly when a jury finds for the defense."

"Objection, argumentative," Patrick said.

"Sustained," the judge ruled.

Ashley adjusted her glasses. "Do you love your job?"

"Yes, I do."

"And why is that?"

"Because I like helping people and seeking justice for those who deserve it."

"Like exactly what you did on the day of October seventh? You actually had a trial conclude that day, didn't you?"

"I did."

"And I'm sure you put a lot of work into preparing for that trial?"

"Yes."

"So you had a long day, you finish up the trial, and then you keep working for a few more hours, is that right?"

"Yes, I didn't leave the office until late."

"And you mentioned getting snacks from the Quick Stop. Had you eaten lunch that day?"

Ashley was even better than Sophie had anticipated. "No. I hadn't."

"Breakfast?"

"Yes."

"What did you have?"

Not a lot. But she couldn't say it that way. "I had coffee and fruit that morning."

Ashley's heels clicked on the floor as she approached the witness stand. "Let me get this straight, to make sure I have everything correct. You were in the courtroom all day for a trial, plus you worked multiple hours after that. You hadn't eaten anything since the fruit you had at, let's call it 6:00 a.m.? Is that fair?"

"That's right."

"And you admit you were hungry, and that's why you stopped to get food on the way home?"

"I was hungry by that point, yes."

"But at the time when you claim you saw my client, you still hadn't eaten anything?"

"Not at that time."

Ashley nodded and let a few seconds of silence pass. "You're obviously a hard worker, Ms. Dawson. In fact, you were just promoted to senior ADA within the past few months, right?"

"I was."

"And you wanted to prove yourself in this new role?"

"I always want to do the best job that I can."

"I assume you were working very hard, preparing for the trial that you were in the midst of when this event occurred. Did you stay up late the night before, working on your closing statement?"

Exactly the argument Patrick had predicted. "I don't recall exactly what time I went to sleep."

"Did you go to sleep at all?"

"Yes."

"And that you're certain of?"

"Yes."

"How can you be so certain?"

"Because all-nighters are very rare for me. I would remember if that had happened." She was thankful Patrick had prepared her for this line of questioning.

"But you can't say for sure how much sleep you got that night?"

"I can't give you an exact number."

Ashley cleared her throat. "Ms. Dawson, you're unclear on how much you slept, you hadn't eaten in over *sixteen* hours, you witnessed two shootings, and yet you want the jury to believe that you are confident in identifying the man you saw as my client?"

She couldn't afford to waver on this one. "I am confident. I saw his face, and I looked into his eyes. It's not something I could ever forget." A chill shot down her back.

"It would be bad for your career, would it not, if it came out that you had misidentified a suspect in a double-murder case?"

"I'm not sure I follow you."

"Answer the question, Ms. Dawson," Ashley said.

"I don't know that it would impact my career one way or the other. What I do in the courtroom on my cases has nothing to do with this case."

Ashley placed her hand on her right hip. "Oh, let's not mislead the jury now, Ms. Dawson."

"Objection," Patrick's loud voice rang out. "Counsel is providing commentary and not asking questions."

"Sustained," the judge ruled.

"Then let me ask you this: Did you know the officers who arrived on the scene?"

"I knew one of them, but not the other."

"And who took your statement?"

"The officer I didn't know."

Ashley turned her attention to the jury. "And didn't that officer offer up my client to you as a possible suspect?"

Where was this coming from? That certainly wasn't how it had happened. "No. The officer didn't offer up anyone. I'm the one who provided all the information and the description of the shooter. Then I identified the suspect through a lineup."

"A lineup that took place three days after the shooting?"

"Yes, because they had to apprehend the suspect first."

"But how did the police determine that they needed to look for my client?"

"You'd have to ask the police that. I provided all of the information I had to them, including the license plate number, and I assume they went from there."

"Before this case, you were aware of my client's brother—Juan Wade?"

"Of course. He has quite the reputation as the leader of one of Atlanta's most dangerous gangs." As the words came out of her mouth, Sophie realized she may have just walked into one of Ashley's traps.

Ashley raised an eyebrow. "That sounds like a prosecutor talking for sure, Ms. Dawson. And wouldn't you agree that it would be an awfully convenient way to get at Mr. Juan Wade by wrongfully prosecuting his little brother? That you and the APD conspired to set him up to take the fall for these shootings to further your own agenda?"

Patrick shot up. "Objection, Your Honor. This is ludicrous. Counsel is testifying."

The judge nodded. "Ms. Murphy, I suggest you reword your question."

Ashley smiled ever so slightly. "Thank you, Your Honor. I'll withdraw that question and move on. Isn't it true, Ms. Dawson, that you have suffered from panic attacks for years?"

Sophie took a deep breath. She had prepared for this one,

but she'd almost thought that she was going to get off the stand without Ashley asking her about it. "I have had panic attacks in the past. They have become more manageable over the years."

Ashley locked eyes with her. "In fact, they were so severe that you saw a psychologist for them, isn't that right?"

"No." *Don't volunteer. Just answer the question.*

Ashley's eyes widened. "Are you saying you haven't seen a psychologist?"

"That wasn't your question." Sophie was proceeding like she'd worked through the issue with Patrick, but even she realized it wasn't coming off well to the jury by the looks on their faces. It was time to shift gears. "I have seen a psychologist over a span of many years to deal with my grief."

"Your grief?" Ashley asked softly.

"Yes, the death of my mother." As she said the words, her stomach clenched, and she fought the feeling that the room was going to close in on her. *No, this can't happen right now.*

"My sincere condolences, Ms. Dawson."

It actually seemed like Ashley meant it, but Sophie knew better than that. She took another deep breath and focused on Ashley. There was no way she was going to succumb to a panic attack right now. *Lord, help me.*

"And were you ever prescribed any medication for your grief?"

This was a tricky question. "I was prescribed medicine, but I never filled the prescriptions."

"And why is that?"

"I didn't think it would do any good."

"On the night of October seventh, were you taking any sort of prescription medication?"

"No," she answered quickly.

"You're positive of that?"

"Yes," she answered.

"You were not drug tested that evening, correct?"

"No, I wasn't drug tested."

196

"Did you have a panic attack that night?"

Sophie thought quickly, trying to choose her words. "Not at the scene."

"But you did later?"

"Once I got home, many hours after the shooting." She'd left that part out in the preparation, and she knew Patrick might kill her. But she didn't want him to think that she couldn't handle all of this.

"But you're certain, even after witnessing that highly stressful event, so stressful that you had a panic attack, that my client is the man you saw?"

Sophie paused for half a second too long. "I'm sure."

"That's all I have for this witness."

And just like that, Ashley had planted a seed of doubt in the jurors' minds—the only thing she needed to do.

CHAPTER
SEVENTEEN

Y ou want to talk a plea deal now, huh?" Ashley looked into Patrick's dark eyes. He'd called her and asked to meet that night. She sat in a Buckhead coffee shop across from him, and she loved to see him squirm.

"You were so out of line in court today, Ashley," he said.

"I was perfectly in line. Just doing my job and what any defense attorney worth her weight would've done."

"By making up outlandish conspiracy theories and trying to poison the jury."

She laughed. "I was doing no such thing. I was just presenting a very plausible fact scenario for the jury to entertain. You couldn't honestly have thought that I was just going to roll over on this one."

"You felt guilty after you came and warned me." His eyes locked onto hers. "And then you did that in court to try to make up for it in your own mind."

"Not at all. You're almost cute when you're angry, do you know that?"

He leaned back in his chair and crossed his arms.

"Don't worry, Patrick. You're definitely not my type." She paused. "So what's your offer?"

"You're mistaken, Ashley. I'm not here to offer a plea."

"Then why did you drag me down here?"

"To warn you that if you pull another stunt like that, I will report you to the ethics committee of the Georgia bar."

Was this guy for real? "Are you kidding me? You're wasting my time. There was absolutely nothing wrong with what I did today. I was zealously defending my client. Maybe if you had a bit more of my passion and dedication, you'd be able to present a better case for the state. You were putting the jurors asleep today with your direct exam of Sophie. Total snooze fest."

"Just when I think you've reached the bottom of the barrel, Ash. You're beyond words. And to go after Sophie over her mother's death."

Ashley tossed her hair back over her shoulder. She'd taken it out of the ponytail after court. "That was completely legitimate. She has emotional issues that directly impact her reliability. She fully admitted that she had a panic attack the night of the incident. You're held back by some weird sense of how you should operate as a prosecutor, and that's what frustrates you the most."

Patrick shook his head. "You've got it all wrong."

"You can't handle the fact that I scored a huge blow today. My chances of getting an acquittal just went up exponentially."

"You sure don't lack confidence, do you?"

"Can't afford to. I deal in life and death. The stakes are far too high." Why was he starting to psychoanalyze her? She was the one who wanted to play the mind games. It was time to cut off this line of discussion.

Then it occurred to her that this whole meeting was a setup by Patrick to try to throw her off.

She smiled. "You're desperate."

"What?" he asked.

"You're getting that feeling. That feeling deep in your gut

200

when the case is starting to slip away. And now you're going to do everything in your power to try to take me down. Don't worry. I've been there too. I know that feeling. It's scary."

His eyes widened. "You're being ridiculous."

"Am I?" She didn't think she was off base. More like right on target.

"I've heard enough of your nonsense." He rose from his chair.

"Patrick, you're the one who invited me for coffee. Not the other way around."

"I've said what I needed to say. See you in court tomorrow morning."

She smiled as he walked away. She'd won the battle today, and she planned to win the war.

Cooper sat on the sofa beside Sophie at the safe house. The TV was on, but he had a hard time thinking she was actually focused on the show.

She'd been uncharacteristically quiet ever since she finished testifying. He understood she was worried about how things had gone, but it wasn't her fault. That shady defense attorney had started hurling accusations. But the problem was that the damage had been done. He'd seen the looks on the jurors' faces—concern, confusion, and the biggest one: doubt.

The revelation about her panic attacks was also shocking to him. He wondered why she had never talked to him about it. In a way, it bothered him that he had been so open with her and yet she'd kept something like that from him. But now wasn't the time to go down that path. What she needed most was his support. He needed to keep Sophie from wallowing in whatever thoughts were surely occupying her brain right now.

"Sophie, talk to me."

She looked over at him and then back at the TV. "There's really nothing to say."

"I think you and I both know that's not true." He studied her and for the first time saw that fatigue had set in.

"Regardless, I don't feel like talking."

He had to keep trying. "It might make you feel better to get it off your chest."

She looked directly into his eyes. "I doubt it."

"Sophie, you're not the type of person to lock up your feelings. It's one of the things I like best about you. If you're thinking something, you say it. Let me help you."

"You've done your job. You've kept me safe. I'm sure you'll be glad when the verdict is rendered and you can move on with your life."

Cooper knew she was hurting, so he didn't take her words personally, but it didn't seem like there was anything he could do about it. "It isn't over yet. The jury could still convict him. One thing Ashley didn't do was convince the jury that you were lying."

"She's the defense. She doesn't have to convince them of anything. That's Patrick's job. She'll just keep poke-poke-poking away until there's nothing left. They all think I'm some sort of unbalanced psycho who needs counseling and has panic attacks. You probably think that too."

He shook his head. "I could never think that about you. You should've told me about the panic attacks, though. I could've been more sensitive, given all the issues you've been going through."

She shrugged. "I didn't want you to think I was weak."

That was the last thing he thought about her. "You're so open about everything else. It just surprised me that you held that back. But I get it." And hearing her explanation, he totally did. Now he felt guilty for even questioning her.

"I don't want you to worry about me any more than you already are." She blew out a breath. "Sometimes I wonder what God is trying to do with my life. Because right now it's a mess."

"Realize that you'll fight another day. That this isn't the end. And that even if this case doesn't go your way, you're still a prosecutor fighting the good fight."

She tilted her head slightly to the side but didn't immediately respond. "I'm trying to have faith that God has it all under control, but right now it's hard. I saw those two people shot and killed in cold blood. Regardless of whether Ricky is young and misguided, he killed those people. I tried to help, and their blood was on my clothes. My hands." Tears started to fall down her cheeks.

Cooper did the thing he knew he shouldn't and put his arm around her. He pulled her closer into him, and she wrapped her arm around his waist, resting her head against his chest.

Holding her tightly as she cried, he prayed that she would stop hurting. But he also prayed for himself. That he could keep the promise he'd made that he wouldn't open a door with Sophie that he couldn't go through. Yes, he wanted to be with her probably more than anything right now. But could he keep her squarely in the friend zone?

Who was he kidding?

After a couple minutes, the crying stopped, and she lifted her head. She looked up into his eyes, her face wet with tears.

And for the first time, he truly wondered if things could be different with her.

The next morning, Patrick walked from his car toward the courthouse, ready to fight. He refused to let Ashley's blatant lies taint his case. Just the smug look on her face last night had been enough to send him over the top.

He'd barely slept as he tried to come up with a strategy to combat her conspiracy theories. Ashley coming to him and pretending to be afraid for his safety was probably all a ploy.

He'd tried to clean things up in Sophie's redirect, but she

had seemed flustered—and rightly so. Neither one of them had been prepared for this specific angle. He'd done so much preparation and put so much thought into it, but there was always the element of surprise.

And then there was the whole panic attack thing. He shouldn't be surprised that Sophie had held back on him a little bit. All witnesses did. But he was still annoyed with her.

Today he'd have to re-call both officers who'd arrived at the scene plus the detective leading the investigation. He wanted the jury to hear it out of their mouths directly that there was no collusion or effort to try to make Juan Wade suffer.

He'd told Sophie that she needed to come to court today in case she had to be examined again. As much as he knew she wanted this nightmare to be over, he couldn't take the chance that he would need her and she wouldn't be there.

A couple hours later, everything was going smoothly. Each of his law enforcement witnesses had testified as he expected—that there was no collusion and no effort by APD to use this case to get to Juan Wade.

He only had one officer left to call back to the stand.

"Call your next witness, Mr. Hunt," Judge Turner said.

"The state would like to re-call Officer Peter Gray."

Officer Gray walked up from the audience and took his place in the witness chair. He was the most junior officer on the in-vestigation and had only been at the APD for two years.

"Officer Gray, thanks for taking the time again, and I will do my best to be brief," Patrick began. "There is just one issue that I want to make sure is clear for everyone."

"Of course."

Patrick looked into Peter's light blue eyes and took a deep breath. This should go off without a hitch, based on the con-versation they'd had last night. "Officer Gray, you testified that you and Officer Wall were the first officers to arrive at the crime scene, is that correct?"

"Yes, sir."

"And you've continued to be involved as an active participant in the investigation?"

"Yes, sir, I have."

"At any point in time, have you experienced anything in the investigation that would lead you to believe the prosecution of Ricky Wade is unwarranted?"

Peter frowned. "Could you rephrase the question?"

That was strange. Patrick had thought it was a softball question. Maybe he had said something weird. "Sure. Let me ask it this way. Do you have any reason to believe that the investigation against the defendant is biased?"

Peter didn't immediately answer, but his eyes diverted to the defendant and then back to Patrick.

Patrick's stomach clenched. He could shut this down now, but Ashley would just pounce. He couldn't tell if Peter was truly confused or if something more sinister was going on.

"That's a difficult question to answer," Peter said.

"Do you have any specific knowledge of bias in the investigation?"

Peter shook his head. "Nothing specific."

This was going off the rails. He could stop now and watch what Ashley had to say. Then he could either try to clean up or figure out another strategy. Rule number one was don't ask a question you don't know the answer to. He needed more time to see how this train wreck was going to play out. "No more questions."

"Ms. Murphy, do you have more questions for Officer Gray?"

Ashley stood up. The tiniest of smiles crept across her pretty face. "Yes, thank you." She walked up closer to the witness stand. "Officer Gray, I think it's apparent to anyone watching in this courtroom that you're uncomfortable with this line of questioning."

His face starting turning red. "I didn't say that."

205

"You didn't have to say it."

"Objection," Patrick said. "Does the defense have a question or is this just more commentary?"

"Sustained," Judge Turner said.

Ashley nodded. "Officer Gray, isn't it true that you do have direct knowledge about misconduct in the Atlanta Police Department regarding this investigation?"

Peter looked down. "I think misconduct might be a strong term."

"Well, I don't want to put words in your mouth. Why don't you tell the jury about any concerns you have about the investigation?"

"Objection, vague," Patrick said.

"Overruled."

Patrick knew that was a weak objection. He was just trying to break up the line of questioning any way he could. He feared he was about to watch his entire case blow up.

"You can answer the question," Ashley said.

Once again, Peter looked down. What Patrick didn't know was whether this was feigned hesitancy.

"It was pretty apparent to me that everyone was taking advantage of this opportunity." Peter fidgeted in his seat. "It's not every day that you have the little brother of the head of one of the most powerful gangs in Atlanta in custody for double homicide."

"Can you elaborate on what you mean by taking advantage of the opportunity?"

Ashley was like a great white shark. Blood was in the water, and there was no way she was going to leave hungry.

Peter clasped his hands in front of him. His face had gone from red to pale. "It seemed to me that we were operating as if the defendant's guilt was a foregone conclusion."

"How so?" Ashley asked.

Peter cleared his throat. "I don't think we seriously considered anyone else for the crime. Ricky was the only suspect we had, and then we pushed hard to get to this trial."

Ashley shifted and turned toward the jury. She didn't say anything. It was just a theatrical move to make them ponder Peter's statements. She wanted it to sink in.

"Thank you for your candor, Officer Gray. I know this was a bit difficult for you given the circumstances. That's all I have."

"Anything else for this witness, Mr. Hunt?" the judge asked.

Patrick had to make a split-second decision. Did he push Peter any more to try to clean this mess up? The risk was that he could just make it worse. The practical response would be to let it go, but Patrick's gut was screaming otherwise. If he was wrong, he'd pay the price, but he had to go there. There was no other option.

"Just one more thing." He stood up and walked up to the witness. "Officer Gray, have you been approached by Juan Wade or anyone connected to him?"

"Of course not," Peter said quickly.

Too quickly.

"I want to remind the witness that he is under oath. Would you like to revise your answer?"

Peter looked up at him, this time making direct eye contact. "No. I have not." His voice sounded unsure, though. It didn't have the same commanding ring as his other answers.

"No further questions." Patrick had planted the seed that Juan was behind all of this, but that was only minimal triage.

This was easily the most awful day in court he'd ever had. And the worst thing was that he'd never seen it coming. What could possibly be next?

CHAPTER
EIGHTEEN

S ophie waited for court to recess for the day so she could talk to Patrick. She couldn't believe what she'd seen play out on the stand. Officer Gray had to be in Wade's back pocket. It was the only explanation that made any sense. He was a newer officer and probably more susceptible to a bribe or threats.

There was no doubt in her mind that she'd seen Ricky Wade shoot and kill two people on the night of October seventh. She refused to think that he could just walk away free and clean. There had to be a way to make sure the families got the justice they deserved.

Sophie looked over at Cooper. "I have to talk to Patrick."

Cooper nodded. "I had a feeling you'd say that. We can keep our seats until he's done packing up."

Most of those in the audience had left or were exiting now. The media presence was still around, swarming like bees. She didn't plan to let any of them get close to her, and she knew Cooper would help in that effort.

Patrick made eye contact with her, then started to walk their way. "Let's go to one of the conference rooms so we can talk," he said.

A few minutes later, she was seated across from Patrick at a table in a private room. Cooper was right outside the door.

"I assume you were blindsided in there?" she asked Patrick.

He loosened his navy striped tie. "Yes. I spoke to all of them last night to ensure there would be no surprises. Something happened. Either he lied to me last night, or someone got to him between then and now."

"Wade's people," she said flatly.

"Who else?"

"We have to figure out a way to salvage this thing," she said.

Patrick sighed. "I know you want to help. The prosecutor in you can't resist, but it really isn't best for you to take on second chair right now."

"I agreed with you on that throughout this whole process, but we're in uncharted territory now. It would seem that you could use my help to brainstorm a way through this."

"That's the thing, Sophie. If we're being realistic, I don't think there's a way we can get a guilty verdict. There are just too many holes. Too many threads of suspicion."

"Put me back on the stand as a rebuttal witness," she offered.

"So Ashley can skewer you again?"

"No. So I can convince the jury of what I saw that night. All of this other conspiracy theory stuff is just smoke and mirrors. If they believe me, then they should convict. That should be our play."

"It's not that simple. And your credibility has already been called into question just by the fact that you're a prosecutor who supposedly wants to get to Juan through his brother."

"If you're right and we're toast, then we have nothing to lose and everything to gain. Please give me a chance to try to make this right." She needed this shot to be able to sleep at night and wanted to do whatever was in her power to know that she had tried her best. She couldn't control the jury's decision, but she planned to make them have to think long and hard about it.

He leaned in toward her. "This means Ashley will take another run at you."

"I'm ready for that. More ready than I was last time."

"All right. I'm going to trust you on this one."

"I won't let you down." She stood up and gave Patrick's shoulder a squeeze before exiting the conference room to find Cooper. He wasn't far, right outside in the hall. But he also wasn't alone. Keith stood next to him in what appeared to be an intense conversation.

"Keith." She strode up to the two men.

"Sophie, I'm glad I caught you. Cooper told me you were speaking to Patrick."

"Yes, trying to do my part to save this case. I'm going to take the stand again tomorrow."

"Good, good. Whatever you can do. For obvious reasons, we don't want or need a loss on this one. It would be a huge embarrassment for our office."

Great, more pressure that she didn't need. She already understood how high the stakes were.

Keith took a step toward her. "I actually wanted to talk to you about something else if you have a second."

"Sure."

"In private?"

"I'll wait right over there." Cooper pointed just down the hallway before walking away, leaving her alone with Keith.

"Is everything okay?" she asked.

His blue eyes narrowed. "I'm not sure. Remember the update you gave me the other day about the Shelton case?"

"Of course."

"I'm concerned that you're going down a rabbit hole. I spoke to Whitney briefly, and she says it's not abnormal for their senior employees to move money between accounts, especially given their level of investments. They also tend to have quite a bit of liquid income."

"So those numerous deposits of less than ten grand over time didn't give her any pause?"

Keith shook his head. "No. She thinks it's quite normal, and I tend to agree."

She couldn't hold back anymore. "With all due respect, sir, I can't help the feeling that SIB wants me to back off. And even more than that, that *you* want me to back off."

He frowned. "Sophie, you need to remember who you're talking to. I don't appreciate your tone or your insinuation. You work for me, not the other way around. Don't forget that."

She had to fight to hold back her anger and frustration. After all that had happened today, this was the last thing she needed. "I'm sorry. I was out of line." Or least that was what she was going to say for now.

His eyes softened. "Put this out of your mind for now and focus on your testimony. Let the jury see the real you, Sophie. I'm confident that if they do, then Wade will go to prison." Keith turned and walked away from her.

Something wasn't right. What she didn't know was whether Keith was just trying to protect his friend or if something more was amiss. She had no intention of offering a plea to Shelton, because she had to find out what was really going on with him and why SIB was so concerned.

Cooper found himself holding his breath as Sophie took her seat in the witness stand for the second time. He was no lawyer, but he knew enough to realize how important this additional testimony was going to be.

It was all on Sophie's shoulders to turn this trial around and convince the jury of Ricky's guilt. He believed deep in his gut that she was more than capable of pulling it off.

He could tell she had been extremely nervous the first time she testified, but he didn't sense any of those nerves now. Not from her. He was another story. His stomach was in knots as he waited for the first words to come out of her mouth. He would do anything in his power to protect her, and he felt incredibly vulnerable right now with her up there and him in the courtroom audience.

She was fiercely determined to tell her side of the story and combat the rumors that the defense attorney was hurling around. He had a strong suspicion that Juan had gotten to Officer Gray, but there was nothing they could do about it now. The jury had heard the testimony, and there was no turning back.

He wondered whether Patrick was really up for this task. Cooper didn't understand enough about the law to know whether these missteps were Patrick's fault or if it could've happened to anyone. There was also the thread of jealously he felt toward the man. Sophie had said there was nothing between them, but he couldn't help his emotional response.

Patrick cleared his throat. "Thank you for coming back again, Ms. Dawson. I appreciate you taking the time out of your schedule."

"You're welcome."

"And just so we're on the same page, you were in the courtroom yesterday and heard all the testimony that was presented, correct?"

"Yes, that's right."

"Then let me cut right to the chase. Ms. Dawson, are you aware of any bias of any type in the investigation that was conducted in this case?"

"I am not aware of any, and I don't believe there was any."

Patrick took a step closer to the witness stand. "Why do you say that?"

"Because this investigation wasn't a black hole. I was there that night, Mr. Hunt. I witnessed the unspeakable tragedy—two people shot—right before my eyes. I described the shooter and gave his license plate number. Then I identified the defendant in a lineup. It was all by the book each step of the way."

"Objection." The defense attorney interrupted Sophie. "Your Honor, I think Ms. Dawson is forgetting that she isn't the prosecutor in this case. It sounds to me like she's presenting an argument, not answering the state's questions."

"Ms. Dawson, just answer the question presented to you, please," the judge said.

Patrick took a step closer to the jury box before looking back at Sophie. "Ms. Dawson, you are a prosecutor, correct?"

"Yes, I am."

"Do you believe that your job had anything to do with how you identified the suspect?"

Sophie turned and looked at the jury. "Absolutely not. One thing had nothing to do with the other. I wasn't a prosecutor that night at the Quick Stop. I was just a person who had worked a long day and wanted a snack."

Cooper smiled as Sophie hit on the key points and themes that she hoped to get across.

"All I can do is tell you and the jury what I saw. And there is no doubt in my mind that I saw Mr. Ricky Wade shoot and kill two innocent people."

"Ms. Dawson, if there was some bias in the APD against the defendant because of his brother, would that impact you in any way?"

"No. I'm certain about what I saw. I didn't know when I identified him who he was. I didn't learn that fact until after the identification."

Patrick turned to the jury. "Let me make sure everyone on the jury understands this. When you made your eyewitness identification, did you have any idea who the suspect was?"

"None. I made the identification based on what I had seen. Once I made the identification, I was told later that the man I had identified as the suspect was Juan Wade's brother."

214

"Nothing further," Patrick said.

Now it was time for Ashley Murphy. Cooper had no idea what her game plan was.

"Ms. Dawson, isn't it a bit disingenuous for you to try to mislead the jury into thinking that your role as a prosecutor didn't cloud your vision?"

Patrick shot to his feet. "Objection, argumentative."

"I'll allow it," Judge Turner said.

Sophie gave a slight smile. "Ms. Murphy, being a prosecutor has shaped who I am today. I believe in the justice system. I also believe in telling the truth. It's what I expect out of every single witness I put up on the stand, and it's certainly what I expect from myself. Your client was the man who shot the two victims."

"And you're sitting here, under oath, testifying that you were not told my client's name until after you identified him as the shooter. Are you certain that's your testimony?"

"Yes. Quite certain. Absolutely certain, in fact."

"What would you say if I told you that Officer Gray is ready to testify otherwise?"

Sophie didn't miss a beat. "I'd say that Officer Gray has been compromised by Juan Wade."

The courtroom erupted at Sophie's accusation.

Judge Turner banged his gavel. "Everyone in the courtroom needs to stay quiet, or I will clear it out. Don't test me on this."

"Ms. Dawson, it's your contention that the APD wasn't biased but that one of their officers has supposedly been corrupted by my client's brother?"

"Yes."

"How can you have it both ways? Claim that the APD was aboveboard in one breath, but admit, even point the finger at one of the officers for corruption of another type?"

The defense had cornered Sophie. Cooper was curious how she would respond.

"Ms. Murphy, I never said the APD was completely above

reproach in all circumstances. My only claim was that in this investigation, I knew of no bias or ill intent, and that I made my identification without knowledge of the suspect's identity. I understand that you might want to confuse the issue because it's beneficial to your client."

"Your Honor, I move to strike Ms. Dawson's last response," Ms. Murphy said.

"On what basis?" Patrick asked.

"It's nonresponsive."

"Of course it's responsive," Patrick replied.

"Overruled," Judge Turner said.

Ms. Murphy's cheeks turned red. She walked back toward counsel's table and picked up her legal pad. Cooper didn't think she was actually reading anything but simply buying herself time.

"I'm done with this witness."

"Mr. Hunt, anything else?" the judge asked.

"No, Your Honor."

"Then, Ms. Dawson, you're excused."

Sophie stepped down, and just like that, she had turned the tide. Cooper now thought they might actually have a fighting chance.

"How could you have screwed this up so badly?" Juan's voice boomed through Ashley's office.

He'd summoned her for a meeting that night, and she knew he wasn't going to be happy. She couldn't say she was surprised at his reaction.

"Juan, you weren't in the courtroom. How could you possibly understand everything that went on?"

"I have my people reporting back to me. They said the prosecutor killed it on the stand today and made you look like a bumbling idiot."

Ashley leaned forward in her seat. "Let's get one thing straight. I've not once in my life looked like a bumbling idiot. You need to get a grip. My goal was to make this thing messy. Messy means that the jury will have doubts. Doubts lead to acquittals. All I need is one of them to have questions to get Ricky off. I never said this was going to be a walk in the park or that it would be pretty. Your brother shot and killed two people, Juan, and we have a respected prosecutor who saw the whole thing."

"You're supposed to make it go away."

"And I'm the only lawyer in town who has a shot at getting that done. My closing statement is going to focus on all of the holes in their case. All the questions that I will put in the jury's mind. Including the fact that we have an officer at the APD basically saying that there was something nefarious going on." She paused. "And I'm certain I have you to thank for that. That whole thing could've blown up in my face. A heads-up would've been nice."

"I thought it was better strategically for you to have plausible deniability."

She blew out a breath. "Juan, your job is not to think of legal strategies. That is my job."

"But how can I trust you and a broken system? You couldn't seriously think I'd let you just take this entire thing on alone. I'm not stupid. We need every advantage we can get."

"I just hope you didn't push it too far. The jury may think that Gray was paid off."

"Nah. I think we're good on that angle."

She laughed. "The only reason you think we're good is because it's something that you had a hand in. But I need to prepare you for the stark reality that we could lose this thing. It's possible."

"No, it's not," he said. "Push me too far, Ashley, and you will see what I'm capable of. To protect my brother, my family, my empire. There are no limits. I warned you about that from day one. If you can't get the job done through the legal system, I will step in."

She had no idea what he had in mind, but it couldn't be good. On the other hand, she didn't want a loss on her record either. How far was she willing to go? Even though Patrick wouldn't believe it, she still had some lines she wouldn't cross. She wasn't like her client. "Closing statements begin tomorrow."

"Then you better get to work." He rose from his seat. "But make no mistake, Ash. If this one goes sideways, I'm holding you personally responsible."

A chill shot down her back. "I understand."

"Good." He slammed the office door on the way out.

Her neck was on the line. She had no doubt in her mind that Juan's version of revenge might include her ending up dead.

CHAPTER
NINETEEN

Sophie wrapped a blanket around her as she sat on the couch. The safe house was always a bit chilly for her taste. Tomorrow was a big day. Each side in the Wade case would give their closings, and the jury would start its deliberation.

She had turned her attention back to Shelton and SIB. Her boss's words kept ringing in her ears. Why was Keith so insistent on her backing off?

The Shelton trial was rapidly approaching, but she couldn't imagine that Leland would ever put Shelton on the stand, so she wouldn't get an opportunity to question him about his accounts. She hadn't even broached the topic yet of calling Whitney as a witness. Keith really would lose his mind then. But at least Whitney would have an opportunity to set the record straight under oath. Still, there was no way Sophie was going to bring that up until the eve of trial, when she had to provide her witness list. That was part of her master plan—or the closest thing she had to one. They were hitting dead ends on tracing the money, so she had scant proof that any money laundering was actually occurring.

A part of her wondered whether she should just put Shelton away for many years and forget about any other wrongdoing that had been going on. But that wasn't her style. She couldn't act like the ostrich that Keith wanted her to be.

She picked up another file of documents and started reading them. She couldn't help but think that the answers she wanted would be in these files. The problem was that there were thousands of pages to comb through. She'd sent Monica a series of emails to make sure she was continuing to work on trial preparation. That part was easier and more appropriate for a newbie attorney.

Her eyes continued to scan the pages. Numbers weren't actually her thing, but in this type of work, she had to force herself to take them in.

Shelton was getting large amounts of cash from somewhere. But that in and of itself wasn't illegal. She had to figure out what he was doing with the money after that.

"House is secure." Cooper walked in and took a seat. "You back to work?"

Sophie set the pages she was reviewing on the coffee table. "Yes. Now that my part in the Wade case is officially over, I want to shift gears. There's nothing more I can do at this point except worry, and that's not going to do me any good. All I've got right now is a theory. I'm not buying Keith's explanation provided through Whitney that it's natural for employees to move that kind of money in and out of their accounts like that. There's something more going on here, and the fact that Whitney is so involved only makes me more suspicious."

"And if Whitney *is* involved, she now knows for sure that you're looking into the money-laundering angle."

"You think I should be concerned about that?" She felt the words rushing out.

Cooper leaned forward, resting his elbows on his knees. "It's just one more factor to be aware of. Unfortunately, we still haven't been able to ferret out what Shelton did with the money. But we'll keep working on it."

"That's why I can't make a direct accusation against SIB. Not until I have something more. And then if I do find more, I have to decide when to bring in the Feds."

"Money laundering is their territory, right?" Cooper asked.

Sophie shook her head. "Not exclusively, no. We have a state money-laundering statute. But the practical answer is that if a bank is involved in something like this, the Feds need to be involved. I can't call them in on my gut instincts and some random deposits that set off my radar. There's still a big piece I'm missing."

"What is that?"

"For this to actually be money laundering, the source of the funds has to have been illegally obtained. It's not enough for me to show that the bank was passing funds without being able to show the purpose."

Cooper nodded in understanding. "You need to be able to demonstrate that the money is dirty. Like it came from some type of criminal enterprise."

"Exactly." Her excitement level started to build. "Which brings up the million-dollar question. Let's assume for a moment that I'm right and SIB is participating in money laundering. What type of criminal activity could SIB be involved with?"

"Based on my experience, I'd say some kind of organized crime or drug cartel. Those entities have both the need to launder money and the means to be able to develop a relationship with a bank like SIB."

Her heart thumped wildly at his words. "We're still a long way from making that leap, but it's something I have to consider. The dirty funds had to come through the bank, get cleaned, and then go back out to the initial source or someone connected to that criminal activity. The issue is how to follow the bread crumbs and determine what's behind the curtain."

"You just need to make sure you can get Shelton convicted." He paused. "How're you feeling about the Wade trial?"

"I've done all I can do, and now it's out of my hands." She looked up into his eyes. "I appreciate your patience with me throughout this whole thing. I know I kind of lost it after I testified the first time. I didn't mean to be on such an emotional roller coaster and drag you along with me."

"You've been a trooper. I can't even imagine how difficult this has all been for you. Don't be so hard on yourself."

Would there ever be a right time for them? While she desperately wanted Cooper to kiss her, she also knew that she'd be taking a huge risk. Would he be able to change his mind about what he wanted? Because if not, then how could she ever give him her heart?

The next few days passed in a blur for Cooper as they waited for the jury to reach a verdict. At the front of his mind was determining what the next steps would be for Sophie. A lot of the security plan depended on the outcome of the case, but he had a nagging feeling that regardless of the outcome, she'd always be on Juan's bad side, and that made him nervous.

But he couldn't provide her around-the-clock protection forever. At least not in the current form.

The other night when he'd taken her hand, it had felt so right. *Lord, what am I supposed to do here? Can I take this leap with her?*

He didn't know what he should do. He wanted to be with her. To develop a real relationship, but he was still scared to death about how that might unfold. Was it worth the risk to both of them?

Sophie walked into the living room, carrying her laptop and a big stack of papers. "What's going on?"

"Just thinking about what's next. Any updates from Patrick?"

"No. But given it's Friday, I suspect the jury will render its verdict today. None of them will want to come back on Monday." She sat down beside him on the couch.

"We'll have to figure out your security situation once the verdict comes down." That was still his top priority.

"If we get a guilty verdict, I suppose Juan could come after me for revenge. But if it's not guilty or a hung jury, why would he care about me?" Sophie placed her hand on her chest.

"Do you think Patrick would retry if it's a mistrial?" Cooper asked.

"I haven't asked him. I didn't want to put that possibility out there just yet."

"Have you prepared yourself for the worst?" He wanted to make sure she wasn't caught off guard. In his opinion, there was a good likelihood they wouldn't get a guilty verdict, even given her great performance on the witness stand. There were too many nagging questions that might impact the jury.

She looked up at him. "Yeah. I've been thinking a lot about it, and I'm ready for whatever comes. I haven't set unreasonable expectations, if that's what you're worried about. I'll be able to keep it together."

"I never questioned that." He took a breath. "Sophie, I've been doing a lot of thinking."

She looked at him warily. "Should I be worried about what you're going to say?"

"I hope not."

Her blue eyes widened. "Tell me what's on your mind."

"You," he said softly.

And instead of trying to explain and backtrack from all the stuff he'd said previously, he decided it was best to just let his actions speak for themselves. He placed his hand under her chin and gently tilted her head up. He hadn't been this nervous about a kiss since his first kiss at age thirteen—which was a lifetime ago. But that was because this meant much more to him than just a kiss.

As he stared into her bright blue eyes, he felt an assurance that he was making the right decision. And when he kissed her, there was surprisingly no sense of fear. Only a huge spark that sent a flood of heat through him. All of his worries and doubts were put squarely out of his mind as he deepened the kiss.

But after a few moments, she pulled away.

"What's wrong?" he asked.

She shook her head. "I'm sorry. I just can't."

It was like the air had been knocked out of him. But it was even worse than that, because he knew why she felt that way. It was because of what he'd told her.

"Unless you've changed your mind?" she asked expectantly. "Unless you can look me in the eyes and tell me that you want the same things I want?"

As much as he wanted to be able to do just that, he couldn't. At least not yet. He couldn't commit to something that he himself wasn't sure of. "As I sit here today, I can't tell you that. I'm sorry. I never should've done this. I let my emotions and the chemistry between us cloud my brain. That wasn't fair to you."

Her eyes misted up. "I'm sorry, too. Maybe for now we should just focus on work."

Guilt ate at him. He never should have kissed her unless he was one hundred percent sure that he could give her what she wanted. He should have been stronger. "My first priority is still your safety, and I'm not going to let down my guard. I think you need to be prepared for multiple contingencies, because we just don't know how this will all play out."

"As long as you stick around, I'll be fine with that."

He wasn't so sure that was true. Especially after what had just happened. "Don't worry. You're stuck with me."

Her cell rang loudly, and she picked it up off the coffee table. After a short conversation, she hung up. "The verdict is in. Let's go to the courthouse."

"Are you sure that's a good idea?"

"I want to be there."

"Let me call in reinforcements." There was no way he was going to take Sophie to the courthouse without backup.

Patrick clenched his fists as he waited for the verdict to be read. They'd overcome a lot of obstacles in this case, but he still had a sick feeling in the pit of his stomach.

He turned and looked over his shoulder into the courtroom audience. Sitting on the defense side in the first row was none other than Juan Wade himself. He'd been conspicuously absent during the trial, but now that the jury had deliberated, it was time for him to flex his muscle.

Patrick made eye contact with Juan, who gave him a menacing wink. A chill shot down his spine. None of this felt right to him. He didn't think justice was going to be served today.

He looked at the defense table, where Ashley sat with an air of confidence about her. Beside her, Ricky slumped, unmoving. Patrick knew the kid had to be worried. But at the end of the day, reasonable doubt was a tricky thing, and he felt sure Juan had done whatever it took to take care of his brother.

Patrick still hoped for a guilty verdict, but he wasn't naïve. This wasn't his first rodeo.

Ashley's confidence troubled him, because it was a bit much even for her. Which in his mind meant she might know something that he didn't. Had Juan bought off someone on the jury?

When the judge entered the courtroom, you could hear a pin drop. Members of the media were present, perched to jump on the story no matter which way it went. There wasn't a single empty seat in the courtroom.

"All right, please bring in the jury," the judge said.

Patrick's heartbeat sped up. Yes, he'd done this a million times, but this case was definitely one of the most unique he'd ever had.

As the jurors filed in, most of them avoided eye contact with anyone. He couldn't read their faces. He'd just have to wait.

Judge Turner cleared his throat. "I've been informed that after ample deliberation, the jury cannot reach a unanimous decision. As such, I have no choice but to declare a mistrial."

The courtroom was abuzz with reaction. The judge banged his gavel a few times to silence the room.

Patrick realized his fists were still clenched. He loosened his hands and looked over at the victors. Ashley wore a broad smile, but Ricky just sat there, expressionless. Patrick could only hope that the kid had learned his lesson, but he wasn't so sure.

The judge thanked the jury, and Patrick sat trying to put on a brave face.

"Patrick."

He turned and saw Sophie walking up to him. He stood, and she wrapped her arms tightly around him in a warm embrace.

"I'm so sorry," she said.

"I should be the one apologizing." Patrick couldn't help feeling like he'd let her down.

"This isn't your fault." Sophie shot a glance in Juan's direction and then scowled. "I knew this was possible, but I was still holding out some measure of hope that justice would actually prevail."

"I feel the same way."

"You know you'll have to face the media."

"Unfortunately, yes. But it comes with the territory, as you know very well."

She looked toward the back of the courtroom. "Okay, Cooper is giving me the eye. He probably wants to get out of here ASAP. The security situation has him concerned."

"Yeah, try to stay out of the media's path. Let me handle them."

"Of course." She nodded and walked toward Cooper.

Patrick turned and started packing up his stuff. He crammed his notepad and his laptop into his bag.

"Can't win them all." Ashley stood in front of him at the table.

Great, let the gloating begin.

226

"I hope you're satisfied with yourself."

She crossed her arms. "I did my job. Just like you did yours. And today I just happened to come out on top. You don't have anything to be ashamed of."

She had some nerve. "Who said I was ashamed?"

"You're clearly upset. You're flushed. You'll want to take a few minutes to calm down before you face the wolves."

"I wouldn't dream of going first anyway. The media is your deal, Ashley, not mine."

"The media serves a purpose. I seem to recall you using them earlier in the case."

"True." She had him there. "So tell me, exactly what did Juan do? Was it direct threats or a payoff?" He could feel the anger bubbling up inside of him as the words left his mouth.

She raised her right eyebrow. "I have no idea what you're talking about."

"I know you'll never admit it, but just know that I know, okay?" He paused. "I need to finish packing up, and you need to get to the press, don't you?"

Ashley smiled. "That I do."

He watched as she walked back over to Ricky and Juan. Patrick had expected after a big victory that they would greet her warmly, but the exchange seemed hostile. Ashley took a step back from Juan as he raised his voice. Then he grabbed her arm before she shrugged him off.

As much as Ashley got on his nerves, he couldn't believe that such a strong woman would put up with being treated like that. And there was a side of him that wanted to intervene. Wanted to go over there and tell Juan to back off and get his hands off of Ashley.

But this wasn't his battle. Ashley had made her bed, and now she had to deal with the consequences.

—◄◇►—

That evening Sophie sat huddled in the living room of the safe house, feeling numb. She'd told herself that she was prepared to lose, but it felt much worse than she had expected. She'd tried to put on a strong face for Patrick because she empathized with how he felt. But today was one of those days where the good guys didn't win.

They'd decided they needed to regroup, so Noah had picked up Patrick so they could discuss their next steps.

"I'd like to go home," Sophie said. "I can't live here forever. And even if Patrick does try the case again, it could be a while before that happens, right, Patrick?"

"This is all very fresh. There are two schools of thought— strike while the iron is hot, or give it some time to cool off and try again." Patrick stared off into the distance. "I also have to weigh whether it makes sense to use the state's resources for a retrial. We all know what we're up against here. Juan only has to get to one member of the jury to make it another mistrial. I don't know how I can fight against that."

Sophie had strong feelings on the topic, which she couldn't help sharing. "Ricky Wade killed two people. I know this isn't my case, but I believe you have to make a second attempt. We can't let criminals think they can buy off the justice system like this. There has to be repercussions."

"On the flip side," Noah said, "I bet Ricky Wade is going to end up on the wrong side of the law again. There may be another opportunity to put him away or at least make him do some solid jail time. The penalties here were so severe, I think that his brother was willing to do anything and everything to prevent a guilty verdict."

She looked over at Cooper, who had been pretty quiet. She wondered what was going on in his head. After their awkward exchange, there had been a lot of tension between them.

Patrick shifted in his seat. "Given all the extenuating cir- cumstances, I think it's safe to say that even if I want to retry the case, it's going to take some time. I'll have to jump through all the hoops, given that I'm a special prosecutor from another county, and everyone will need to be on board. Even if I pushed as hard as I could, I'd say we're at least a month or two out from going at it again. And that's the best-case scenario. I'd also need time to deal with the APD and Officer Gray. That kind of thing can't happen. Regardless of the outcome here, I'm going to suggest an internal investigation into Officer Gray."

"That's something," she said. "But everything you're telling us just supports my position that I should go home and get back to work. Juan won this round. Who's to say he even cares about me anymore?"

Patrick nodded. "Possibly. You're already on record, so he can't do anything about that. That testimony is set in stone. But he doesn't strike me as the type of man to just forget the fact that you testified against his brother."

"Or that you prosecuted him," she added.

"True. But that comes with the territory." Patrick stood up. "I've got to get some things done. I'll leave you all to discuss how you want to handle Sophie's situation. My two cents is that she's probably as safe as she's going to be. She's right that she can't stay locked up forever. If Juan wants to come after her again, he could wait her out for months or years. I think life's too short to live like that."

"I'll take you back," Noah said. "Cooper, I'll call you later."

Once she was alone with Cooper, Sophie took a seat beside him on the sofa, making sure not to get too close.

"I'm sorry about how this all turned out," he said.

"It's not your fault."

"I know how much this meant to you."

She nodded. "Yes, but like you said, I was prepared for this. It sickens me, though, that men like Juan can run roughshod over justice." She leaned her head against the couch. "I want to go home."

"I know you do. We'll see what we can do."

Sophie turned her face toward him. "My father won't like it. I'm just warning you."

Cooper gave a weak smile. "I figured as much. I know you think I'm being overly protective, but there are a lot of unknowns right now."

"I'm not suggesting that you just drop me off at my doorstep to fend for myself." She wanted to clear the air between them. "I don't want things to be weird between us. You've been so good to me throughout this, and you're great at your job. I feel safe because of you."

He nodded. "That means a lot to me. Let's just continue to work together on your SIB case and try to put the other stuff out of our minds."

"Sounds good."

But she wondered how she'd ever be able to put it out of her mind. Because while she hadn't allowed herself to fully act on it, she had developed some serious feelings for Cooper.

TWENTY

Juan sat in Ashley's office, wearing a smug grin. "I held up my end of the bargain."

"I did too," she shot back.

"Well, that remains to be seen. I need you to do something else for me."

She hated to think what he had in mind now. "What?"

"I need you to convince that prosecutor not to retry the case. We need to put this awful mess behind us."

"In case you didn't notice, I'm not Patrick's favorite person right now. Getting a mistrial stinks. I'm sure he's still wrecked over the decision."

"All the more reason to get him when he's vulnerable. I've seen the way he looks at you. I think he has a thing for you."

She laughed loudly. "The thing he has for me is hatred, Juan. Nothing more. He thinks I'm disgusting."

Juan shook his head. "No way. He's a man, isn't he? He can hate you and still want to—"

"Enough," she snapped. She didn't need to hear what he was going to say. She'd always been objectified by men like Juan, but she wouldn't allow him to do it in her office. She was near her breaking point with both brothers and ready to put this case behind her.

"No need to get all testy. I get that it was a stressful trial. And I appreciate what you've done." He reached into his jacket.

She gripped her chair, fearful that he was pulling a gun. But when she saw the envelope, she let out a breath.

"Here's your payment. It's cash. Hope that's not a problem."

"Of course not." She tried not to think about the fact that it was dirty money. She'd signed on to this life, and she had to deal with it. No judgments. "But I haven't sent you my bills for the trial yet."

"I think this payment should more than cover it. If it doesn't, you know where to find me."

She accepted the envelope. "What's next for you? Are you going to lay low? And what about Ricky?"

"I'm sending Ricky out of town. He needs to get out of the ATL. I'll go about business as usual."

She had to bring it up, because it was on her conscience. "I assume now that we have the mistrial, you're going to lay off Sophie Dawson?"

"If she doesn't mess with me, then I have no reason to mess with her. But if this case goes to trial again, I can't say the same thing. If you have some interest in her well-being, that's all the more reason for you to convince the prosecutor to put this one to bed. I have no doubt you can be very persuasive about this." He stood up. "Hopefully I won't need your services again anytime soon, but you know how it is. I'm sure we'll be talking again in the near future."

Juan walked out of her office, and she opened the envelope. As she started to count the cash, she wondered if she could believe him. Would he really just leave Sophie alone? And now she had the added problem of him wanting her to get Patrick to lay off. Juan was delusional if he believed Patrick had a thing for her. She knew when men were into her, and Patrick was just the opposite.

But maybe Juan was right about one thing—maybe it was best to go to Patrick sooner rather than later. But her interests didn't align with Juan's. She needed to figure out what was best for her. She'd catered to Juan for far too long.

The last thing Patrick wanted to do was have a meeting with Ashley, but she wouldn't take no for an answer. He made her come over to his turf, though. If she wanted the meeting that badly, then she'd be willing to come to him.

He figured she probably wanted to gloat, but it took a lot of guts to request a meeting just for that purpose. The more time he'd had to think about things, the more convinced he was that Juan Wade had played a role in the hung jury. Yes, his case had experienced some setbacks, but the gang leader had no qualms about taking drastic action. The attacks against Sophie had shown that.

A deep feeling of conflict was brewing inside him. On one hand, he wanted to get back to his other cases and put this whole ordeal behind him. But on the other hand, it infuriated him how Juan had worked the system. He didn't want to be a coward and back down. But the result could be the exact same the second time around, and he'd be powerless to stop it.

When Ashley walked into his office a few minutes later, he tried to put on his best poker face. "Have a seat," he told her.

She sat down and looked at him. "How're you doing?"

"I doubt you came here to check on my emotional state. So let's cut the crap and get down to it."

She leaned forward. "I know you think I'm some sort of monster, but that's the furthest thing from the truth. Just because we chose different sides of the law doesn't mean I'm evil. Far from it."

"So now you're patting yourself on the back? Having a guilt trip, maybe, about what you've done?" He couldn't stop the words from coming out. There was no doubt he was still raw about the whole thing.

She shook her head. "Absolutely not. But I am here to give you some friendly advice—lawyer to lawyer."

"I can only imagine what that's going to be." He figured she was about to put on the hard sell to make sure he didn't re-try the case.

"You're not going to win this one. Walk away from all of it."

"Of course you're saying that."

She laughed. "Actually, it's better for me personally if you do retry the case. More exposure, and it keeps me relevant. But my clients' needs are my top priority."

One thing he grudgingly admitted about Ashley was that she was a fierce advocate for her clients. "I haven't made a decision yet. I need some time to think about it and regroup. Especially after Juan got to Officer Gray."

Ashley crossed her arms. "You don't have a shred of evidence to support that."

"Not yet. But when APD is finished with their investigation, I think it will be crystal clear what happened. And don't even get me started on the jury tampering."

Ashley placed a hand over her chest. "Patrick, I didn't tamper with the jury."

He was quickly losing his patience. He knew as a prosecutor that he should take the high ground, but she was making that very difficult. "Really, I don't know why I waste my time talking to you. What do you want from me?"

Ashley's eyes softened. "I'm not the enemy, Patrick."

"You sure seem like it." He paused. "If you really want my opinion, you should drop Wade as a client. I've seen the way he treats you. He's not worth it. No amount of money is worth putting your self-respect on the line."

She blew out a breath. "It's always so black and white with you. My life is much more complicated than that. My law practice is shades of gray, not one extreme or the other."

"But it's your own practice, and you have the freedom, especially at this point in your career, to make choices."

"Don't act like you're immune to the issues I deal with," she snapped. "Don't you have your sights set on something much higher? Maybe being *the* district attorney one day? Ambition basically oozes out of you."

"You have guts, I'll give you that much. But what do you think Juan would do if he knew you were here now in my office?"

"He's the one who ordered me to talk to you."

"I bet his orders involved you talking me out of re-trying the case. Right?"

"Obviously. But know one thing—if you do decide to re-try, I'm not going to go soft on you. I'll put everything I have into it."

He found himself smiling. "I've come to expect nothing less from you."

As she exited his office, he struggled to figure out what Ashley really wanted.

Sophie felt energized as she walked into the District Attorney's office. It hadn't been that long, but to her it felt like forever. Yes, the Wade case had completely gone sideways, but that only motivated her more to work on her own case—the Shelton case. Which in her mind had expanded to become the SIB case. But if she said those words to Keith, he would pull her off so fast, her head would spin.

"You're back."

Harrison was lurking in the hallway near her office.

"Yes, I'm back."

He reached out and patted her shoulder. "Too bad about

the Wade case. They always say that lawyers make the worst witnesses."

Instinctively, she took a step back. She hated it when he touched her. "I did all I could do. We knew it would be a tough one."

"I talked to Keith. It seems like it won't impact your review, from what I could tell."

Anger simmered beneath the surface, and she could feel her nails pressing into her palms as she clenched her fists. "And why would my performance review be any of your business, Harrison?"

He held up his hands. "No need to get testy. I thought I was doing you a favor."

"I don't need favors from you. Now, if you'll excuse me, I have a lot of work to do."

"Just make sure you don't screw up the Shelton case. You can't afford to have two losses back to back. I'm ready to offer my services if you feel like you're in over your head."

Furious thoughts ran through her mind. *Lord, please give me the strength to hold my tongue.* She brushed past him and into her office, then slammed the door.

It took her a few minutes to get her emotions in check. She knew better than to let Harrison get under her skin. What she needed to do was get back to work and not spend any more time letting him bother her. She dialed Monica's number and asked her to come down.

A few minutes later, Monica opened the office door and greeted her warmly with a big smile. "I'm glad to see you back."

"It's wonderful to be here. We've got a lot of work to do."

"How're you doing? You've been through so much." Monica's dark eyes showed her true concern.

"It was a trying situation, but I did everything I could. It's actually a good lesson and reminder for all of us. The justice system isn't perfect, but it's the best thing we've got. This time justice didn't prevail, but one of two things will probably happen. Either this experience will cause Ricky Wade to straighten up and change his life, or he'll commit more crimes and get caught again. I believe it will all work out in the end."

Monica smiled. "I like your positive outlook. A lot of people would've just thrown in the towel or gotten really upset about the outcome."

"That doesn't help anyone. Which leads me to our next topic. We have to get down to the bottom of what is happening at SIB."

Monica leaned forward. "I'm ready. I reviewed all the documents you sent me, and I agree that there's a pattern. I found some additional deposits to Shelton as well, but I feel like it's almost impossible to track all of his output. He makes some cash withdrawals, but that's where the trail goes cold."

That wasn't surprising. "Keep looking."

"What do you think is actually going on?" Monica asked.

"Nothing legal. But right now, I can't prove anything. My own personal speculation isn't going to get us very far. That's why we need evidence."

Monica stood up. "I'll get back to work, then."

Sophie turned her attention to her email for a bit to get caught up. She'd gotten lost in her work when she looked up and saw Keith standing at her door.

"Welcome back," he said.

"Thank you. I'm glad to be here."

"I'm sorry about the Wade trial. I know you put it all out there. I think Juan Wade got to someone on that jury."

"I do too." But of course, they couldn't prove that either.

"Don't be hard on yourself. I know I probably put a bit of pressure on you, but this wasn't your fault. You did your job and made the office proud."

She smiled. "Thanks, Keith. It means a lot for you to say that."

"I imagine you're still champing at the bit on the Shelton case?"

She didn't want him to know just how focused she was. "I'm ready for trial. We're in good shape."

"And what about the other things you were looking into?"

"That's still in the preliminary phase." She needed more time to get her ducks in a row. "Shelton's trial is my first priority."

"All right. Well, try to wrap it all up so we can get you onto your next big case."

"Yes, sir. And also, it may take me a little time to acclimate back to the office after everything that has happened."

His eyes noticeably softened. "Of course. I didn't mean to come off as cold. Take as much time as you need and re-immerse yourself slowly. You've been through quite a lot over the past few months. I didn't mean to imply that you had to be back up to full speed right away."

She felt a little guilty for playing the sympathy card, but it seemed like the best move. He gave her a reassuring nod and left.

As she sat there with her notes on the SIB case in front of her and thought about her next steps, she couldn't help but wonder if she'd just traded one set of dangers for another.

CHAPTER
TWENTY-ONE

T ad took a gulp of his coffee and watched from his car as Cooper Knight walked toward his SUV, which was parked in Midtown. He'd found out that Cooper was the co-owner of K&R Security. What he still hadn't figured out was whether he was Sophie's boyfriend or if there was a business relationship there—or both.

The fact that Sophie had finally gone back to work was good for him, because it gave him more access to her. But the underlying problem remained. As long as Sophie kept pushing the Shelton case, then SIB was at risk.

He figured Sophie might be in the office for a few more hours, so he took the opportunity to tail Cooper and see where he was headed. Tad was pretty sure SIB was up to its neck in dirty money. He needed Whitney to open up to him, and he felt like he was getting close.

He tailed Cooper down to the K&R Security office and waited. He pulled out his laptop, connected to his mobile hot spot, and started doing more research. Even though he wasn't young, he had a thing for technology, and that had served him well.

He'd asked and Whitney had given him access to all of the files she'd turned over to Sophie. He had gotten the impression that Whitney hadn't intended for Sophie to find some of the connections in the documents. That was the problem with a large data dump. Yes, it would make the other side's life difficult in wading through all of it, but there could very well be something damaging in there too.

If Sophie was hot on the trail and focused on SIB's illegal activities, then his timetable to complete his assignment was accelerated. Fortunately, he didn't back down from a challenge.

Cooper sat with Landon and Noah in their main conference room at K&R.

"Do you really think it's wise for Sophie to jump into the deep end on this after all that's happened?" Landon asked.

"Believe me, I pointed out the same thing to her, but she's stubborn. She's not going to let this go, and I'd much rather be closely involved if she's going down this path than have her go it alone." That wasn't an option for him.

Noah typed on his laptop. "We haven't made much progress on tracking the funds. Since that avenue is dry, I've been thinking it's time we come at this differently. I say we start working our sources and see what we can find out about any possible links between SIB and any criminal enterprises. Between all of our contacts, someone has to know something."

That sounded like a good plan. "Based on everything, if you had to speculate, what would you say?"

"I'd say cartels," Noah said.

Landon nodded. "I agree. The cartels have the powerful connections and the cash flow to pull off an elaborate scheme."

Cooper had an idea. "I think we need to cross-reference the key cartel figures in the area with Whitney Bowman and see if we can find any connection."

"I'm on it from the tech side," Noah said. "Plus, I'll reach out to my ATF contacts."

"And I'll help too," Landon said.

"I'll talk to my APD contacts. Between the three of us, I think we can bust this one wide open."

"And then what happens with Sophie?" Noah asked.

"I have to keep her safe. That's the bottom line." He took a breath, feeling the responsibility weighing heavily on his shoulders.

"Am I sensing something more between the two of you?" Landon asked with wide eyes.

"I know it's not like me, but she's really gotten into my head—in a good way. But things are super complicated. We both have issues we have to work through, and I might have blown it."

Landon gave his back a hearty pat. "You're in deep, man. Welcome to the club."

"I just don't want to screw this up any more than I already have," Cooper muttered.

"Then don't," Noah said. "You've tortured yourself over your father for way too many years. It's time to let someone in."

Cooper looked at his friend. It was rare for Noah, the quiet one of the group, to speak so openly about something like that. "I'm trying. It's a big step for me." He paused. "But enough about that. Let's get to work."

"Order some pizza for lunch, and you've got a deal," Landon said.

Cooper laughed. "Two maxed-out pizzas coming up."

He had a feeling that they were going to pull this off, but he feared what they might find.

"Why did you invite me to dinner?" Patrick asked Ashley.

She had several motivations for wanting to have dinner with him, including getting him in a social setting away from the office. She had a business proposition for him that she knew was going to blow his mind. "I thought it would be nice to talk away from our offices and all the baggage that comes along with it."

He took a sip of his sweet tea. "Ashley, I don't think you really want to hang out with me, so just tell me what's on your mind."

Patrick really sold himself short. He was a smart and very attractive man. But she wasn't playing the romance card with him. This was all business and on the up-and-up. "You don't give yourself enough credit. You're more than pleasant company when you want to be, but you're right that this isn't exactly a social visit."

"Then what it is? I'm sick of thinking about the Wade trial, so if that's what you're here to talk about, I'd rather not."

She still hoped that he wouldn't re-try the Wade case, but she'd come up with something even more interesting for them to talk about. She couldn't believe she hadn't thought of it before. "I've gotten to see you up close and in action throughout the Wade case."

"Yes, that's how it works."

"I'll just put it all out there, because there's no point in trying to dance around this." She took a deep breath. "I want to offer you a job."

Patrick had just taken another sip of his drink and started coughing loudly. She'd clearly taken him off guard. The last thing she needed was for him to choke to death.

"Patrick, are you okay?"

He cleared his throat and nodded. "Just give me a second," he said in a raspy voice. He drank some more and took a moment. "Are you joking?"

"I see how you might think that, and I admit the idea does seem a little crazy and completely unconventional. But it came to me the other day after I left our meeting. I was thinking about what a powerful team we could make if we were on the same side."

He crossed his arms. "And why in the world would I become

242

a defense attorney? Isn't that the basic problem here? We play on completely different teams."

"A few reasons," she said bluntly. "Working with me, you'd make multiples of what you ever could as a prosecutor. Plus, you'd get tons of exposure. A man like you isn't someone on a crusade. You thrive off the power and influence you have. I could tell it from our interactions and from watching you in the courtroom."

He cocked his head to the side. "You really think I'm that driven by money and power?"

Wasn't everyone, if they were being honest? "Patrick, you don't have to put up these pretenses with me. It's perfectly acceptable for you to want something more. I'm not judging you for that—just the opposite. I'm trying to encourage you to embrace it."

She watched as he sat quietly, his dark eyes focused on her. She wished she could figure out what was going on in his head. Had she pushed him too quickly?

"I honestly think I'm at a loss for words," he said. "That may be a first for me."

"You don't have to decide right now. Take whatever time you need to think about it."

He started laughing. "Ashley, I have no words because this is the most ridiculous proposal I've ever heard in my life."

She sucked in a breath. "You're just being stubborn. Don't deny the brilliance here."

Patrick shook his head. "Yes, I'm ambitious, but that ambition is in the context of fighting for justice in the courtroom."

"I think that's just what you want to believe. If you're honest with yourself, you'd love the challenge of switching sides. The adrenaline rush. It takes being an attorney to an entirely different level."

"What you're not understanding here is that I like being one of the good guys. I can't see myself on the defense side.

And that's putting aside the fact that you and I would kill each other."

"We're not getting married, Patrick. This is purely business." She wasn't going to beg, though. She'd make her case, but in the end, if he turned her down, he'd be the one losing out.

"I'm sorry to disappoint you, but you should put this idea out of your head. Better yet, we can pretend like this conversation never happened."

Could she have misread him so badly, or was he just lying to her? How could he not want more than what he had right now? No, she didn't believe him.

He stood up. "I think it's best for me to go. I'll see you around, Ashley."

She sat stunned that he had rebuffed her like that. She'd given him a chance that she'd never offered to anyone else. Once he had some time to think, he'd come to his senses. There was no way he could turn down her offer.

It had been a good first day back in the office once she'd gotten over her annoying welcome from Harrison. She caught up on a lot of administrative matters that needed her attention, and she mapped out a game plan for the Shelton case.

Monica was proving to be very helpful and resourceful. Sophie wondered if she was that on top of things herself when she was a rookie prosecutor. Regardless, it was nice to have the help and have someone in the office who was committed to pushing through with the case. Even if Monica didn't really have a choice, since Sophie was calling the shots. But Monica seemed to genuinely care. Being invested in a case was important.

"You seem deep in thought," Cooper said.

They were back at her house, sitting at the kitchen table. "Just thinking about how glad I am to be back. I know things aren't completely normal, but it's a big step in the right direction."

"Good. I have an update for you on what the guys and I are doing. Our working theory at the moment is that there is some connection between SIB and one of the area drug cartels. We're trying to see if we can get any tangible evidence of that."

"Why a drug cartel?"

"For this type of money laundering, we all think it makes the most sense. It could also be some other organized crime group, but we're starting with the cartels' key players first and trying to see if there are any links between them and Whitney Bowman."

Her mind started to fill in the blanks. This could be huge. *Could be* was the operative term, though. They didn't have anything yet and might not even be chasing the right theory. "That sounds like a solid plan."

"Here's the thing, though."

She waited for him to keep going.

"The guys and I are worried that this investigation could get very dangerous. If you start poking your nose around the cartels, they don't take kindly to that. I think it's best if you let us take the lead on this part of the case. See what we can find. I don't want you out there asking questions. Let us do that."

She nodded. "Well, I don't even have the connections you guys do. I have APD contacts, obviously. I could reach out to them."

"No, let me. You never know who you can trust."

"You're worried about dirty cops?"

"I'm worried about everything, and the last thing I want to do is to put you in the line of fire."

She wanted to reach out to him for reassurance, but she stopped herself. She had to remind herself where the two of them stood. "I don't want to be a target again either, but I also want to crack this case. But I'll do as you ask and focus on other parts of the investigation. Monica and I are creating a detailed chart of all of the transactions. When you lay it all out, there's no denying that something fishy is going on."

"Have you heard from Patrick?"

Cooper was all business tonight. She was flooded with a mix of relief and disappointment. "Yeah, he called me today. He hasn't made up his mind yet. He seemed a little off. I think the mistrial really got to him. I'd be the same way in his situation. I'm upset, and I wasn't even the prosecutor. I wanted to take the pressure off, so I told him I would stand behind whatever decision he makes."

"But don't you want justice for those families?" he asked.

"Absolutely, but I'm not sure if we'll ever get it. Juan has proven that he has the ability to impact the legal process. He did it once, and I'm sure he'd do it again."

"That is so frustrating."

"Tell me about it."

"Everything else go okay at the office today? Did you stay inside all day as I asked?" He seemed to have a laser-like focus on following protocol right now.

"Yes. At some point, I'll want to be able to go out, but I know it's still early. Do you really think Juan would still come after me now?"

Cooper nodded. "Unfortunately, there's a risk. And now with the SIB angle, we have to be vigilant."

Everything seemed to be hanging in the balance.

CHAPTER
TWENTY-TWO

One advantage of being a retired police officer was that Tad had a lot of connections. And those sources let him know an extremely troubling fact. Cooper and his partners were asking around about Whitney's connection to drug cartels.

Everything was coming to a head. He'd considered his options, but given that he now had this knowledge, he felt he had to take it to Whitney. She needed to be warned about what was happening and then make her decision.

He waited for her to arrive at a table in the back corner of the coffee shop in Colony Square. It was only a short walk from the SIB building. He thought it best that they have this conversation outside of the corporate office.

Whitney joined him a few minutes later. She looked classy, as always, today wearing a white pantsuit. "Do you have something for me?"

"I do." He had gone over in his mind the best way to play this, but now that her icy blue eyes were locked onto his, he was having second thoughts.

"Well, what is it?"

"The guy I told you about who has been hanging around

Sophie has a private security business. He and his business partners have been asking law enforcement some questions."

"About what?"

Best to just say it. "More about who. You, specifically."

Her eyes widened. "Tell me everything you know."

"They're nosing around, trying to find out if there's any link between you and the drug cartels."

Whitney sucked in a breath. "Are you serious?"

"By your reaction, it seems that this comes as a surprise to you. But I don't know if your surprise is that they found out about it or that they suspect it at all. Is there anything behind this whole mess that could make them think you're wrapped up with the cartels?" He watched her carefully to see if she had any tells.

She looked down and then back up at him. "Are you certain they're doing this? I have a source inside the prosecutor's office, and nothing like this has been brought to my attention."

He thought it telling that she didn't deny the accusation. "Ms. Bowman, to be able to help you here, I need to know the truth."

Whitney looked away again. "I don't know if that's such a good idea."

"What have you gotten yourself into, Ms. Bowman? Remember, I'm no longer in law enforcement. You hired me, and I'm bound by confidentiality."

"We may have a bit of a problem," she said in a hushed tone.

"Why don't we start with who you're doing business with."

"Manuel Smith," she said softly.

And there it was. Smith was one of the heavy hitters in one of the major cartels that worked the Southeast. A fact Tad knew very well. But he wanted to hear Whitney's side of the story. "How in the world did you get mixed up with Smith?"

She let out a sigh. "It's a long story."

"Is the bottom line that the cartel is using your bank to clean its money?" He figured why not just lay all the cards out on the table.

"We have to put a stop to this inquiry right away."

"They're already asking questions. It's probably just a matter of time before they find out."

She shook her head. "We've been so discreet."

"What's Shelton's connection to all of this?"

"The weak link, obviously. He got greedy and started to go rogue with his completely separate money-making schemes. If he had stuck to the plan, we wouldn't be having this discussion right now. Shelton was just a pawn I used to move the money."

"He knows about the connection to Smith?" It was important to determine what Shelton knew.

"He doesn't know everything, but he knows enough to cause me great concern. He processed the transactions, but he didn't know what they were for initially. Then he started asking questions and doing his own digging. I can't be certain how much he knows, which is another reason I'm trying to squash this case before it goes to trial. I told Smith that Shelton was completely in the dark because I thought I could contain things. Now I'm not so sure."

Wasn't that an interesting tidbit. There was more exposure here than he'd initially thought. The cop in him made him ask, "Why did you get involved with Smith in the first place? I'm sure you're already making significant money in your CEO position."

She rolled her eyes. "I don't make nearly as much as those CEOs at our larger competitors. We're a regional player at best."

He leaned forward over the table. "Do you have any idea how dangerous Smith is?"

She shrugged. "There's nothing I can do about that now. I crossed that bridge a long time ago."

"If he gets a single whiff that you are going to double-cross him, he will not hesitate to kill you."

Her cheeks reddened. "But why would I turn on him? That would implicate myself."

"He may fear that you'll try to cut a deal."

"I wouldn't do that," she said quickly.

Almost too quickly. "I just want to make sure you understand how serious this all is." He needed to hear it from her own lips.

"Then what would you suggest?"

He sighed. "You need to let Smith know before he finds out from anyone else that your secret may be exposed." He wanted to present her with the option and see how she played it.

"Why would I do that when we don't even know if they're going to be able to determine who he is and the connection between us?"

"Because if you take the risk and stay silent and Smith does find out, it won't end well for you."

She tucked a stray piece of hair behind her ear. "But what I think I'm hearing from you is that you don't think this is going to end well regardless."

He knew she was a smart woman. "You're in a difficult situation. I just want to set you up for the best chance of success."

"Let me sleep on it."

"Don't wait too long. The hounds are onto a scent, and I don't think they're going to just walk away."

"Understood. I've got to get back to work."

As he watched her leave the coffee shop, he wondered if she really had enough guts to come clean with Smith. He hoped so, because he'd grown to like Whitney. And her life might depend on it.

Sophie had made it through her first week back at work. As she packed up Friday night, she was looking forward to the weekend. Cooper had called and said that they needed to talk, but that he wanted to have the conversation in person.

So once they got back to her house, they sat down in the living room, and she anxiously waited to hear what he had to say.

"You know me and the guys have spent this week working all of our sources."

Her heartbeat started to speed up. "You've got something?"

"It's not definitive, but yes. We think we've found a possible link. I say *possible* because we haven't been able to corroborate it all yet, but it's definitely a big first step."

This was just what she had been hoping and praying for. A major break in the case. "Well, don't make me wait any longer. What is it?"

Cooper pulled a folder out of his bag. He opened it and placed it on the coffee table in front of her. He pointed to a picture. "This is Manuel Smith. One of the leaders of the Sanchez Cartel. According to our contacts in the DEA, Atlanta has become a major hub for the Mexican drug cartels. Product is held here and then shipped out for distribution. So big money is moving through the city."

She tried to process this new development. "And you found some link between this Manuel Smith and SIB?"

"More specifically to Whitney Bowman. She and Manuel Smith grew up together in the same neighborhood. Turns out Whitney didn't come from money. It was a pretty rough part of town. Smith got linked up with the Sanchez Cartel and has been managing their Atlanta operations for the past five years."

"Just showing that they knew each other isn't enough."

"I know. But we have a major lead now. We also have a major problem."

"What?"

"It's like I was telling you before. These cartels don't mess around. I'm sure Smith is responsible for more deaths than you could wrap your head around."

"I wouldn't be going after Smith, though. I'd be targeting the bank and Whitney Bowman. Leave Smith for the Feds to handle."

He shook his head. "I don't think Smith cares about those

distinctions. To be able to get to Whitney, you'll have to prove the connection to Smith and the cartel. So he'll be involved any way you cut it."

"And you're concerned it's too dangerous."

He nodded. "Now that we've uncovered this possible alliance, Whitney's innocence is highly suspect. And I have to say this."

"What?"

"Given how Keith has reacted to your investigation the entire time, we have to seriously consider that he's involved too."

No, that couldn't be. "You think the *district attorney* for Fulton County is working with the drug cartels?"

"Think about it, Sophie. Why has he warned you off so much? Why did he want you to stop the investigation and just offer Shelton a plea?"

Her heart sank, and a wave of nausea washed over her. "I don't even know how to process that." But even as she said the words, her mind went back to all the conversations she'd had with Keith about this case.

Cooper leaned toward her, his gaze sympathetic. "I know it's a lot to take in, but this could be a lot more complicated and dangerous than we anticipated. This isn't the story of a one-off rogue bank employee. This is so much more than that."

That was an understatement. "I need hard evidence of all of this."

He sighed. "Even hearing everything I said, you still want to proceed?"

"I know it's dangerous. But if what you say is right, this is a huge corruption ring that has to be brought down. This isn't about me or my ego or career. This is about doing the right thing. We can't have the DA colluding with the cartels. We can't have a major bank laundering their dirty money."

"If you're dead set on this, I think you absolutely have to go to the Feds."

She considered his point carefully. "You're probably right."

They sat there silently for a few moments while she mulled things over.

"Can we shift gears for a minute?" Cooper asked.

"Sure. Hopefully to a happier topic?" All the doom and gloom was starting to weigh on her.

"I hope you think so." He looked at her.

"All right. Now you have me curious."

"I've been doing a lot of thinking." Cooper wrapped his arm around her, and she straightened in surprise. "I don't want to lose you, Sophie."

"What're you saying?" Deep inside of her, hope was building. A hope that maybe he had changed his mind.

"I don't know what the future will hold. But I do know that I don't want to be blinded to what we could be because I'm afraid. I don't want to close myself off anymore, Sophie. I want to explore what we could have together."

She fought back the flood of emotions running through her. "Why? Why did you change your mind?"

"Because of you. The person you are. You make me want to give it a try, even given my concerns and fears. I've thought about it, prayed about it, worried about it. And at the end of the day, I can't deny what's going on between us."

Her eyes misted up. "I didn't come into this looking for anything with you. But I'm the type of person to follow my heart, and my heart is telling me that I need to give us a chance."

"I feel the same way."

She looked up into his kind blue eyes and knew she'd never be the same again. He pulled her closer to him, and she heard herself let out a sigh.

As he pressed his lips to hers this time, there was no apprehension on her part. There was no worry or second-guessing. Just a desire to be completely in the moment with Cooper. His lips were soft yet strong. His touch steadying, comforting . . . electrifying.

She kissed him back, and this time she didn't end things abruptly but enjoyed each moment of his lips on hers. If she was going to go down this path, then she was all in.

Sophie hated asking Monica to come into the office on Saturday, but she'd worked countless Saturdays in her career, especially when she was a young prosecutor.

There was an adrenaline rush when you were working on a big case and were getting close to breaking it open. She knew she couldn't trust Keith. It was too risky. But she needed Monica's help to run through the documents again to see if she could find any link, no matter how remote, to Manuel Smith and his business interests. There was no way she could do it alone.

On top of that, Leland had pushed for a quick trial date, so as interesting as the new developments were to her, she still had to prosecute Shelton for the crimes that he was arrested for. That meant getting ready for the trial, which would start in less than a month.

Monica had been such a great asset that Sophie was going to make her official second chair. It would be big for a rookie, but much deserved after the long hours she'd been putting in.

When Monica arrived shortly after Sophie did, Sophie gave her the briefing on everything she knew—which admittedly wasn't a lot.

"You think there's a connection between this drug cartel guy, Smith, and Whitney Bowman?" Monica asked, eyes wide.

"I know it's hard to believe that a CEO of a reputable bank would get involved with someone like that, but we can't ignore the facts. It would also provide an explanation for all the money moving in and out of Shelton's accounts."

"Do you think Shelton was in on it, or was he just doing her bidding?"

"I have no idea. I know this case is a bit unusual, but I can't get everything done alone."

Monica grinned. "No, don't be sorry. This might be one of the most impactful and exciting cases of my career."

Sophie smiled at Monica's enthusiasm. "I remember feeling so energized when I first started working here."

"You don't anymore?"

That was a good question. "I do, it's just that with time, if I'm being completely honest, it's hard not to get a little jaded. The Wade case is a prime example. The system doesn't always bring about justice."

"I get that." Monica leaned forward, oozing earnestness. "But you need to focus on all the amazing work you've done over the years. There's nothing that you could've done differently in the Wade case."

"Thanks. Enough about all of that. We have a ton of documents to review. You ready?"

"You bet. Let's nail this guy."

They worked until midafternoon, and then Sophie sent Monica home. She didn't want to ruin her entire weekend, and there was stuff she could accomplish on her own.

When there was a loud knock at her door, she didn't even have time to answer before Keith stepped inside. His face was red, and she immediately knew something was wrong.

She stood up and walked over to him. "What it is?"

"I'm afraid I've got some troubling news."

A million awful thoughts ran through her head. "Tell me."

"The police just contacted me." He took a breath. "Glen Shelton was found dead in his apartment. It appears he killed himself."

Sophie sucked in a breath and placed her hand on the back of a chair to steady herself. "Are you sure?"

"Shelton's definitely dead, and preliminary analysis is that it's suicide. They'll do a thorough investigation, of course." He took a step toward her. "I'm sorry to be the one to tell you.

But let me make sure that you understand that his actions are purely his own. You had nothing to do with this."

Keith was worried that she might feel guilty, given she was the one pushing the case. But she didn't feel guilty. She felt worried. But she didn't want to talk about everything with Keith just yet. She needed some time to process this. "I understand. Sorry, there's just a lot going through my head right now."

"Of course. Sophie, you've had a rough go of it lately. I think it'd be a good idea if you took a little time off."

Maybe he was right. She wasn't sure about anything right now. "Let me think on it."

Keith left her office, and she immediately went back to her desk and picked up the phone to call Cooper.

"Hey," he answered. "What's going on?"

"Glen Shelton is dead."

Patrick still couldn't believe that Ashley had actually asked him to work with her. As he sat at home on Saturday night, finishing his Chinese takeout, he replayed their conversation in his head. Why had she even offered the job to him?

It still bothered him, because he simply couldn't figure her out. One moment she seemed like pure evil, and the next she seemed like she might actually have some good in her. Could it be that she was just that complicated?

Women were often complicated, as evidenced by the fact that he was almost forty and still single. But he couldn't help but wonder if Ashley had a deeper plan she was trying to put into motion. He'd been so unprepared for her proposal, all he could do was laugh it off. Now that he'd had some time to think, though, he had to admit that he couldn't just reject the idea out of hand.

He grabbed his cell off the table and found Ashley in his contacts. He pressed call and waited for her to answer.

"This is Ashley."

"Ashley, it's Patrick. I hope I'm not interrupting your Saturday evening plans."

She laughed. "I'm still at work. Have you had second thoughts about blowing me off?"

"I must admit you threw me for a loop."

"Sometimes curve balls are just what you need. But you did laugh in my face the other day. If you've changed your mind, then you need to do some groveling first."

Why had he called her? Why did he think he could keep up with her games?

"Are you still there?" she asked.

He ran a hand over his hair. "Yeah. Ashley, you have a way of confusing me."

"On this topic, that isn't my goal. I was serious in my offer. After you re-try the Wade case, of course. I wouldn't want to impede your ability to do that if it's what you really want. Although I hope I convinced you otherwise. It's a waste of your time for a variety of reasons."

"You really are a piece of work."

"Is that a slam or a compliment?"

"Maybe a bit of both." And wasn't that the truth? He was almost developing a love-hate relationship with this woman. He feared he'd never be able to compete with her, though. She was willing to go so much further than he ever would.

"I should say one thing. Thinking back on it, I realize I probably didn't present the opportunity to you in the best way. And I know I caught you off guard."

"I still don't understand why in the world you'd want to work with me." He truly had no clue. The partnership didn't make sense to him.

"Patrick, you're a very gifted attorney. I watched you during the trial, and I think you have skills that complement my own. You and I are very different, but sometimes you need someone opposite of you to balance you out."

He still wasn't completely buying her story. Ashley was doing great on her own. "I just find it hard to believe that there isn't something more going on here. If you really want me to consider your offer, you have to be straight with me."

Silence passed between them for a moment before she answered. "You don't believe that I just want to expand my practice by hiring you?"

"No," he responded quickly. "I don't. There has to be something else going on here. I need to know what that is, or this conversation is over." He wished he was having this conversation face-to-face so he could see her expressions.

"You're the first lawyer I've ever gone up against that I actually felt could be my equal."

That was saying a lot for her, considering how big her ego was. "Thanks, I think."

"I'm a smart businesswoman, and I think we could do great things together if I could get you to abandon your pie-in-the-sky aspirations. You'll be more challenged and have more fun on the defense side. Clients would like you because you provide the experience of being on the other side. That's a great marketing tool we could use for the business generation. I'm offering another way that you could thrive and seek out new challenges."

There was a strange kernel of truth to what she was saying. That he was even listening to this made him question his sanity. "I need to think."

"You'll come around, Patrick. The fact that you called me back lets me know that I made the right decision in making the offer."

"I'll talk to you later."

He ended the call and stared down at his phone. Could he really switch sides?

TWENTY-THREE

Sophie looked at Cooper and felt her eyes well up with tears. She'd been through a roller coaster of emotions lately.

She was anxious to get the final report on Glen's death. The timing seemed highly suspicious to her, but then again, Cooper had pointed out that it was completely possible that Shelton could have taken his own life. He was facing serious allegations and major prison time. A man like him wouldn't fair that well in prison.

But this Sunday morning, she was trying not to focus on Shelton and all the awful things that she dealt with in her job. Instead she was trying to be thankful for what God had done in her life.

She sat in the pew beside Cooper. It was the first time she'd been back to church since the shooting, but today was even more special because the man she cared so much about was sitting right beside her, holding her hand. It was a day she had prayed about for what seemed like forever.

Lord, you have truly answered my prayers and sent Cooper into my life.

There was no doubt in her mind that they could build something wonderful together. And now she was having a hard time not getting emotional, because there were so many feelings flooding through her.

As they stood for the closing worship song, she belted it out. She wasn't going to win any awards for her voice, but she could carry a tune. Not unexpectedly, Cooper wasn't singing, but that was okay with her. There was a calm strength about him that steadied and grounded her. He was the pragmatist while she was the dreamer. But together they brought out the best in each other.

After the service, he leaned down and whispered in her ear. "Are you okay?"

"Yes. It feels good to be back here. Just a lot of overwhelming emotions."

"You've been through a lot."

"Thanks for sticking by me. Even now, when we have more uncertainty to face."

He squeezed her hand. "I'm not going anywhere."

He'd come to her church, and she was excited for him to meet her friends. She'd promised that she would go with him to his church another time. The thought of them deciding on a church together made her heart warm even further. "I'd like to introduce you around."

"Sure."

They lingered for quite a while, talking to people she knew and to the pastor. Cooper easily held his own in conversation with a wide range of personalities. It was obvious that he felt very comfortable. By the time they were ready to leave, the parking lot had cleared out.

"That was nice." Her spirits were high after all the interaction.

He leaned down and kissed her on the cheek. "I love seeing you smile. There hasn't been enough of that lately."

She realized she couldn't stop smiling, and she didn't want

to. "I know we're facing tough times, but today has felt like a respite from the storm. I find strength here with these people and with you." She tightly grasped his hand.

His blue eyes locked onto hers, and for a moment they just stood right outside the front entrance.

Finally, Cooper broke the silence. "What do you want to do for lunch?"

"I'm starving, but I'm up for anything. Although an omelet and a big fat biscuit sounds awesome."

He laughed. "I think we can swing that."

She walked with pep in her step and Cooper by her side, thinking about how they'd spend the rest of the day together. They were almost at his SUV when she dug into her purse and realized that she'd left her phone somewhere in the church. "Cooper, wait, I gotta go back and get my phone."

"No worries. I'm in no rush."

"Thanks." They turned to start walking back toward the church. "I'm glad I noticed before we left."

But she'd only gotten a few steps when a loud blast shattered the air, and she was thrown forward, hitting the ground hard. She couldn't catch her breath as smoke pushed into her lungs, and she couldn't hear anything but a high-pitched ring that caused a blistering pain to go through her head. She tried to take another breath, but the pain in her ribs prevented her. Then she closed her eyes and gave in to the pain.

"Sophie!" Cooper called. He staggered to his feet, trying to steady himself. His ears kept ringing from the bomb blast. A plume of smoke rose from what was left of his SUV. His vision was blurred, and it was a few seconds before it cleared enough that he could see Sophie lying on the ground a few feet away from him. The blast had propelled her a lot farther than it did him.

He knelt beside her. *Lord, please let her be alive.* He checked for a pulse and found it steady. *Thank God.*

Sirens started to sound off in the distance. A few people ran toward him, including the pastor he'd met just minutes ago.

"I called 911," the pastor said. He knelt beside Cooper and started praying.

Cooper couldn't tell the extent of Sophie's injuries, but at least her breathing seemed even, although very shallow, and her pulse was strong. Maybe she'd just been knocked out.

The paramedics arrived, and he stepped back and let them work on her.

"What in the world happened?" the pastor asked.

"It was a car bomb. If Sophie hadn't forgotten her phone in the church, we'd both probably be dead right now." As he said the words, he clenched his fists by his sides. Was this an act of revenge by Wade? Or had Smith and Whitney found out that Sophie was on to them?

Either way, Sophie was lying on the ground and being administered medical attention. And this bomb wasn't meant to intimidate or scare. It was meant to kill. Although it also occurred to him that it was *his* SUV. And he had been the one asking around about Smith and SIB.

Could he have been the intended target? The thought made him sick because the last thing he wanted was to put Sophie in danger. Everything he'd been doing was to keep her safe.

One of the paramedics started to check him out, even though he told them he was fine. It was no use arguing as they strapped the blood pressure cuff on his arm and then shined a light into his eyes. They bandaged a cut above his left eye. They asked him a series of questions about what hurt. But his main concern was Sophie's condition.

What was he going to tell the police? At this point, he didn't have enough actual facts or evidence to start pointing fingers at Smith or Whitney or anything connected to the bank. But the police would all be familiar with the Wade trial, and once they realized who Sophie was, that was sure to be of interest to the APD.

Cooper was a bit relieved when one of the responding officers was someone he knew.

"Cooper, man, what happened?" Officer Roberts asked.

He quickly recounted the story to Roberts and another officer he didn't know. But as the paramedics were getting ready to take Sophie to the ER, he wanted to go with her. "That's it, guys. I need to ride with Sophie."

He hoped she had regained consciousness. Thanks to Officer Roberts, the EMTs let him ride in the back of the ambulance. When he saw her bright blue eyes open, relief washed over him. *Thank you, God.*

"Sophie, I'm right here. You're going to be fine."

"Are you okay?" she asked.

They'd started an IV, and her skin was pale, but at least she seemed coherent.

"Yes, just a little banged up. You got it worse than I did." She grimaced. "My ribs hurt."

The EMT looked at him. "She may have some broken ribs. We'll need to get her into X-ray right away."

He understood why the EMT's dark eyes were serious. It wasn't the ribs themselves that was concerning. He'd seen situations where broken ribs led to internal bleeding, and that could be life threatening.

"Was anyone else hurt?" Sophie asked.

It was just like her to be more concerned about others than herself.

"No. Most everyone else had already left, and only a few people, including the pastor, were left in the church. The pastor called 911 and got help."

"Who did this?" she asked.

He leaned down closer to her. "I don't know. But I'm not going to leave your side."

"Please don't." Her voice cracked.

As he locked eyes with her, he realized that he was falling in love with Sophie.

The next morning, Patrick practically barged into Ashley's office. "I couldn't believe I was actually starting to believe some of the bull that you were feeding me."

She looked up from the papers in front of her and took off her glasses. "Patrick, what are you talking about?"

"The bomb. That's what I'm talking about."

Her dark eyes widened. "What bomb?"

"Don't play stupid, Ashley."

"I really have no idea what you're talking about."

When he'd gotten the call from Cooper last night, he almost couldn't believe it. Wade was obviously trying to get his revenge against Sophie, even if his brother had gotten off scot-free. And Ashley was in thick with him.

"The car bomb attack against Sophie. Did you not see the news?"

"I've been cramming on another case and haven't even looked at the paper or TV today. Is she alive?"

"Yes, thankfully." He studied Ashley carefully. She truly did seem caught off guard. Could it be that Wade acted without her knowledge? "Look me in the eyes and tell me you had absolutely nothing to do with this."

She made direct eye contact with him. "I did not. I would never advocate violence. Believe it or not, just because I represent questionable characters doesn't mean I am one myself. I hold myself to high standards. And think about it. Why would I want my client to do something that stupid? We got a hung jury—we won. Revenge is just plain idiotic at this point." She leaned back in her chair.

She sure sounded convincing, but he was still skeptical. "You're telling me that Juan would have decided to take this action all on his own?"

"I don't control him. He has a mind of his own." She paused. "And have you considered that it could be someone else entirely going after her?"

"Who else would do something that drastic?"

"I don't know, but I'm sure the APD will be looking closely into that. One thing I can assure you of, Patrick: this is not of my doing or with my blessing. And I find it highly unlikely, based on every discussion I've had with Juan, that this would be his doing. He's moved on to other things. He would have absolutely no reason to take her out."

"Then consider this a courtesy visit." Patrick looked down at his watch. "APD should be picking up your client just about now, if they haven't already."

She mumbled under her breath. "I better get going, then."

"Don't worry. I'm sure, given his experience, he knows not to talk without you there."

Her nostrils flared. "Patrick, I hope you didn't instigate this little stunt."

Actually, he hadn't. "No. The wheels were already put in motion. I was just informed this morning."

"We'll talk about this more later." She stood up and shoved her laptop into her bag. "Come on. Get out of here."

She kept mumbling under her breath, and for a moment he almost felt a little sorry for her. What was wrong with him?

"I need to speak to my client before you start peppering him with questions." Ashley stared down the lead detective she had just met.

"Fine," Detective Manley said.

Once she was alone with Juan, she wanted to strangle him. But before she could say a word, he started dropping the f-bomb. "I did not do this, Ash. I swear to you. I'd own up if it was me."

"You're saying you had nothing to do with the bombing? Just like you told me you didn't have anything to do with the assault or the drive-by?"

He shook his head. "That was different. The trial is over. My baby brother is free. I've moved on. Like you said, I don't need the heat right now. I want to grow my business, not be hassled even more by the APD. And now I have them banging down my door this morning, spouting off crap about a bomb!"

"Juan, they're looking at you because you are the most likely suspect. Men like you are known to hold grudges and act in revenge."

He leaned forward. "I didn't do this, and I need you to make sure these charges don't stick."

"Do you have any experience with explosives? Either personally or for hire?"

"Nope. You can check that out. There won't be anything or anyone tying me to that stuff. Blowing people up is not my thing. I've never gone down that road."

No, he just beat the crap out of them or shot them. But she wasn't going to say that. "All right. The cops will question you. But you know the drill. I'll be here and step in as needed. Don't volunteer information. Keep it short and sweet."

"I got it."

"If you're being straight with me, then you have the truth on your side, which is actually the most powerful defense—and to be frank, Juan, it's not one we have the luxury of having all that often. Use it to our advantage. If you're clean on this, there won't be any evidence tying you to the crime."

"I'm clean."

"Then let's get started. The sooner we do, hopefully the sooner I can get you out of here."

—◁◇▷—

On Monday evening, Sophie opened her eyes from a much-needed nap. Once she had been released from the hospital, Cooper had insisted on taking her back to Noah's safe house instead of her own home. Given the circumstances, she'd complied.

Thankfully, she'd just suffered a cracked rib. It hurt like crazy, but she knew it could have been so much worse.

"You're awake." Her father walked into her room, carrying a tray. He had insisted that he come and help take care of her, and she welcomed his presence. Especially after everything she'd been through. Cooper had fared better than her, but the thought of that bomb having almost taken them both out was enough to make her sick.

"What did you bring me?" she asked her father.

He sat down on the edge of the bed and placed the tray in front of her. "One of your favorites. Pimento cheese sandwich, tomato soup, and sweet tea."

Initially, all she'd wanted to do was sleep because the pain was so bad, but now the thought of food did seem at least somewhat appetizing. "Thank you. It looks so good. You know me so well. I remember you making this for me when I was little and got sick." She'd always cherish those days when her father had worked from home so he could stay with her while she was ill. She couldn't have asked for a better dad.

"How are you feeling?"

"A little better. The doctor said it would take time."

"Yes, and remember that you're supposed to be taking deep breaths even through the pain."

"I know." The doctor had warned her that coughing and breathing deeply would hurt, but it was part of trying to prevent the development of pneumonia.

She picked up the sandwich. "And how're you?" She knew this whole ordeal was weighing on him.

He looked intently at her. "This scared me half to death. The thought of losing you is too much to bear. I've already lost so much." His voice cracked at the last few words.

The last thing she wanted was to cause her father any more pain or distress. "I'm here, and I'm going to be perfectly fine. That's what you have to remember."

He snapped his fingers. "One second. That's all it takes to change everything. I've lived through that pain before, and I cannot take it a second time."

She laid her hand on his arm. "Everything is going to be okay. I've got plenty of security now, as you can see, and no one knows where I am."

He smiled, and it surprised her.

"What is it?" she asked.

"You know, I couldn't help noticing how you and Cooper have been looking at each other."

She felt her cheeks redden.

"So I was right." His smile widened. "I'm so happy to see you happy. It's obvious that you care for each other." He paused. "But if he hurts you, he will have to answer to me."

Now it was her turn to smile. "Don't worry, Daddy. I've got this under control."

"I bet you do, sweetheart."

A knock on the door was followed by Cooper walking into the room. "Hope I'm not interrupting. I just talked to the police and wanted to update you."

"I'll let you two talk." Her father rose from the bedside. "I'll be downstairs if you need me. And make sure you finish that sandwich, Sophie."

"I will."

Her father left the room, and it was just her and Cooper.

"What are the police saying?" she asked.

"They brought Juan in for questioning."

"And?"

"They have zero evidence linking him to the bomb, and he

wasn't in the vicinity of the church on Sunday. He was about an hour away at the time, and he has plenty of people who were with him as an alibi. That's not to say he would've ever done it himself anyway, but the police are a bit skeptical. They let him go because they didn't have anything to charge him on, and you know Ashley Murphy was all over that."

"It doesn't make sense, does it? Unless it was just a pure revenge move. Or . . ."

Cooper looked directly into her eyes. "Juan wasn't even behind it."

That was exactly what she was thinking. "The gang isn't exactly known for bomb making, are they?"

"No, that's one of the facts the police are digging into. Juan has never had any connection to explosives. The gang doesn't buy or sell them and has never used them, as far as anyone knows."

"Which means this could be completely unrelated to Juan."

"And related to SIB."

In her gut, she feared that scenario. But it made a lot more sense than a revenge play from Juan. "Is this just an APD operation at this point?"

"No. They've looped in the FBI, given the bomb. Noah was able to use his ATF contacts to get in with the FBI. Preliminary analysis shows that it's a well made explosive but pretty standard fare."

She knew what she needed to do. "We also should bring in the DEA. Let them know everything we know."

"I didn't want to make that call without you, but I think you're right."

"This is a lot bigger than my initial case against Shelton ever was. And now that he's dead, things only seem more dangerous." Her head started to pound. "Have you heard from Keith?"

"Yes. He acted concerned about you, but I'm suspicious. Patrick is also involved, because he was running down the Juan angle."

"I assume you've been tight-lipped with both of them?"

"Yes. I don't trust anyone at this point. Even the Feds are a stretch, but we have to have federal law enforcement assistance."

"I would like to talk to the FBI and DEA as soon as possible. My case against Shelton died with him, but the Feds can still work on the larger issues. They'll need my help getting up to speed, and I plan on giving that to them."

"I'll get that set up. In the meantime, you should finish eating and then get some more rest."

"Cooper," she said, catching his hand. She had so much she wanted to say. Needed to say. But there were no words that seemed adequate for the wave of emotions that flowed through her. She felt hot tears streaming down her cheeks.

He moved closer to her. "You're safe here, Sophie. We have extra security, and nothing is going to happen to you."

"It's not just that." She tried to find the words. "Before the bombing, I remember being so happy. A lot of that is because of you and what you've brought into my life. Then, in one second, everything changed. If I hadn't left my phone in the church . . ."

He held tightly to her hand. "I know. All I can say to explain it is that we survived by the grace of God."

"He was watching out for us, Cooper. But it's a reminder that life can change in the blink of an eye. And I don't want to take you for granted." She hesitated. "I know things are moving quickly, but my feelings for you are already so strong. You've been by my side through all these ups and downs, and you've taken the time to get to know me as a person. Embracing all sides of me, not just the good parts."

"I know. I feel the same way. Let's just get through this battle, and then we can figure out what's next for us. But I'm by your side, no matter what."

Now that she had found Cooper, she refused to let him go.

TWENTY-FOUR

Tad's palms were sweating. He'd heard the news that Sophie Dawson was the target of a car bomb in her church parking lot. His gut told him that Manuel Smith was behind this. He'd warned Whitney that Smith was dangerous, but now he needed to confront her and get an idea of where things stood so he'd know what his next move should be.

Oddly, she'd invited him over to her place, which was a condo in a large high-rise in Buckhead. He'd had to get the doorman to let him in the building, then proceeded up to the penthouse level. When she'd called him, she seemed freaked out. He planned to get to the bottom of things.

He rang the bell of her condo, and Whitney opened the door. It was the most casual he'd ever seen her dressed. No suit this evening, just a light pink blouse and khakis. "Come on in. Can I get you anything?"

"Coffee would be great."

A few minutes later, they were seated in her large living room, which had a much too modern flair for him.

"I assume you're here because of the bombing," Whitney said.

"Yes. First things first, though." This was very important.

"Did you give Smith the heads-up like I told you to try to smooth things over?"

"No. I know you suggested it, but I just wasn't comfortable making that move."

"That means he found out through his own sources and decided to take action. Unless you had anything to do with the bombing?"

She shook her head. "No, of course not. I thought I would be willing to take some drastic actions, but I'll be honest, this has shaken me up. I never dreamt he would do something like this. Maybe try to scare her or something, but a bomb? And at a church! I don't know about you, but I was raised here, and a church is one place you don't mess with." Her face reddened as she clutched her ivory coffee cup. "But I'm in so deep, I don't know what I can do now."

"Listen, you've gotten in way over your head. It's only a matter of time before this whole thing is exposed. Too many people have different pieces of the puzzle, and I bet they won't quit until it's all put together." This was the cop in him talking. But he was right. "We're not talking about some minor fudging of books here. You got in bed with the Sanchez Cartel."

Her head snapped up. "You don't have to remind me of that fact. Believe me, it's not something I'm ever going to forget."

"You need to make contact with Smith and try to make this right. Time is not on your side here. The longer you wait, the more at risk you are. He's the only one who can offer you any kind of protection right now. It's not the cops."

She rubbed her temples. "You're pressuring me. I need to think."

"Who all knows about this?"

"No one knows everything but me, and I guess we'll never know how much Glen knew."

"I notice you're not crying any tears for him."

"I've got bigger problems," she said flatly.

"Okay, besides you and Shelton, is there anyone else?" It was crucial he found that out.

"I have a source inside the prosecutor's office who knows something."

"A source you don't want to name?"

"No. It's better you don't know."

"Everyone is at risk here. Anyone who has touched this thing."

"You've given me a lot to think about. I need some time."

He rose from his seat. "The clock is ticking."

The next afternoon, Sophie made herself presentable and waited in the safe house kitchen, sitting at the large table, for a meeting with the Feds.

She realized she should have probably brought them in sooner, but she'd wanted her case to continue. That had not only been selfish but potentially dangerous. *I should've known better*, she thought.

But there was no use beating herself up now. She had to get everyone plugged in and present the case as she currently knew it. She grimaced as she took a deep breath. She refused to take the painkillers and was instead only taking the over-the-counter anti-inflammatories the doctor insisted she needed for the first week.

Cooper joined her and gave her a reassuring kiss. "They're almost here. You ready for this?"

"Yes." At least, she hoped she was.

A few minutes later, she heard voices. A woman and a man entered the kitchen with Noah.

The tall woman, her dark hair pulled up in a ponytail, stepped forward first. "I'm Special Agent Terri Nix with the FBI."

Sophie shook her hand and then turned her attention to the man.

"And I'm Agent Jacob Rivera with the DEA." His dark eyes

met her own. He was built like a hulk. She'd hate to get on his bad side. At least he was one of the good guys.

"Please, everyone take a seat," Cooper said.

"Why don't we start at the beginning, Sophie," Agent Nix said.

"It's a long story. I started working on a case against SIB Senior Manager Glen Shelton. As I'm sure you're aware, he was overcharging his customers and pocketing the money. That in and of itself is enough to prosecute him."

"But Sophie started to get pushback from her boss," Cooper said.

"Yes, the DA, Keith Todd. He knows SIB's CEO Whitney Bowman. Keith wanted me to strike a deal. Whitney also encouraged that, but she did turn over a ton of documents. We're talking thousands and thousands of pages. I think she thought I would get lost in the sheer number and never find anything. But I started wading through them, and I found some strange deposits to Shelton's personal accounts, all under ten grand. The further I dug, the more it seemed like there could be some money-laundering activity. Because there has to be some underlying criminal activity to entail money laundering, I enlisted Cooper and his security firm to help work on that piece."

Cooper nodded. "That's when we started working the cartel angle, to see if there was any connection between Whitney Bowman and a criminal enterprise."

"And you found the personal connection between Bowman and Manuel Smith you told me about on the phone?" Agent Rivera asked.

"Exactly," Cooper said.

It wasn't so neatly tied up in a bow, though. That was Sophie's issue. "Then Shelton committed suicide, or at least that's still the word out of APD."

"We're going to follow up on that too," Agent Rivera said.

"All of this information puts the Shelton suicide in a different context."

Sophie was glad they would be looking into it. "Thanks. It's a loose end that's really bothering me. Also, we don't have any evidence to link Manuel Smith to the transactions. And we haven't been able to trace the source of the deposit funds or what they did with the money once they withdrew it. That's why I need your help. This has gone far beyond what I can do from my office as a Fulton County prosecutor." She paused, hating to make the next statement. "And I don't know whether our office has been compromised. From day one, Keith urged me to offer a deal and put this case to bed. He and Whitney are close. I'm not sure if there's anything nefarious going on, but it's enough to concern me."

"Let's talk about the bombing," Agent Nix said. "The bomb was planted in Cooper's SUV, right?"

"Yes," Cooper said. "I honestly don't know if I was the target, Sophie, or both of us. I had been snooping around and asking a lot of questions about Smith and Bowman."

"APD doesn't think Juan Wade was responsible. What do you think?" Agent Nix asked Sophie.

"I don't think it was him. I believe he was behind other things that happened to me, but this one doesn't fit his MO. And it doesn't make sense, after the mistrial."

Agent Nix nodded. "I agree."

"One more thing," Sophie said. "There were a couple of other incidents that might not be tied to Wade at all." She went on to explain everything else that had happened to her, including the hit-and-run.

"Thanks for telling us that," Agent Nix said. "It could be that Smith or those operating at his direction tried to derail your investigation, and when those initial efforts failed, he decided to step up his game. Rivera, what do you think?"

"Manuel Smith is the top dog of the Sanchez Cartel in this

area. Cooper, I know you were asking around about connections between Smith and Whitney, but I assume you and your guys kept it really vague and high-level?"

"Very high-level. Just to see if there was any link between the two of them. We didn't mention anything about the case or investigations or anything like that."

Agent Rivera turned and looked at Sophie. "Then we need the names of everyone who knew that you were investigating a possible money-laundering scheme at SIB."

"It's a short list," Sophie said. "In my office it was just me, Keith, and my rookie prosecutor, Monica Lacey." She thought for a minute. "It's also possible that Keith told another senior level prosecutor named Harrison Westgate."

The agents took down the names. "Anyone outside of those people and K&R Security?" Agent Rivera asked.

"No," she and Cooper said in unison.

"We know Keith floated the discovery of the deposits to Bowman because she said it wasn't that unusual an activity," Cooper added.

"Bowman could've tipped off Smith," Agent Rivera said. "Then Smith could've decided to take matters into his own hands, and he's smart enough to cover his tracks. Plus, he had a built-in cover story with Juan Wade. Smith couldn't have asked for a better setup to keep his hands clean in this."

"Where does this leave us?" Sophie had to ask. She was trying to keep calm, but when she looked down, she realized her fists were clenched tightly by her sides.

"I definitely think you need to stay put in the safe house," Agent Nix said. "It's way too risky for you to go back home right now. Since their effort failed, Smith will make another run at you. He has no idea that you've already brought in the Feds. And even if he did know, he's the type of man to take revenge regardless of the circumstances."

"And what about Whitney Bowman?" she asked.

"We're going to reach out to her," Agent Nix said.

"You did the right thing by coming to us," Agent Rivera said. "You don't want to tangle with the cartels."

"I feel like it's too late for that," Sophie said softly.

"You're in a secure spot," Agent Nix said. "Just lay low and let us handle things from here on out. Also, you should cut off all communication with everyone at your office. Use the bombing as a reason to take a leave of absence, and we'll sort this all out."

"No communication at all? What if Keith calls?" Sophie asked.

"Radio silence. Understood?" Agent Rivera gave her the stare down.

"Yes." As she spoke, pain hit her again. She glanced over at Cooper, trying her best to try to hide her discomfort.

"Anything else you need Sophie for? I'm sure sitting isn't very comfortable for her right now," Cooper said.

She let out a breath of thanks.

"I think we're good. We'll start our investigation right away," Agent Rivera said.

Sophie prayed that the Feds could bring Smith down before it was too late.

Wednesday night, Tad was starting to get nervous. He'd called Whitney multiple times, and she was ignoring his calls. He'd already visited the SIB building multiple times today, and her secretary said Whitney hadn't come in. Which had been unexpected but not completely out of the ordinary, according to her secretary.

He didn't think Whitney had appreciated him being so blunt about her options. But once you started working with the cartels and they thought you could expose them, then all bets were off. He'd tried to give her the best chance possible by encouraging her to go directly to Smith to work it out. Hopefully, she'd come to her senses.

Since he knew where she lived, he made his way back to her condo and convinced the same doorman to let him in the building. After he rang the bell a couple of times, Whitney opened the door. Her eyes were bloodshot, and she looked disheveled—her silk blouse was wrinkled and untucked, and her hair was unruly. This was not the CEO he'd become accustomed to.

"You didn't answer my calls or texts." He walked by her and into the living room.

She shut the door and followed him. "I've needed time to think. I feel like everything is about to come crashing down on me." She sucked in a breath. "I think I'm going to leave the country. Figure out a plan once I'm gone. I don't trust Manuel not to come after me. I've been doing a lot of thinking about everything."

"And?" Her answer would mean a lot.

"I'm going to turn over the evidence I have against Manuel to the authorities. Anonymously, of course. I was hoping I could actually enlist your help on that."

This was even worse than he had thought. "You want me to rat out Manuel Smith?"

Whitney hands began to shake. "I need to get him off my back, and if he's focused on the Feds and they're focused on him, then I can just disappear. I'll be off the grid. I've pulled serious cash, and I'm all packed."

She was completely serious about this. He would make one more attempt to talk her out of it, because he felt like it was the right thing to do. He walked over to her. "Whitney, you can't outrun the cartel. If you walk out that door, you're as good as dead."

A big tear rolled down her cheek. "Tad, I'm not stupid. I know I'm as good as dead no matter what. But at least this way I get a fighting chance." She took a few steps back and turned to stare out the living room window. "If you're not comfortable turning over the evidence, I can make other arrangements."

He took a deep breath. "Give me the evidence."

Whitney left the room and came back a minute later with an envelope. "There's a USB drive in there with everything I have."

He took the envelope from her hands.

"You'll get that to the FBI, right?"

"No. I won't."

She frowned. "What do you mean?"

He took a step toward her. "I know that you thought I was working for you, Whitney. But I actually report to Manuel Smith."

Bright red blotches crept up her thin neck and onto her face. "No, Tad. That can't be right."

"That referral you got for me was all arranged by Smith and his people. He sent me here to keep an eye on you. He knew that he had exposure, but he wasn't sure how much. Now I understand exactly how much." He paused. "I tried to get you to go to him and come clean."

"He would've killed me regardless, though, wouldn't he?"

He didn't want to lie to her. Not now. "Probably. But now I have no choice."

"You wouldn't kill me." She held her head up in defiance. "You're not a killer. You used to be a cop."

"Shelton didn't commit suicide."

Her eyes widened, and she took a step back. "You killed him."

"I'm in deep with Smith. If I let you go, I'll be dead before the night's over." Smith had blackmailed him since back when he was still a cop. He'd made some stupid decisions, and now when the cartel called, he answered. Every single time. No matter what they asked. His life depended on it.

The color started to drain from her face, and her eyes darted across the room.

"There's nowhere for you to run, Whitney. Don't fight me, and this will be a lot easier." He wouldn't get any joy from killing her.

She screamed.

He pulled out his gun, which was equipped with a silencer, and shot her squarely in the head. She dropped to the ground, the life instantly gone from her body.

There had been no other option. He'd liked Whitney, but the choice had been between his life and hers. And that was an easy decision to make.

He pulled out his phone and sent one simple text.

It's done.

Cooper couldn't believe the words he was hearing from his APD contact on the other end of the phone. He asked a few questions, most of which the officer couldn't answer yet, and then hung up.

He walked up the stairs to Sophie's room, where he found her lying down, reading a book.

She sat up. "What's going on?"

"I just got a phone call from the APD."

"What's wrong?"

"Whitney Bowman was found murdered in her condo."

"What?" Sophie nearly shouted before frowning in pain.

"The details are sketchy, but there's no doubt it was murder."

"How did she die?"

"Gunshot wound to the head."

Sophie looked down. "I should've done something to stop this sooner. Things have gotten out of control. Shelton, the car bomb, and now Whitney's murder. This is beyond anything I could've ever imagined."

He sat on the bed and carefully put an arm around her. "This isn't your fault, Sophie. When you start doing business with the cartels, there are risks."

"But why would they kill Whitney?"

"Maybe they think she ratted them out and made a deal? Or they started to see her as a liability or loose end? She was just another strategic move or play that had to be made. Their moral compass isn't like yours or mine. They act completely out of self-interest and to make sure their business and power remain intact. All the normal rules are thrown out the window."

"It's about money, isn't it?"

"It's always about money. And power. And the fact that these guys don't deal well with anyone they feel is in their way. Whitney served a purpose for them. And now, whether it was to cut their losses or out of revenge, it's done."

"This only furthers the argument that we're really onto something. They wouldn't be acting like this if there wasn't something big going on."

"And the Feds will get to the bottom of it."

She deflated slightly. "I know."

He empathized with her. He knew how much she wanted to be involved and how hard she had worked on this. "I get how you're feeling. You did all the legwork, uncovered the entire scheme, and then the Feds swoop in and take over. It's natural to be upset about that. But remember that the DEA and FBI are equipped to handle circumstances like this. They deal with the cartels and can manage the risks in ways you can't. You're just one person."

She nodded. "I'm trying to keep my ego in check. I know this is much larger than me and my career. Whitney's death certainly proves that."

"What's most important is that you're safe here," he said. "Cases come and go, but your life is more precious than any of that." He could've said a lot more, but he stopped himself. He didn't feel like now was the appropriate time for any grand gesture. Not after the news of Whitney Bowman's death.

"What about Keith? If he is involved in all of this and was working with Whitney, then doesn't that make him a target, too?"

He'd had that same concern. "Already talked to Agent Nix

about that. She's on it. They also talked to Harrison Westgate, although he didn't seem to have any information outside the Shelton case."

"Harrison is very sly. Hopefully they push him. I've gone back over everything in my mind, starting with the messed up search warrant. What if Harrison was in on it from the beginning?"

"Leave it up to the Feds. They'll put together the pieces." She nodded.

"They're also working on a plan for Monica too. They don't think anyone would know about her working on this, but they aren't going to take any chances."

"Good. The last thing we need is more blood spilt over this."

Cooper's phone rang, and he rose off the bed as he answered. "Yes," he said.

"It's Agent Nix. We've got Keith Todd safe in custody."

"Good." That was one less thing he had to worry about.

"He was very distraught over the news about Whitney Bowman so we haven't gotten very far with him yet. But my gut says this guy may be clueless. He seemed totally taken aback by the initial line of questioning."

"Really?" Now wasn't that interesting.

"Yeah. But we'll know more once he pulls himself together and can be fully questioned."

"Thanks. Keep me posted."

"How did Sophie take the news?"

"As you might expect." He looked at Sophie who was staring off into space. He knew her well enough to know that she was taking it hard.

"Remember. Don't let her out of your sight, and no leaving the safe house. This could all come to a head very quickly. We've also got Monica secured in an FBI safe house. She was completely freaked out about the whole thing, but I think one of my agents got her calmed down. We should be squared away on that front."

"Roger that." He ended the call and walked back over to Sophie. "That was Agent Nix."

"Do they have Keith?" she asked.

"He's safe and sound. But she says he's torn up about Whitney. Could the two of them have had something going on?"

"You mean romantically?"

"Yeah."

She paused. "That thought never occurred to me. He said they were old friends, but I guess it's certainly possible. That would add an additional twist to this mess," she said softly.

"A couple other things. Agent Nix said her first impression is that Keith may be clean."

"Really?"

"Yeah. I thought you'd like to hear that." She needed at least one piece of good news, given all the bad that had been happening.

"Maybe I just made the leap based on the wrong assumption. What if Keith wanted me to put on the brakes to help Whitney because they were involved? Or maybe because he wanted them to be involved?"

"That's a very good point. I'll make sure they go down that line of questioning with him."

"You know that only makes my point about Harrison even more viable."

"The Feds spoke to him once, and I'm sure they'll talk to him again if they feel like they need to." He noticed that she was frowning. "What's wrong?"

"I don't know how this all gets resolved."

"Hopefully with the arrest and prosecution of Manuel Smith."

"Won't the cartel just replace him with another man who can still run the business in the city?"

He nodded. "Yes, but it takes time to build up a power base."

She looked up at him. "Do you think I'll ever be safe?"

"Yes. If they can capture and put away Smith, that's a big

part of it. Plus, the Feds will get the heat for the take down and prosecution. Not you."

"That's true. But I don't want anyone in harm's way."

"Speaking of harm's way, Monica's secured in an FBI safe house too. So you won't have to worry about her."

She let out a huge breath. "We're going to get through this, right?"

He wrapped his arms tightly around her. "Yes."

He was going to do everything in his power to ensure her safety. Not only because it was the right thing to do, but because he knew he loved her.

CHAPTER
TWENTY-FIVE

Ashley was relieved that the police had released Juan. Beyond pure speculation, they had no evidence tying him to the car bomb. But she still had a bad feeling about the whole thing. If Juan wasn't behind it—which she didn't think he was—that meant someone else was after Sophie Dawson. And while she wasn't friends with Sophie, it bothered her greatly when attorneys were under attack.

She wasn't naïve. One day it could just as easily be her in danger.

Patrick had asked to meet her in Piedmont Park. It was a sunny and warm fall afternoon in the city. The park was filled with dog walkers and joggers.

She didn't have to wait long before he arrived.

"Walk with me," he said.

"What's going on?"

He smiled. "You're going to think I'm crazy."

"I already think that. So what's up?"

"This situation with Juan and the car bomb has really gotten me thinking."

She wasn't sure what direction he was going with this. "What's on your mind?"

"I so quickly jumped to the conclusion that he was behind it. I was blinded by my emotional reaction and by the fact that the case against Ricky had gone sideways."

She raised her eyebrows. "I can't believe you're actually 'fessing up to all of these feelings. And especially to the enemy."

"That's the thing, Ashley. I became a prosecutor because I wanted to be on the side of justice. I wanted to put criminals behind bars. And, of course, I wanted to excel in my career. But all it took was this one case to make me turn against those values and jump on Wade for a crime I don't think he committed."

"Are you apologizing to me?"

He shook his head. "Not exactly."

Now she was really confused. "Patrick, you've lost me."

They walked through the park for a minute in silence before he spoke again.

"I turned into exactly the thing I am supposed to be fighting against. Granted, I don't agree with a lot of your tactics, but this has shown me that I've had a bit of a blind spot."

She couldn't believe where this conversation was going. "Is this your roundabout way of saying you want to be my partner?"

"I haven't ruled it out."

She surprised herself by giving him a tight hug.

He laughed. "I wasn't expecting that."

"I think this could really be something great," she said, taking a step back.

He held up his hand. "I haven't accepted yet, and we haven't even talked specific terms."

"We can negotiate the agreement. But what I hear is that you're very close to *yes*. I'll take that. And I'm happy because you've realized that everything is not so black and white. Everyone deserves representation in our criminal justice system. So many innocent people are incarcerated."

"And that's exactly what I wanted to talk to you about specifically."

"All right."

"I don't want to take the cases like yours. I don't want to defend heads of gangs and drug lords. I want to defend the people who are at the bottom of the rung, who have zero shot at getting a fair trial unless they have competent counsel."

She grinned. "I can work with that. But there will be times when I need you to work a high-profile case. The two of us as a team could be a powerful combination, and we could hook some huge cases. Remember, that's how we make the money, by taking on clients who can pay the hefty fees."

"I could live with that. As long as you understand that day-to-day, that's not what I want to do. If I'm going to cross over to the defense side, it has to be on my terms. And I don't need an exorbitant salary. I'm not doing this for money."

"You really are an odd man, Patrick." In her experience, most everything in life came down to money. She figured he would come to his senses at some point. Right now he was still in do-gooder mode. He'd shifted sides in the fight, but the bottom line goal was the same for him.

"Do we have a deal, then?" Patrick stretched out his hand.

She took his hand in hers. "When can you start?"

Sophie hung up the phone after speaking with her father. Since she was feeling better, he'd decided to go home. But she'd been concerned about his well-being, so one of the K&R Security employees was providing him around-the-clock protection as well. He had insisted that it was overkill but had accepted because of everything that had happened.

While she didn't think Smith would go after her dad, it was a risk she wasn't willing to take. Meanwhile, she was still holed up at Noah's safe house with Cooper while the Feds did their thing.

Cooper walked into the living room and took a seat beside her.

"Any updates?" she asked.

"The Feds can't locate Smith, which isn't that big of a sur-prise."

"And Keith?"

"He's still a mess, according to Agent Nix. She got him to admit that he was in love with Whitney, but it doesn't seem like she ever reciprocated. Although Nix said it wasn't clear whether Keith ever actually told her how he felt. That might only be adding to his angst."

"It's hard when something happens to someone and you haven't told them how you really feel. My father says that as awful as my mother's death was, at least she knew how much he loved her. He didn't hold back."

Cooper took hold of her hands. "Do you think I'm holding back?"

"I think we're still figuring things out. One step at a time. And I'm okay with that. As long as I know that we're still tak-ing steps together." There was no doubt in her mind how she felt about Cooper, but the last thing she wanted to do was rush him. He'd already opened up so much to her and revealed the struggles he was facing.

"Sometimes I wonder what you could even see in a man like me."

"Everything," she said without hesitation.

He smiled, and before she could say anything else, his lips were on hers. There was so much going on all around them, but as he kissed her, she didn't think about all the turmoil. Her only thoughts were about Cooper.

The next night, Sophie tossed and turned as nightmares in-vaded her dreams. She'd finally gotten back to sleep when she was awakened.

"Sophie, get up." A hand nudged her shoulder.

It took her a moment to realize she wasn't dreaming but that it was Cooper.

"What's wrong? Is my dad all right?" Her thoughts immediately went to the worst. Why else would Cooper be waking her up in the middle of the night?

"Your father's fine. I just called and checked. Landon has him on lockdown and has called in reinforcements just to be safe."

"Why?" Her mind was still groggy.

"Because there's been an incident at the FBI safe house where Monica was staying."

She sat up. "What? Is she okay?"

"She's slightly injured, but one of the FBI agents in the house is in critical condition. There was some type of explosion."

"In the FBI safe house?"

"Exactly. Which means the FBI could be compromised. Noah is going to bring Monica over here. We can't risk moving her to another FBI safe house if they've been compromised. He's going to ensure that he's not followed. First they're going to get her patched up, but that won't take long. I thought you would want to be up to greet her when she gets here, given the circumstances. I think she's really shaken up."

"Of course." She ran a hand through her hair.

"I'll give you some privacy. I'll just be downstairs waiting for her."

Cooper left the room, and she threw back the large comforter and groaned. She was so thankful that no one was dead, but she felt directly responsible for Monica's safety. The young lawyer didn't deserve to have this happen to her. Sophie couldn't even imagine how she would have handled a situation like this right out of law school. It was still hard for her now.

She brushed her teeth and pulled herself together. It was almost four in the morning. There would probably be no going back to sleep for her tonight.

As she walked downstairs, she heard voices, and she rushed

the rest of the way down. When she saw Monica, her stomach sank. Monica's eyes were red and puffy from crying.

Monica ran over to Sophie and grabbed her in a tight hug. "It was so scary."

Sophie tried to ignore the pain in her side. As she held the shaking young woman, she made eye contact with Cooper. He nodded, seemingly trying to reassure her that everything was going to be all right.

"Monica, I'm so sorry this happened to you. How're you feeling now?" Sophie asked.

Monica took a step back. "This is all insane! You didn't tell me that someone would try to kill us." Her voice shook.

"I didn't know they would either. And I definitely didn't think they'd have any reason to come after you. But you're safe here. This isn't an FBI safe house. They have no way of finding us. We're completely off the grid."

Monica sniffed. "I honestly don't know if I'm going to be cut out for this kind of work."

"Sit down and let me get you some water."

"I'll get the water," Cooper said.

Monica took a seat on the couch, and Sophie sat beside her. "I know you probably have a ton of questions. I'll do my best to answer them, but I'm largely in the dark, just like you."

"The FBI told me I needed to go to the safe house because of the SIB case. But I didn't get a lot of details. Then the next thing I know, some explosion happens, and I'm rushed out of there and over here."

"This is all about the Sanchez Cartel. We think at this point, given everything that's happened, that Whitney Bowman was definitely working with the cartel."

"I just don't get it."

"I still don't know why a powerful CEO of a well-established bank would decide to work with a cartel, but maybe that will become known in the investigation."

"What happens now?"

"The Feds are all over this. It's out of our hands completely. They're even talking to Keith."

"Keith? What could he have to do with this?"

Sophie hated to talk about her boss to her young colleague, but she couldn't deny it. "There's some question as to whether he was involved in any way. Or whether he just had a personal relationship with Whitney that caused him to push us off the Shelton case."

Monica closed her eyes and leaned her head back on the couch.

"I know you must be exhausted," Sophie said. "Why don't I show you where you'll be staying, and you can lie down?"

"I'd appreciate that." Monica stood up. "And I'm sorry if it seemed like I was blaming you for all of this. I know it's not your fault. It's just been a rough few hours."

"That's completely understandable."

Sophie got Monica settled into one of the bedrooms and came back downstairs to find Cooper in the kitchen.

"How's she doing?" he asked.

"About how you would expect. But she's strong. She'll be able to handle everything."

"She has a good role model on that front."

Sophie poured herself some coffee and sat down beside Cooper at the kitchen table. "Everything still okay with my father?"

"Yes. Safe and sound."

"I know I might be paranoid, but I can't help it, as far as he's concerned. He's the only family I have. And after what happened with Monica, I can't take any further chances."

"I promise we have it under control."

She wanted to accept his words as true, but she couldn't help but wonder if she could believe him.

⊰◇⊱

Ashley had asked Juan to her office so she could face him on her turf. She'd had a few sleepless nights thinking about her future, and Juan was a piece of that. It was time to take a different road, and she was about to do something she should've done a long time ago. It was strange, because Patrick calling her out on the Juan situation had really been the catalyst for her taking action. She'd made excuses for Juan's behavior for far too long.

Juan sauntered in a few minutes later, wearing a smug smile. He had no idea why she had asked him there.

"You wanted to talk?" he said. "I thought the police cleared me in the bombing."

"Yes. They did. They're going down other avenues right now that have absolutely nothing to do with you."

"Then why are you frowning?"

She took a deep breath. She could do this. "Juan, I think it's best for us to part ways."

"What?" he asked with a raised voice. "Why?"

"I've gone above and beyond the call of duty for you. I've gotten you through hard times, including Ricky's trial. And I got you out of this bombing mess. Not to mention all the messes I've cleaned up for you over the past couple years."

Juan threw up his hands. "That's all good. It shows we work well together."

She shook her head. "No. It shows I'm great at my job, but I refuse to be treated badly by you and those around you. I don't deserve it."

He leaned back in his chair and crossed his arms. "You're talking crazy. I don't mistreat you. I paid you on time."

"I'm not talking about the money. I'm talking about how you treat me on a day-to-day basis. The yelling, the physical threats and contact. That's what I'm talking about."

He scowled. "People don't leave me. Ever. I'm a lifetime commitment. You should've realized that from day one. There's no leaving this life. Leaving me."

"Juan, listen to me. I am not going to work for you anymore. It's as simple as that. I am not your lawyer going forward." She kept her voice steady and didn't break eye contact. There could be no hint of indecision or weakness on her part.

"I treat you well."

She couldn't help but laugh. "That is a lie and you know it."

"Is this your way of trying to get a raise out of me?"

"Nope. I simply don't want to work with you anymore."

Juan leaned forward, his dark eyes narrowing. "No one walks away from me. You should realize that better than most, after all we've been through together. You understand that?"

"I do understand. Which is why you can say whatever you want about why you're hiring a new lawyer. I don't care. But you will have to hire a new attorney, because I quit."

He cursed and lunged over the table, wrapping his strong hands around her neck. He squeezed, and she started to choke. For a moment she thought he might actually strangle her right there. Using her legs, she was able to break his grip by shoving her swivel chair backward and away from the desk.

She placed her hand on her neck and sucked in a few breaths. The skin burned from his violent grasp. But this outburst only confirmed her decision.

"You're dead," Juan said, leaning threateningly over her desk.

She smiled, trying to play a convincing role. "No, I'm not. Because if anything happens to me—and I mean anything at all—I've made arrangements to release all of your dirty laundry. Every single sordid piece."

His dark eyes widened. "You wouldn't do that. That's unethical."

"Try me."

"You're out of line," Juan said.

"Then stay away from me, and you'll never find out all the dirt I have on you and your family. I've given you fair warning, and I'm making this as easy for you as possible. But absolutely nothing you say at this point will change my mind. Your normal threats and intimidation tactics won't work on me."

He cocked his head to the side. "I have to admit, Ashley, I vastly underestimated you." He stared off into space for a minute.

"This doesn't have to end badly for either of us." She slid a piece of paper across the table. "Here's a list of top-notch defense lawyers who would love to have you on their roster of clients. But for me, I'm done. Do we have an understanding?"

Juan stood up. "Yes." He walked to the door and then turned around. "You're going to regret this."

"I don't think so."

As he walked out the door, she blew out a breath. She'd stood up to him. Now she could only hope he wouldn't call her bluff.

CHAPTER
TWENTY-SIX

P atrick arrived at Ashley's office at about ten in the morning. He'd put in his notice first thing that day. Everyone might think he had sold out and gone to the dark side, but it really wasn't like that at all.

It was like his eyes had been opened to a completely different area of the law that he'd never considered. Maybe he could do his part to make sure that defendants got fair trials. That thought inspired him more than anything else had lately. Ashley was right. He was in a serious rut, and this would provide him the means to make a difference in a way he had never contemplated.

He would have to come to grips with the fact that he'd still have to defend people who committed crimes, but he'd been up front with Ashley that he wanted complete control over his cases.

She had asked him to swing by to discuss an important matter. She probably wanted to make sure he hadn't changed his mind, but he was completely at peace with his decision. Even more than that, he was actually filled with excitement. Like he wasn't just going through the motions anymore.

He greeted Ashley's assistant and then walked back to her office.

"There you are." Ashley stood to greet him.

"What's so urgent?" He sat down. "Is everything okay?"

"I've been doing a lot of thinking, especially after our conversation in the park, and there's something I want to fill you in on."

"Tell me." His mind raced as he waited for her to respond.

"I had a meeting with Juan last night."

"How did that go?"

"I'm glad you're sitting down, because you won't believe this. I told him that he needed to find a new lawyer."

"What? Why?" That was the last thing he had expected to come out of Ashley's mouth.

"Because you were right. I don't deserve to be treated that way by anyone. It doesn't matter that he pays the bills. I have plenty of business without him. I went the extra mile time and again for that man. I don't owe him anything more."

Patrick stared at her. "I hope you didn't do that purely on my account?"

She shook her head. "No. But you did help spur me into action. I shouldn't have to suffer at the hands of my clients. Not after all the work I do for them."

"How did Juan take it?"

She laughed. "About like you would imagine. After he choked me and threatened to kill me—"

He held up a hand to stop her. "What? Are you hurt?"

"No. My neck is a little bruised, which is why I'm wearing this high-collared shirt. But I told him that he needed to back off. He gave me the whole *no one walks away from Juan Wade* speech, but I stood firm."

Patrick ran a hand over his hair and tried not to gape at her. "Did he really threaten to kill you?"

"Yes. But I told him if anything happened to me, I had made arrangements to pull all of his skeletons out of the closet."

"Did you really do that?"

"No. But I think I thoroughly convinced him that I would play hardball."

He didn't think he'd ever met anyone with as much spine as Ashley Murphy. "How did you leave it?"

"I gave him a list of new lawyers to consider, and he told me I'd regret my decision. I doubt I've heard the last from him."

"Do you think you're in danger?"

"No. I actually think once he cools down and gets a new lawyer, I'll be a distant memory."

"For what it's worth, I think you did the right thing." He was really proud of her for standing up to the gang leader. She deserved better than Juan.

"There will be other clients like him, though. That's the nature of the business and something I also wanted to talk with you about."

"Okay."

"I want us to be able to work together well and for neither of us to have issues with clients the other brings in. I was thinking maybe we could briefly consult on clients that may be of a more sensitive or high-profile nature to make sure we're both comfortable with them."

He couldn't believe she was actually considering his opinion on things. Maybe this really could be a successful partnership. "You continue to surprise me, Ashley. I agree with you. For this to work between us, we have to be honest about what cases we want and how we want to handle them. As long as we keep an open line of communication, I think we'll be fine." He smiled. "Also, I gave my two weeks' notice at the DA's office today."

Ashley grinned. "I've got the additional office all set up for you. Whenever you're ready."

"In two weeks." He couldn't wait to start the next phase of his life.

—◁◇▷—

Tad pulled up in front of a large abandoned warehouse in College Park on the south side of the city. This was where he usually met Manuel Smith. Tad had held up his end of the bargain by taking out Whitney. Smith had promised him a little something extra, and it was time to pay up. But for Tad, it was even bigger than the money. Smith had also floated the idea of a promotion. If Tad had to be stuck in the cartel, he might as well make the most of it by working his way up the ranks.

Smith's black Escalade was parked in front of the warehouse. The lights of the SUV shone brightly, lighting up the surrounding area. Smith rarely went anywhere alone and always had a driver.

Tad put his vehicle in park and opened the door. He knew Smith would expect him to make the first move. Then one of Smith's men would check him for weapons, as was standard operating procedure. They could never be too careful.

As expected, a man got out of the Escalade and patted Tad down. He'd left his weapon in his SUV. He knew the drill.

The man gave a thumbs-up toward the Escalade, and Smith got out of the car and walked toward Tad.

"Give me a minute," Smith told the hired hand.

The driver nodded and went back to the car.

"You did good." Smith patted Tad on the shoulder.

"Thank you, sir." Tad felt a sense of pride even though he'd hated having to kill Whitney. But now wasn't the time to start forming sentimental attachments. It was all part of the job.

"What did Whitney say to you when you confronted her?" Smith asked.

Tad took a breath. "She was actually about to split town." He debated about telling Smith the entire story, but thought it best not to hold back. It was the same advice he'd given Whitney, but she hadn't taken it. "She also said she was going to tip off the cops about you."

Smith laughed. "Why would she have done that?"

"I think she hoped it would be a diversion and that she could disappear."

Smith shook his head. "There's no such thing as disappearing."

"I agree." Tad's palms felt sweaty. He was anxious to discuss his promotion and put all this Whitney business behind him.

"Tad, you've been very loyal since we crossed paths a few years ago."

That was an interesting way to describe how they'd met. Tad considered it more like blackmail, but he'd learned long ago to hold his tongue with Smith. "I'm glad you can appreciate that. I've always had your back."

"And I want you to know how much that is valued."

Now would come the good news. The new position would definitely involve more money.

"Here's the thing." Smith looked Tad in the eyes. "Shelton is gone, Whitney is gone, and there's nothing linking me to any laundering scheme. Right now all the cops have is a wild theory and speculation. No hard evidence at all. There's just one piece of unfinished business."

"I thought I'd taken care of everything, sir." Tad had been meticulous in covering his tracks and making sure Smith was clean. The laundering scheme had been highly effective.

"Not quite." Smith took a step toward him. "You're the only person who could ever tie me—and more importantly, the Sanchez Cartel—to this scheme."

"But I work for you." Tad's voice cracked.

"I know. Which is why you have to understand that I can't take the risk of you flipping on me one day." Smith paused. "It's not personal."

As those words came out of Smith's mouth, Tad realized he was as good as dead. He kicked himself for not seeing it coming. What an amateur move on his part. He almost deserved to be killed for being so blind. And all because of the lure of more money and power. His pulse started to thump wildly. "I wouldn't flip on you."

"That's what they all say. But you have been a very good and loyal soldier to the organization, so we'll make this as easy as possible."

Tad stood there, unmoving. There was no point in trying to run. Then he'd just get shot in the back. He took a moment and contemplated his life. He didn't think there was anything to look forward to. Death was final. But he'd given it a good run. "Just do it, sir."

Smith nodded and pulled a gun out of his jacket.

Tad took one final deep breath before he heard the loud crack of the gun.

Sophie and Monica sat on the couch, watching a movie. Sophie had suggested a comedy to keep things light. Cooper had opted out of the movie and was grabbing a quick nap after dinner. Maybe she had overloaded him with too many carbs with the big Italian pasta dish she'd made. But cooking was one of the few things she could do here to keep her mind off the situation.

Monica had been highly appreciative of the home-cooked meal. It seemed she wasn't that handy in the kitchen, but she'd been a big help with cleanup.

Sophie closed her eyes for a moment, not that interested in the movie. The volume on the TV went up, and she opened her eyes.

"Sorry. I thought if it was louder, it would stop me from falling asleep," Monica said. "I want to get a decent night's rest tonight, but if I fall asleep now, that won't happen."

"Sure. Turn it up as loud as you want." She watched without much interest as the movie passed by. Her mind was far away, wondering what the future held. For her cases, for Keith and the office, and most importantly, for her relationship with Cooper.

300

A few minutes later, Monica's phone rang.

"They gave me a temporary cell, and I gave the number to my mom. She's completely worried about me. I should take this." Monica stood up and walked toward the stairs.

It was exactly times like this when Sophie really missed her mother. She'd talked to her dad earlier that evening before dinner, and he was doing fine. But she understood that there was nothing else quite like having your mother in your life. She tried to hold back her emotion, but it was no use.

She was an emotional person, and that was never going to change. As she wiped the tears away, she hoped she could pull herself together before Monica got back. She was clearly more vulnerable right now, given everything that had happened. Usually the mere mention of someone talking to their mom wouldn't have any effect on her. But right now, she was battling too many things at once.

The loud laughter emanating from the TV was in direct contrast to her mood. She wished Cooper was awake to provide some comfort, but that was selfish of her. He deserved some rest.

Instead she walked into the kitchen and tried to locate some chocolate. A couple minutes later, as she was rummaging through the cabinets, she heard footsteps.

"Monica, I just found some chocolate, if you want to share." She turned around with the large chocolate bar in her hand, and then dropped it to the floor.

Monica stood in front of her with a gun drawn and pointed right at her head.

"Monica, what're you doing?"

"We're going outside. Our ride will be here any minute."

"You can't do this. Are you working for SIB?"

Monica shook her head. "Of course not."

If she wasn't working for Whitney, then who had hired her? The answer was too awful to fathom. "The cartel?"

"I couldn't believe you never put two and two together. I thought so many times that you might be on to me."

How could Sophie have been so wrong? "And Harrison?"

"He has nothing to do with this."

"Are you even a lawyer?" A million questions flooded through her mind.

"Yes. But I had to get my hands a little dirty for the family business."

Monica was a member of the Sanchez family. The news just kept getting worse. "What did you do to Cooper?"

"He'll wake up at some point. I dosed his Coke at dinner with a sedative. The organization doesn't really care about him."

"But they care about me?"

"Yes. It's because of you that this entire deal went sideways. You had to go poking around instead of just taking Shelton and putting him away. It's personal."

"Why not just kill me now?"

"I'd prefer to have someone else do it." Monica took a step forward. "But don't try me. I will pull the trigger if I have to."

As she looked into Monica's dark eyes, Sophie believed her.

"Now move slowly toward the front door. I'm right behind you."

"Cooper!" Sophie screamed.

"Stop it! We're already behind schedule. Now move."

She couldn't let the cartel remove her from the safe house. She had to stall. "I'm not going with you. Why would I knowingly walk to my death? You're just going to have someone kill me."

Monica's eyes widened in surprise at Sophie's statement. She clearly hadn't anticipated any resistance.

Sophie did the only thing she could think of. She lunged at Monica, trying to knock her off balance. Sophie towered over Monica, but unlike the younger woman, Sophie had never been trained in any kind of fighting except a basic self-defense course her father insisted she take her first year of college.

Sophie went at Monica again, grabbing her right arm, and the gun dropped to the floor.

"Enough!" A deep voice rang out.

Sophie turned and saw a man standing in the doorway. She'd only seen pictures, but she recognized this bald man with a dark goatee as Manuel Smith, and her gut clenched in fear. His dark eyes focused in on her.

Smith walked closer to her, gun in hand. "You're coming with me."

What could he possibly want to do to her? Punish her and seek revenge? The scenarios were too awful to imagine.

Monica's words rang through her head—*It's personal.*

Sophie wasn't going to budge. She could only pray that he wouldn't pull the trigger.

He fired a warning shot into the air. That got her attention, but she still feared the repercussions more if he took her out of the safe house. A quick death now seemed preferable to torture or worse.

"You need to cooperate," Smith said.

He fired the gun a second time, this time hitting Monica in the leg. Monica crumpled to the floor.

"Why did you do that?" Sophie shouted. "Are you crazy?" She knelt beside Monica, who was moaning in pain. Even though Monica had been working against her, Sophie didn't want to see her hurt.

"She'll be fine," Smith said. "Just a little nick to help maintain her cover. We've worked too hard to get her into the prosecutor's office to pull her out now."

Smith pulled Sophie off the ground with one hand while keeping the gun in the other. His fingers dug into her arm. "Leave her there," he barked.

Reluctantly, Sophie took a step.

He pushed her forward. "Walk."

The gun pressed into her back. She screamed as loudly as she could, hoping and praying that Cooper would wake up.

"Stop it!" Smith demanded. He smacked the side of her head hard enough to make her stagger sideways, and then shoved her forward.

They walked to the front door. She figured this might be her only chance to make a move.

"Open the door slowly," he said.

Sophie did as he asked, but once the door was open, she lifted her right foot and slammed it as hard as she could down onto his foot.

As he yelped, she sprinted out the door. She knew there was a risk that he would just shoot her in the back, but it was one she had to take.

Sophie ran as quickly as she could, her heart pounding in her chest and her ribs aching. But she couldn't let the pain get the best of her now. She ran around the side of the house, desperate for any place to take cover. Since the house was tucked at the end of a private cul-de-sac, she wasn't sure she could outrun him to the nearest house. If the neighbors were even home. And what if Smith just killed them too? Her best bet was to find a place to hide. The darkness gave her an advantage.

Smith couldn't be far behind, but she kept running, her feet pounding on the ground. She grimaced through the searing pain shooting across her right side from her rib injury.

She could hear him gaining on her. When the first shot rang out through the night, she pushed herself to keep going. There was no turning back now.

The next round of shots came in rapid succession. She didn't look back as she continued to run. She had to make a decision whether to keep going straight or to loop back toward the house. Because Cooper was still inside, she ran back toward the house, though she feared that as Smith got closer, he was bound to hit his target—her!

The next thing she knew, loud heavy footsteps were right behind her. Far too close. Then she was tackled hard to the ground. She tasted a mix of grass and blood in her mouth, and she screamed in pain at the impact to her ribs. Her side was on fire.

Smith was on top of her. He flipped her over and punched her hard in the gut. She saw stars and couldn't breathe. She had ticked him off, and now he was out for his dose of revenge. Shooting was too easy. He wanted to make her feel real pain.

He let out a string of curses as he slapped her hard across the face. She tried her best to fight back, but she was no match for him.

As he reared back and was about to hit her again, a few loud gunshots pierced the darkness. Smith fell hard onto her, crushing her down into the wet grass. He didn't move.

Instinctively, she bucked and rolled him off of her then lay still on the ground, trying to catch her breath, staring up at the few stars in the dark night sky.

"Sophie!" Cooper's voice rang out. A second later, he was on the ground beside her. He gathered her up in his arms and held her tightly.

She could barely catch her breath. The pain was so intense. She looked to the side and saw that Smith was unmoving. "He's dead?"

"Yes. He can't hurt you anymore." Cooper looked down at her. "You're bleeding. We've got to get you help."

"I think some of it is his blood too." She felt disgusted thinking about it. But her face was definitely bleeding from his attack. "Monica also needs medical attention. He shot her in the leg. She was working for him."

Cooper kept Sophie in his arms, but pulled out his phone and dialed 911. "They'll be here any minute." He pushed the hair back from her face. It felt like she was caked in blood.

"Monica said she put a sedative in your drink at dinner."

"That explains why I was so tired. I should've realized something was off, but it came on so quickly that I thought I was just exhausted. I'm so sorry, Sophie."

"You still made it in time."

"Barely. But I'm not going anywhere now. It's going to be okay."

She closed her eyes, knowing what he said was true.

The next morning, Cooper waited for Sophie in her kitchen. He'd only slept a few hours, but that was enough for him. He could tell she was thrilled to be home after being discharged late last night from the hospital. Thankfully, she had sustained no major injuries, and Smith had missed her cracked rib by a hair. It could've been so much worse.

He'd just had two calls with the Feds and the APD, and it appeared that he didn't have anything to worry about regarding Smith's shooting. It was clearly justified, and his law enforcement background gave him credibility on that. Taking a life was never easy or something he took lightly. But the alternative of that man killing Sophie was unfathomable. He'd prayed for the Lord's forgiveness, and he felt he was at peace.

Now he hoped that he and Sophie could put all of this behind them.

She walked into the kitchen, and anger bubbled up inside him as he saw her beautiful but bruised face. The only solace he had was that the man who had done that to her could never hurt her or anyone else again.

"How did you sleep?" he asked.

She leaned against the kitchen counter. "Once I got to sleep, I actually slept better than I have in a while. It helped knowing you were here with me."

"I'm sorry again that I didn't wake up sooner last night."

"It's not your fault. Monica drugged you." She let out a breath. "Have you heard anything on her condition?"

He nodded. "Yes, she's perfectly stable. I think the Feds are set to question her this afternoon."

"I can't believe they had someone on the inside the whole time. I would've never in a million years suspected her. She seemed so young and innocent."

"She is young, but not so innocent. It appears she took on a new last name years ago to distance herself from the Sanchez family. I bet they always planned to have her play a role on the outside. It's like she was groomed for it."

"And everything was okay with the shooting, right? Do I need to talk to them again?"

"No. It's all fine." He stood up and walked over to her. "Sophie, if I hadn't woken up . . ."

"Don't talk like that. You did wake up. You saved my life."

He gently wrapped his arms around her waist, pulling her close to him. When she smiled, it was like a huge load was lifted off his shoulders. "Last night was so surreal. I was afraid I'd lost you."

"Right before everything went down, Monica told me her mother was calling. It was probably Smith, now that I think about it, but at the time, it hit me hard. I'm a bit emotionally fragile right now. I know you say I wear my heart and my feelings openly, and that's always been a struggle for me." She took a breath. "But I don't want you to think I have any doubts about us."

"Really?"

"No. If anything, last night reminded me of my father's story. And about how at least he hadn't lived with regret, because my mother knew she was loved."

He lightly cupped her bruised cheek in his hand. "I don't want to have regrets either. I had thoroughly convinced myself that I could never have a wife and loving family. That it would be easier to just go it alone. That I was bound to end up like my father—an addict with a violent streak that couldn't be tamed. But through God's grace and the love you've shown me, I know now that I was wrong. And I also know that I've completely fallen in love with you."

"Cooper, I love you too. It's as simple as that. You created your own special way into my heart, and I wouldn't change a thing about you. We can work through our issues together, hand in hand."

"I wouldn't want it any other way."

He leaned down and kissed her gently. A promise of many things he hoped were still to come, if he had his way.

EPILOGUE

Over the past six months, Sophie's life had changed in many ways. But the best of ways was that she was in a wonderful relationship with Cooper.

They'd spent time really getting to know each other and working through the obstacles that stood in their way. She'd even convinced him to reach out to his father—who was still maintaining his sobriety.

She didn't think Cooper and his dad would ever be close, but it was an important step for him to be able to heal. Her own father had really taken to Cooper, and it made her heart so full seeing them together.

They sat outside on her porch, enjoying a beautiful Atlanta spring day, the sun shining brightly down on them. Her life at work had returned to a much more normal routine. Keith was still in his job after taking a brief leave of absence. He'd been cleared of all wrongdoing, and she was thankful for that. Harrison was still gunning for Keith's job, but he mostly left her alone.

Although Patrick had decided not to re-try Ricky Wade, she'd come to terms with it. She'd even visited the victims' families on occasion. They seemed to have moved on, so she needed to do the same. Even a guilty verdict wouldn't have brought their loved ones back.

Oddly enough, Patrick was giving the defense bar a try, and he seemed refreshed to be taking on a new challenge. They had remained in touch and had even had a case against each other. She couldn't imagine switching sides, but it seemed like the right move for him.

"So I've been thinking," Cooper said.

"Is this about the dog again?"

He had been pushing for rescuing a puppy. She'd given him a hard time about it, but secretly she was totally excited about the whole thing.

"No. Not exactly about the dog. Not just yet anyway."

"Why not? I thought you had your heart set on one of the lab puppies at the humane society?"

He smiled. "Why do I get the sneaking suspicion that your heart is also set on one of those puppies?"

She laughed. "Okay. I'll 'fess up. They were adorable. The thing is, I know it sounds silly, but at this point it would feel like your dog instead of our dog. The pup would be staying with you. That's really my only hesitation."

"What if that all changed?" he asked, his blue eyes sparkling.

"What are you saying?"

Cooper scooted off of his chair and knelt beside her as he pulled a sparkling diamond ring from his pocket. "Sophie Elizabeth Dawson, you are the love of my life. I want to be with you and take each step of this crazy life with you. I want to have that family with you that I know you've always wanted. The family that you've made me want. I love you with all that I am." He took a breath. "Will you marry me?"

Happy tears flowed down her cheeks. This wasn't like she'd imagined over and over since she was a child. It was even better. "Of course. I love you, Cooper."

He slid the ring on her finger and scooped her up into a big hug. "I love you too. But one thing. Please don't kill me."

"What?"

He looked down at his watch. "Our engagement party is going to start any minute."

"Here? Now?" she asked.

"Yeah. Our fathers are coming first. Then the rest of our friends."

"Our fathers?" She started to cry again.

"Yeah. They're right inside. You've convinced me that I have to keep pushing forward with my dad so that I don't ever go back to that dark place again."

"I won't let you go there, Cooper." She kissed him with everything she had and wrapped her arms tightly around his neck—until she heard someone clear their throat.

"Save that for the honeymoon."

She turned around and saw her father. He walked up onto the porch and gave her a huge hug. "Your mother would be so happy for you," he said.

"I know, Dad. I'm so glad you're here for this."

"I wouldn't miss it for the world."

She watched as Cooper and his father seemed to have a pleasant conversation. Pretty soon the back porch was full of people, including Kate and Mia.

"Let me see the ring!" Kate squealed.

Sophie showed them both the princess cut ring that sparkled on her finger.

"So I guess this means I'm the last woman standing," Mia said.

Sophie wrapped her arm around her friend. "Don't worry. Mr. Right will come along when you least expect him to."

"That's what they say," Mia responded. "But I'm not a dreamer and a romantic like you, Sophie. I'm not sure what's in store for me." She paused. "But tonight is not about me. It's about you. Let's celebrate."

A couple hours later, as the party was winding down, Sophie stood beside Cooper and rested her head on his shoulder.

"So about that puppy," he said. "I hope you were serious."

"Why?"

"Because we're picking her up tomorrow."

She laughed as she looked into the eyes of the man who had stolen her heart. "Guess that means we'll have to get started on the wedding planning right away."

"Whatever you want," he said. "I'd marry you right here and now."

And she knew he meant it. "Let's not get too crazy. I am going to have that dream dress."

He kissed her again, and she couldn't wait to start her new life with him. Cooper wasn't the man of her dreams, but the man she never could have dreamed of. And that made it so much better.

ACKNOWLEDGMENTS

Many thanks to those who helped make this book happen. To my agent Sarah for your constant support and encouragement. To Dave, Jessica, Noelle, Amy, and everyone in the Bethany House family for your hard work. I truly appreciate all that you do for me.

Thanks to my family for the continuous love and support. Tog, thanks for being such a huge supporter of my books. Mama, I love you and hope you enjoy this book as much as the first. Aaron, thanks for being a part of this writing journey with me. I love you.

Teresa, thanks for taking the time to provide me with your keen insights into the world of being a prosecutor.

Rachel's Justice League, you continue to be a source of joy and encouragement for me. Thank you for everything you do.

I praise and thank the Lord for all He has done for me, and for each day that I'm able to write and share my stories with the world.

Rachel Dylan writes Christian fiction, specializing in legal romantic suspense. Rachel has practiced law for over a decade, including being a litigator at one of the nation's top law firms. She enjoys weaving together legal and suspenseful stories with a romantic twist. A southerner at heart, she now lives in Michigan with her husband and five furkids—two dogs and three cats. Rachel loves to connect with readers. You can find her at www.racheldylan.com.

Sign Up for Rachel's Newsletter!

Keep up to date with Rachel's news on book releases and events by signing up for her email list at racheldylan.com.

More from Rachel Dylan

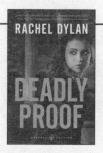

Attorney Kate Sullivan has been appointed lead counsel to take on Mason Pharmaceutical in a claim involving an allegedly dangerous new drug. She hires a handsome private investigator to do some digging, but when a whistleblower is killed, it's clear the stakes are higher than ever.

Deadly Proof by Rachel Dylan
ATLANTA JUSTICE #1

BETHANYHOUSE

Stay up to date on your favorite books and authors with our free e-newsletters. Sign up today at bethanyhouse.com.

Find us on Facebook. facebook.com/bethanyhousepublishers

Free exclusive resources for your book group! bethanyhouse.com/anopenbook
anopenbook

You May Also Like . . .

When a terrorist investigation leads FBI agent Declan Grey to a closed immigrant community, he turns to crisis counselor Tanner Shaw for help. Under imminent threat, they'll have to race against the clock to stop a plot that could cost thousands of lives.

Blind Spot by Dani Pettrey
CHESAPEAKE VALOR #3
danipettrey.com

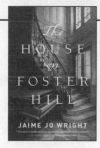

Fleeing a stalker, Kaine Prescott purchases an old house with a dark history: a century earlier, an unidentified woman was found dead on the grounds. As Kaine tries to settle in, she learns the story of her ancestor Ivy Thorpe, who, with the help of a man from her past, tried to uncover the truth about the death.

The House on Foster Hill by Jaime Jo Wright
jaimewrightbooks.com

When Tox is shot at a picnic, he discovers the bullet is a strange invitation to join a Special Forces buddy's quest for revenge for their fallen team. Despite his injury, Tox feels sympathetic to the cause, recognizing a growing darkness within himself. But after he learns Alec is using a deadly ancient artifact in his plan, Tox must fight the monster without becoming one.

Crown of Souls by Ronie Kendig
THE TOX FILES #2
roniekendig.com

◊BETHANYHOUSE